THE DEAD SANG OFF KEY

A VISCOUNT WARE MYSTERY #4

J. L. BUCK

KENMORE, WA

A Camel Press book published by Epicenter Press

Epicenter Press
6524 NE 181st St.
Suite 2
Kenmore, WA 98028

For more information go to:
www.Camelpress.com
www.Coffeetownpress.com
www.Epicenterpress.com

Author's website: janetlbuck.com

All rights reserved. No part of this book may be reproduced or transmitted in any form or by any means, electronic or mechanical, including photocopying, recording, or any information storage and retrieval system, without permission in writing from the publisher.

This is a work of fiction. Names, characters, places, brands, media, and incidents are the product of the author's imagination or are used fictitiously.

The Dead Sang Off Key
2024 © J. L. Buck

Library of Congress Control Number: 2023950946
ISBN: 9781684921690 (trade paper)
ISBN: 9781684921706 (ebook)

Printed in the United States of America

Acknowledgments

Many thanks to my editor Jennifer who asks all the right questions and to the faithful readers who keep me going.

Chapter One

Seaford, England, 13 June 1813

Lady Anne Ashburn shifted her black parasol to a better angle as she picked her way along the pebble beach, her black skirts swishing round her sturdy boots. The sun bore down on this warm day, but the breeze coming off the water cooled her flushed cheeks. Unlike the more popular shoreline around Brighton, Seaford's beach had more rocks than sand, and for the moment, she and her maid Jenny had this part of the rugged coastline to themselves.

"You were right, my lady," Jenny said, fanning herself with one hand. "There is a breeze down here, and once we get out of the sun, it should be cooler."

Lady Anne nodded, the gentle movement stirring the curls dangling on each side of her cheeks. The rest were piled high on her head like a fashionable fair-haired halo. She insisted on a proper toilette each day even though they were in the middle of nowhere—well, truthfully, not nowhere, they were only a few miles from the popular seaside resort of Brighton, but it felt like isolation, and she had already had months of that.

After a long illness, her mother had passed last November. Winter and spring had been dark months of grief, wandering the silent halls of Chadley, the seat of her father's earldom in Warwickshire. Anne had welcomed his decision to hire a house near the coast for the summer months. She had hoped it was a sign his gloom was lifting, that he was coming to terms with their loss, and indeed his face had lightened over the past month, his steps growing brisker. When he received word a week ago that he was needed in the House of Lords, he had packed his bags and gone, exuding a sense of purpose that had been missing since last autumn.

Anne had felt similar stirrings within herself. She still ached with loss each day, but grief no longer consumed every waking moment. Chadley had held so many memories that hadn't had time to transition from painful to cherished. Away from there, her spirits had gradually returned, and she was getting bored with the quiet village of Seaford—especially with her father in London. Beyond a few townspeople she'd met during her limited morning calls, she had no friends in the Seaford area. Her mourning clothes kept people away, and propriety prevented her from attending the few social events the village offered.

Stepping around the point of the cliffs that nearly barred her way as it jutted close to the water's edge, she stopped to enjoy the shade on this side. She tilted her head to get a better look at the impressive white walls that towered above her.

"They are beautiful, are they not?"

"Yes, my lady. I've never seen anything like them."

Anne picked up a small pebble and tossed it in the water. "My friend Daniel used to skim rocks across the water on a pond back home, but it would never work in these waves." She turned to look at the cliffs again. "Is this not where the Singing Cave is supposed to be?"

"Yes, ma'am. According to Ben, the stable boy, it's on this back side of the rock point, but you have to climb a bit to get there." Jenny peered at her mistress suspiciously. "You aren't thinking of going inside, are you, my lady? Is that why we walked this way?"

"It *would* be interesting to see, do you not agree?" Anne shaded her eyes from the glare of the sun reflecting off the higher portions of the cliff wall and studied the huge surface for crevices or fissures large enough to be a cave opening. Exploring it would be the most daring thing she had done in many months. "How far up?"

"Ben didn't say, but he told me to look carefully, and I'd see a path that the smugglers used." Jenny took a step toward the cliffs, brushed her light-brown hair away from her face, and peered upward. "I cannot see it, my lady. Can you?"

"Perhaps we need to walk a bit farther." Lady Anne moved closer to the cliffs and kept scrutinizing the walls as she walked. "What about there?" She stopped and closed her small parasol, sticking the closed end of it in her reticule, stretching the soft knit material into a long bag, and tentatively stepped onto a narrow ledge, brushing away loose pebbles and white dust with the toe of her right boot.

"My lady, are you sure about this?" Jenny's hazel eyes narrowed with concern. "What if you take a tumble?"

"Why would I? But if I do, I have you to go for help," Anne said practically. She kept walking, studying the surface beneath her feet. "It is definitely a path. The farther I go I can see it has been worn by use…maybe over a long time." Anne turned her head and looked behind her. "I believe someone tried to conceal the path by throwing those pebbles over it near the bottom. How very interesting. I wonder why."

She couldn't stop now. As she continued to climb, the path angled to the right with a gentle incline. After ten feet or so, Anne reached a crack in the cliff face that was not easily visible from the beach below.

"Oh, we have found something." She slipped through the fissure opening and looked around. The crack ran part way up the cliff and was open enough at the top for light to filter inside. Ahead of them the path grew wider and steeper. Definitely intrigued now, she ventured on. Only a few steps farther, she looked up and gasped at the dark opening in front of her.

"Oh, my lady," Jenny whispered and scrambled up beside her. "That must be the cave, but I don't hear singing, do you? Nor ghostly sounds. I suppose Ben was just giving give me a fright with talk of the ghost of Singing Cave."

"Perhaps one has to go inside to hear her sing."

"*Are* we going inside? It's so dark."

"Look here." Anne picked up an oil lantern and flint box set beside the cave opening. "Who could have left this—local lads who play here or curious walkers, like us?"

"Maybe it's smugglers. What if they catch us here?" Jenny whispered, looking behind them as though French bootleggers or pirates might appear any moment.

Anne gave her a startled look. "Why would you ask that? Has someone said they are active around Seaford?" She *had* wondered if there was smuggling in the area. On the few local calls she'd made, Anne had noticed an abundance of French wines, and a preference for French lace. It was not unheard of for small coastal towns to turn a blind eye on smugglers for the pleasure of procuring wines, silks, and other coveted goods from the Continent.

"Ben did, but later he took it back, saying he was just fooling."

"Not a worry then. Shall we look inside? Just a ways, not too far."

"What if we run into the ghost?" Jenny said, giving the black entrance a wary look.

"Presuming I believed in ghosts—which I do not—why would she bother us?" Anne asked. "I heard she starved herself to death while waiting in vain for her seafaring lover to return. A sad story but hardly frightening."

"That's only one version," Jenny said ominously. "Another says the sailor was married, and the girl was murdered by his wife. She haunts the cave and even walks the beach at night seeking revenge for her death."

"Oh, well, yes, that is a gruesome tale," Anne said. "But I do not see why she should worry us."

"The murdered cannot move on until they've had revenge against *someone*. That is what Ben said."

"He was teasing you again," Anne said with an indulgent smile. She lit the lantern. "Stay here if you would rather. I am going to look around."

"I can't let you go by yourself."

"Then come along and quit upsetting yourself with thoughts of ghosts and smugglers. Neither should be around during the day. This is just another adventure."

"That is what I'm afraid of," Jenny murmured.

Anne smiled to herself and pretended she had not heard. Indeed, a couple of their prior adventures *had* turned rather perilous.

She held up the lantern, and they ducked through the opening. The path was narrow enough they walked in single file for several feet until it widened into a small chamber approximately six feet wide. It was empty, and Anne moved on into a tunnel at the rear, the swinging lantern creating shadowy figures on the walls that had Jenny grabbing her arm more than once.

"It is nothing," Anne reassured her. "There is no one here except us." She stepped past a pile of large rocks and into another chamber, no wider but longer than the last. The walls were slightly moist here where the dry heat of the day had failed to reach, and it smelled musty. Anne moved forward again, headed toward something dark on the cave floor.

"What's that?" Jenny asked, stopping abruptly.

"A pile of rags, I believe."

As though their voices had triggered a response, a strange sound, somewhere between a moan and a whistle, came from deeper in the cave. Anne flinched at the sudden sound, and Jenny squeaked.

"Oh, my lady! It's the ghost." Jenny clamped a hand over her mouth to stifle a scream and backed away.

Anne took a deep breath and relaxed as she realized what it was. "Nonsense, Jenny. It's the wind. My father told me of visiting a singing cave many years ago. He said the strange sounds had something to do with the air going in and out of small openings. There is no ghost."

"I'm not so sure, my lady."

Anne started forward again, Jenny lagging behind. The lantern glow reached the bundle on the floor, and this time Anne stopped, staring at what the lantern light revealed.

Jenny came up beside her and pointed with a strangled scream. "How do you explain her?"

"I cannot, but she is definitely not a ghost."

The body of a young woman wearing a well-made blue gown that implied she was gently born was crumpled on the floor, her black hair pulled loose and covering part of her face. She lay on one side, her legs twisted awkwardly.

Anne's heart pounded in her ears, her breath rapid. What should she do? For she was nearly certain the woman was dead. She wanted to run away, but that would hardly be practical. What would Lucien…um, Lord Ware, do if he were there? His inquiries for the War Office made her friend more acquainted with this kind of situation than she was—although this was not her first dead body. The woman was so motionless she could not be alive, but Anne knew Lord Ware would begin by confirming the death.

She moved forward and crouched beside the body, reaching out a trembling hand to place it on the woman's neck. It was unnaturally cold to her touch, and Anne steeled herself to keep from snatching her hand away. She felt no hint of pulse or breathing. She noted what appeared to be bruises on the neck and the girl's cheek. Glancing over the rest of the body, she froze at the sight of blood on the lower chest. Anne rose and scanned the cave floor. No weapon, unless it was under the body…and she was not going to look.

"Is she dead?" Jenny asked.

"Yes, most decidedly so." Anne returned to her maid. "Jenny, you must go for help, while I stay with her."

"No, my lady, I will not do it."

"Whyever not?" Anne asked with a puzzled frown.

"I would not be doing my duty, if I left you here alone."

Anne was taken aback. "Are you implying being alone with a dead body might compromise me in some fashion?"

Jenny gave her a pointed look. "I am not daft, my lady, but what if the killer comes back with you here all alone?"

"Oh." The thought gave Anne a chill on the back of her neck. Thinking this was just a pleasant seaside walk, she had not brought the pistol she often carried in her reticule. Anne had been in the hands of cutthroats once before and had vowed never to repeat that horrible experience. What made Jenny assume the woman had been murdered? Had she been close enough to see the blood on the victim's chest?

"All right. We shall both go. I suppose there is nothing we can do for her by staying."

They scrambled back down the path…and to say they hurried across the beach was an understatement. They were running long before they reached the cliff top and spotted Timothy with the carriage.

He hurried to meet them. "My lady, what is amiss?"

"We must find a constable," Anne said, taking a deep breath in an attempt to regain her composure. "A woman has had a terrible accident." There was no reason to tell him it was a probable murder. That was information for the constable.

Reacting to the urgency in her voice, Timothy helped Lady Anne and Jenny into the carriage and whipped the horses into a gallop.

• • •

"I am certain she is dead," Anne said firmly to Constable Harald Harrison, a pleasant-faced, earnest young man. He was no more than two years her elder, putting him in his mid-twenties. "And I fear it might not be an accident. Do you need me to point out where she is?"

He shook his head. "No, my lady. I am familiar with the cave. You've had quite a shock. I suggest you go home and have a cup of tea. I'll collect some mates, and we will see to the body."

Anne let out a breath of relief. "Very well. I confess I was not keen to go back, but you will tell me who she is and what happened, will you not?"

"Yes, my lady. As soon as I know myself."

Anne returned to her carriage and did as Constable Harry had suggested, except when Jenny brought tea to the parlor, Anne added a small splash of brandy from the sideboard.

As the day wore on, the sun settled low in the west, and still Anne heard nothing from the constable. Perhaps she was too impatient. It would take time to move the body, and then he would have to notify the poor woman's family.

She couldn't put the incident out of her mind. The image of the dead woman haunted her. Although she hadn't said so to Jenny, she agreed with her that the woman had been murdered. Anne couldn't say whether she had been shot or stabbed, but the blood on her chest and the bruises were more than suspicious.

Anne tried knitting, took a stroll in the garden, wrote a letter to a friend back home, and then played the pianoforte for a while. Finally, she heard a knock at the door. The local butler hired for the summer announced Constable Harrison, Justice of the Peace Martin Colby, and Sir Timothy Mansfield. All three men were stern-looking, and they stared at her as though…well, she could not put a name to it, but something was gravely amiss. Rather wary, she raised her chin.

"Gentlemen, please have a seat," she said.

"We won't be staying long," Constable Harry said. "Uh, my lady, are you sure you were in Singing Cave?"

"Why, yes, I believe so. Just past the point where the cliffs stretch across the beach, and several feet up the cliff wall. There is a faint path. We even heard the eerie whistling it makes."

"Just where was this body?" asked Justice of the Peace Colby, a middle-aged man with short graying sideburns, a slight paunch, and prominent jowls.

"Where? Did you not find it? It was in the second chamber. We went through the first chamber, down a short tunnel, and then into the second room, much longer than the first. The woman lay in the middle toward the far end."

"She is not there now."

"I do not understand."

"Neither do we." Colby lowered his brows. "Nor do we enjoy tromping around the cliffs because city folk are having their fun with us."

"Sir," Anne rose to her feet indignant at the accusation. "I assure you, finding a dead body is not my idea of fun. Nor am I from the city, not that it matters. The victim was a young woman, with black hair, and from good family if I am not mistaken. Someone will surely miss her and come forward to report it. I cannot fathom why you could not find her."

"Because she was not there, young lady," Colby said, speaking with all the authority of his office. "I am not convinced she ever was."

Chapter Two

London, 13 June 1813

Lucien Grey, Viscount Ware, and his fellow agent, the Honorable Andrew Sherbourne, crouched in a pitch-black alley among the stench of rotting food and human refuse. They'd been following Mr. Oscar Hensley, a suspected French traitor, that evening and had been forced to take cover to avoid discovery when Hensley had suddenly turned to look behind him.

Lucien held a handkerchief to his nose. He had been in foul-smelling places before, but this was like standing in a wastewater drain. He doubted if his valet would ever get the smell out of his clothing, and his boots were unspeakable.

Sherry stirred beside him. "Let's get out of here before I cast up my accounts."

"You'll have no argument from me. In any event, I am sure he is gone by now."

They picked their way carefully toward the light at the end of the alley. Once they'd reached the end, Sherry walked a short distance away to stomp his feet without splashing the offensive sludge on Lucien. "That was revolting."

"I agree, but forget about it. Our efforts might not be a total loss. We are only one street over from the home of the Spanish diplomat. If we can catch Hensley coming out, we can confirm Whitehall's suspicions that the embassy is the source of the leaked information."

"And we can turn this damnable matter over to Lord Rothe for the politicians to settle," Sherry finished with a show of enthusiasm.

"Exactly. We must hurry."

"Hold on. You mean we are going to hang around in these clothes, waiting for him to come out?"

"'Fraid so. If we take the time to change, our efforts may be for nothing."

"Bloody hell." Sherry hurried to keep pace with his partner.

Half an hour later, Lucien grinned at Sherry from their hiding spot behind the hedgerow. "That does it," he murmured, watching the short, squat figure of Hensley stealthily exit from the embassy's rear entrance. "Caught him."

"Now can I go home and change clothes?"

"Since neither of us is fit to call upon Rothe tonight with our report, yes, home it is. We'll meet at Whitehall in the morning. Say, ten?"

"It is an ungodly early hour, but since this is a matter of urgency, I shall be there."

They cut over two streets and found Finn, Lucien's small, red-haired groom, waiting with the curricle outside a pub where its presence would not have drawn notice.

"Take us home, Finn," Lucien said as the two men climbed aboard the small, open carriage.

"'Gor, milord." Finn instinctively took a step back. "Where ya been? Pardon, gov, I dint mean—"

"Never mind," Lucien said. "We know how bad the odor is. We're dropping off Sherry first, but we shall not dawdle on the way. I am looking forward to a bath."

"Washin' the carriage will be easy, but Talbot ain't gonna like what y' done to them boots," Finn predicted, ducking his head to hide a grin.

"I am very sure you're right," Lucien owned with a sigh.

• • •

After placating Talbot and taking a long bath until the water grew cold, Lucien slept soundly. His normally unflappable valet remained distant the next morning. Lucien suspected it had been a short night, as Talbot had been determined to save the boots.

Indeed, they gleamed as though new, and Lucien failed to detect even a whiff of the alley's foul odors.

"Good morning, Talbot."

"My lord. I thought perhaps the puce jacket today." He spoke stiffly, his slender but deceptively strong figure—no more than two inches shorter than his six-foot master—held rigid as well.

"Oh, did you?" Lucien turned to eye him with a raised brow. "I thought I told you to get rid of it. I find the hue offensive."

"It seemed appropriate attire, sir, if you intend to spend time in the alleys of Seven Dials."

"Lighten up, Talbot. That is an order." He spoke casually, but he saw his valet's brief flash of concern. Lucien was on rather friendly terms with his servants, perhaps more so than he should be, and he occasionally had to draw a line. He was no longer amused by Talbot's sulking.

"Would you prefer the green jacket, my lord?" Talbot asked, his tone much improved, even deferential.

"Most assuredly. What did you do with yesterday's clothes?"

"They are being aired, my lord. I have not given up hope."

"Very good. Thank you," he said as Talbot helped him into the chosen jacket. He gave a last tweak to his cravat and shot his cuffs. Before leaving the bedchamber, he gave his valet a faint smile. "I shall attempt to return this jacket in better condition. I am quite fond of it."

• • •

Their timing could not have been better—Lucien halted his curricle outside Whitehall just as Sherbourne was dismounting from his saddle horse. "I doubt if we will be long, Finn, but if the team or Sherbourne's big bay get restless, walk them up the street and back."

"Aye, milord. General looks a mite frisky this morning," he said, watching Sherry's gelding snort at a passing carriage.

"He needs exercise," Sherry said. "I have promised him a jaunt in Hyde Park after this meeting."

Finn grinned. "Ifn he gets too twitchy, I'll remind 'im."

Lucien and Sherry headed into the government building of Whitehall, taking the stairs two at a time. They had been reporting to the Marquess of Rothe for two years now, since their return from spying for England on the Continent. Their official assignment to Wellington's army was over, but both men had been recruited to the Prince Regent's private spy unit, aimed at eliminating domestic infiltration by foreign spies. Their official status was unofficial, but neither Rothe nor Prinny seemed to remember they were no longer under orders each time a new problem arose.

Lord Rothe's outer office was busy as usual—clerks and under-secretaries reading and writing reports and the latest communications from Wellington or others on the war front; the codebreakers in the side office were poring over encoded messages.

Mr. Sloane, Rothe's personal secretary and keeper of the spy unit's files, rose to greet them, pushing his wire rim glasses into place. "Gentlemen, his lordship was just leaving for an appointment."

Wasn't he always? Rothe spent much of his day running back and forth from the Palace or Parliament. "This will not take long," Lucien said.

"Very well. It would not do to keep the Prince Regent waiting."

"Understood."

Sloane tapped on Rothe's door, entered and announced the two men. Rothe looked up. The tall, lean marquess, wearing the elegant gray he preferred—coat, waistcoat, and long trousers—rose from the desk and gestured with one hand. "Do come in, by all means. Do we have confirmation yet?"

Lucien nodded. "Yes, sir. We followed Hensley from White's Club last night, lost him briefly one street over from the Spanish Embassy, and then spotted him leaving Envoy de Leon's rear gate thirty minutes later. I believe that is enough, sir, for you to take it to the top level."

"Yes, by Jove." Rothe sighed with relief. "I am delighted and disappointed at the same time. How could the Spaniards be so careless—particularly after their ambassador was recalled for his disgraceful conduct with Lord Lancaster's daughter just one year ago? I doubt if this is de Leon himself, but someone under his charge must have met with Hensley. I am talking with the Prince Regent shortly on another matter, and I shall inform him of your observations. The matter should be dealt with by the end of the day."

"Excellent, sir. If that is all, Sloane warned us not to keep you long."

Rothe smiled. "It is good he looks out for me, or I might never be on time. Thank you for yet another task well done. I shall be in touch."

The three gentlemen walked down the stairs together, then Rothe strode off toward the palace. Lucien watched him go, thinking how grateful he was that Rothe was the one who must deal with their unpredictable prince. Prinny could be pleasant enough when things went his way, but only a select few dared to take him bad news. Rothe was one of the few, but upon this occasion, the prince would have no reason to direct his displeasure at Whitehall.

"Where are you off to tonight?" Lucien asked Sherry as they approached their horses.

"Boodle's, I think. I'm in the mood for cards, and I like their dealers."

"You could always play Hazard with Mr. Cade's guards," Lucien teased. During a misunderstanding over a woman's death last autumn, Sherry had spent several days hidden in a private suite at Cade's Club, a gentleman's establishment owned by Charles Cade, the Gentleman Thief, London's most elegant crime lord.

"I actually considered it," Sherry said. "For criminal types, they are not bad fellows."

Lucien laughed. "I cannot contradict you, not after they kept you safe—and occupied, without fleecing you completely—when you were on Bow Street's wanted list."

"Let's not talk about that," Sherry said. "It was a dark time for me. Do you want to join me tonight?"

"I cannot. I have an invitation to dine with Lord Walter and Lady Castlebridge."

"Sophia? Is that wise?"

"I believe she wishes to make a point, signaling to the world that the freedom of her widow days are behind her now that she and Castlebridge have wed. Besides, Sophy and I ended our affaire almost three years ago." Except for one near-mistake six months ago, but Lucien and Sophy had agreed it was a moment best forgotten and not spoken of again. "We are merely good friends now, and I hope Castlebridge will allow us to remain so."

"I wouldn't," Sherry said.

Caught by surprise, Lucien lifted a brow. "You would not trust *me*? Or are you referring to just anyone?"

"I might trust you, because I know you well. I also know my Emily, and she has never been your mistress," he said, referring to Miss Emily Selkirk, the young country woman Sherry had been courting for nearly two years, "but I wouldn't care for any man being close enough friends with my wife that he was seeing her alone."

Lucien frowned. Now that he thought about it… "You may have the right of it, Sherry, although that does not seem to be the manner of things in many households. Nonetheless, I shall keep your words in mind. I have no desire to trouble Sophy's marriage. I shall be most circumspect, giving neither Castlebridge nor the gossipmongers reason to take notice."

"Moreover, you wouldn't want such gossip to reach the ears of Lady Anne."

Lucien gave a derisive snort. "I doubt if the latest London on-dits make it to Warwickshire, not unless they are of such magnitude that they make the news sheets."

Sherry lifted a brow. "Have you not heard? Her father is back in Parliament, and Lady Anne is said to be staying near the seaside, not too far from Brighton."

Lucien hid his surprise. He had, of course, heard of Lady Chadley's death near the end of last year, but nothing about the earl or his daughter since then. It was odd his own father had not mentioned Chadley's return to the House of Lords, but perhaps Salcott was cautiously staying out of Lucien's business. Not long ago, the Earl of Salcott and his heir were barely speaking beyond mere civil discourse—it was just as well he'd said nothing. Lucien and Lady Anne were merely friends, and yet he found it strangely unsettling to know she was again so close to London.

• • •

Lucien arrived at the dinner party that night determined to keep his distance from Sophy. He need not have worried for there were forty guests, and Lucien was seated well down the table, next to Julia Castlebridge, the wife of Lord Castlebridge's second cousin. She was a pretty woman in her mid to late twenties, calm and self-assured, with rich dark-brown hair, and a soft, charming laugh. She was an interesting, intelligent dinner companion, and Lucien enjoyed talking with her. Nevertheless, he was mindful to spend equal time conversing with the older spinster seated on his left. She too was an amiable conversationalist, the food was good, and Lucien was most impressed with how Sophy had settled into her new life and hostess duties.

After dinner, music was provided by several of the young ladies, and occasionally a gentleman would join in to sing to the accompaniment of pianoforte or harp. Once again, Sophy had chosen her musicians well, nothing jarred the ears.

He saw Lady Julia Castlebridge sitting by herself and joined her. "Do you not play or sing, Lady Castlebridge?" he asked.

"Heavens, no. They would all leave early if I made the attempt. But you really must call me Julia. All my friends do, and it is much too confusing to have two Lady Castlebridges in the same room."

"Ah, my lady, we are such new friends that I cannot feel it is right to take that liberty. Perhaps we can compromise with Lady Julia."

"If you must. I rather like it." She laughed. "As I was saying, my only artistic ability, if I should be so bold to call it that, is in my watercolors and sketches. It pleases me to dabble about, and others seem to enjoy my efforts…unless they are only giving me Spanish coin."

"What does Sophy say about them?"

The lady in question spoke from behind them. "I say they are wonderful. Julia thinks I love them only because she is family, but that is not true."

Lucien smiled at Lady Julia. "I have known your new cousin-by-marriage for several years, and she offers no false praise. Perhaps one day I shall be able to view your work in an exhibit."

Lady Julia gave a soft laugh. "You give me entirely too much credit, my lord."

"You can see one of them now," Sophy said. "She did a sketch of me one day while we were just talking. I liked it so much I have hung it with our portraits. Come and see."

"You shall make me blush, Sophy," Lady Julia said, but she and Lucien rose and followed their hostess down the hallway to the gallery.

"There," Sophy said pointing to a framed drawing. "Is it not splendid?"

Lucien surveyed the very realistic sketch. "Indeed. This was done in a matter of minutes?"

"No more than twenty," Sophy said.

"Remarkable." The artist had not only caught Sophia's features but her vivacity. "You have an extraordinary talent, Lady Julia."

"Thank you, my lord," she murmured. "I am truly honored."

Sophy gave her cousin a self-satisfied look. "Told you so."

When they returned to the drawing room, Sophy left to attend to other guests, and Lucien chatted with Lady Julia about her drawings another quarter hour before excusing himself. As Sherry had reminded him, he might become a subject of gossip if he showed overly-much attention to any woman, married or not. He joined a group of men talking politics and remained with them until he felt he had stayed long enough to meet social standards of politeness. He excused himself to his host and hostess and departed.

Once outside, Lucien smiled to himself. Sophy had told him this marriage to an older, rather staid gentleman would give her a good life, and he'd had some doubts at the time. No longer. She had clearly embraced her position as Lady Castlebridge with grace and ease.

He looked back at the house and said a silent good-bye to the Widow Stine. They'd had good times together, but she had wished to be married again, had longed for children, and they had amicably parted. He was delighted to see her happy and contented.

Lucien sighed, knowing as heir to the Earldom of Salcott he was expected to marry and produce an heir of his own—but he was not yet ready. He had too much that interested him, too many secret inquires for the Crown yet to do.

He flicked the reins. "It is time for home, Finn. Lord only knows what Rothe will send our way tomorrow."

Chapter Three

Seaford, England, 15 June 1813

Anne paced across the Persian rug of her parlor, the folds of her skirt swishing angrily around her. She glared at the floor, a deep frown lowering her brows. She had just returned from the village, where she'd hoped to follow-up on the body in the cave, and instead she had encountered nothing but suspicion and doubt. Botheration! Oh, everyone was polite to her face, naturally, but they were talking about her—and not very kindly. She's seen the furtive looks, heard the hushed words. She shook her curls, her emotions swaying between anger and frustration.

Of course, she understood Constable Harrison's problem—without a body it was hard to investigate the woman's death—but did he, and especially Justice of the Peace Colby—the pompous popinjay—have to be so patronizing? They did not believe her and had not the good grace to keep their opinions to themselves. She gave an unladylike snort. As though she, or anyone, would make a mistake—or tell a plumper—about finding a dead body.

What would happen to that poor young woman now? Did no one care who she was, where her body was, or why she was dead? Would her murder go unpunished?

Anne dropped onto the window seat, absently smoothing her gray gown with one hand. The expected six months of mourning for a parent had passed, but her loss felt so fresh that Anne had not discarded it entirely. She had lightened her gowns to a sober gray. Her outward appearance might just as well suit her mood. Her gentle mother would wish for her to resume her former social life, yet Anne simply was not ready.

The discovery in the cave was the first thing that had distracted her since last October when she had provided Lord Ware with information that helped solve two murders. That story was one of the last things she had shared with her dying mother. Anne brushed away a tear that trickled down her cheek.

She had to stop this. Maybe another inquiry was just what she needed. If Harrison and Colby would not follow up on the missing body, or at least identify the woman so her family could mourn her, then Anne would.

She stood abruptly and pulled the bell for Jenny. A lady could not go around unescorted, even in the country. Besides, two minds were superior to one, and she could use a partner in her endeavors.

• • •

"But, my lady," Jenny said, frowning when advised of her mistress's plans, "where do we start?"

They were sitting high on the seaside cliffs, looking out over the English Channel. This area had no paths down to the beach—in fact, there wasn't much beach below them. Neither of them wanted a second look at the cave or to be anywhere near it. The recent find was still too vivid.

"I don't exactly have a plan," Lady Anne admitted. "But I know we have to do something."

"Do we not need to know her name or where she is from?"

"Those would be good, yes," Anne conceded. "That is where we shall have to start. I think we should inquire if there is a family in the area with a young daughter with black hair. I would guess her age about seventeen, but she might not be out of the school room yet."

"Would the parents not have told the constable if their child was missing?"

"You would think so, but no one has come forward, so…maybe the family was involved in her death. Until we know more, we must be very careful in asking questions, showing just a casual interest in the young ladies of the area."

"Be discreet, you mean."

"Very. I doubt the community would approve of our inquiry, so I'd rather keep it as quiet as we can. Besides, I don't wish to draw the attention of the killer."

"What if he comes after us?" Jenny asked quietly.

Rather startled by hearing the thought aloud that she'd tried to push away, Anne glanced at her maid's downcast eyes. "Perhaps you should leave the matter to me. I don't want you in danger, and if you are not seen as a threat, you'll be free to watch out for me."

"Oh, no, my lady. I want to help." She smiled at Anne. "We can look out for one each other, and between us we shall find out who the lady is."

"Are you sure? Not if it makes you uncomfortable."

"Well..." Jenny put a finger beside her mouth and gave an impish smile. "I can't really say it is comfortable, but it does give me a little tingle inside. You must let me help."

"Silly goose. Very well. Perhaps we should start at the village market and if that does not yield the information we want, I may have to come out of mourning and make a round of social calls. I know Mother would approve. She was as intrigued by mysteries as I am. But no need to worry about that now. Tomorrow we shall attend the market. I suppose I should check with Cook to see what supplies we need."

"Won't she consider it strange that you want to do the marketing?"

Anne smiled. "Not once I explain how very bored I am." Which would only be the plain truth.

• • •

Anne and Jenny were riding toward Seaford in an open carriage before nine the following morning. After all, Anne thought, as they bounced along the uneven road, everyone knows you have to get to market early to get the best produce. She wore a lavender-gray gown, the most appropriate in her wardrobe to signal she might be ending her official mourning—in the event she had to make those social calls.

It was a mild summer day, sunny but not hot. There had been a shower overnight. Anne closed her eyes and breathed in the light breeze tinged with the scent of the sea. It was wonderful to be doing *something*, even if the marketing was all they accomplished.

She opened her eyes as she heard the sounds of a busy market, the hawkers calling out their wares, the laughter of children playing while their mothers or nannies haggled over prices. "Pull over, Timothy. We shall get out here."

Climbing down, she handed the shopping basket to Jenny, opened her parasol, and they wandered through the stalls and among costermongers' carts, picking up items here and there. By the time the basket got heavy, Timothy had made arrangements for the care of the horses and had joined them.

"Take the basket from Jenny," Anne instructed him. "I think we have everything that cook wanted, now I'd like to go shopping for myself. I saw a material that caught my interest and a matching lavender lace. Oh, and a few other items. And perhaps we should sample the variety of breads and other baked goods making these wonderful smells. Please take the produce home and return to pick us up in an hour or so?"

"Yes, my lady. I'll come find you."

Anne watched him walk away, then turned to Jenny, her eyes sparkling. "Now that our errand is done, let us see what we can learn about our neighbors. I see the local vicar over there." She nodded toward the gentleman dressed in black with two narrow bands attached to the front of his collar, denoting his religious position. "He would be an excellent place to start." She had met Mr. Dodson a few weeks earlier, and she waved to him now.

"Lady Anne," he said, coming to meet her. "How nice to see you out on this fine day."

"It is lovely weather, is it not? We came to do a bit of shopping."

"I don't even have that excuse," he said confidentially. "I am here merely to share a bit of idle chat with friends. How is Lord Chadley?"

"My father was called to London on Parliament business."

"Oh, dear, and you are alone? We must have you to dine, if you would feel comfortable at a very small dinner party, maybe ten or less."

"That would be delightful. I intend to put off my formal mourning soon, and spending time with new friends might make the days more bearable."

"Then we shall do it right away." He beamed at her, a genuine gesture of good will. "I will talk with my lady wife when I get home and we shall get it arranged. Would tomorrow be too soon?"

"I have nothing but time on my hands, Vicar. I would be delighted whenever, so let us allow your wife to pick the date." Anne gave him a warm smile, but in truth she felt rather guilty over his generosity considering her own agenda.

"I am certain she will be honored," he said. "If there is an unforeseen impediment, such as another commitment I have forgotten, I shall send word. Otherwise, shall we say six?"

"Perfect. I shall be there."

"Then I shall run home, confirm with my wife, and see if she needs anything special from the market."

After saying their good-byes, he hurried off at a brisk pace, and Anne continued on, well-satisfied with arrangements. A dinner party would be the perfect place for a newcomer to ask questions about the neighborhood.

A few minutes later, Anne met up with Mrs. Mead, a lady well-known for her well-meant but nosey interest in everyone's business. Anne halted when the woman called to her. "Lady Anne, oh, Lady Anne. Yoohoo." Anne stifled a laugh and put a welcoming smile on her face.

"Mrs. Mead, I did not see you there. How are you today?"

"Very well, my lady, but I hear you had a dreadful fright. Finding a body, and then it vanished. My, my." Mrs. Mead's eyes grew big. "Some say it was the ghost. Did you hear her?"

"We did hear something, but I am rather doubtful it was a ghost. Where did you hear of our discovery?"

"Mrs. Colby. She says there was no body, but she never knows what she is about." Mrs. Mead sniffed.

Anne stifled her annoyance. Not only did Justice Colby doubt her word, but he had recounted the story to his wife.

"Never you mind, my dear. No one will listen to her." Mrs. Mead pursed her lips hesitantly. "If it wasn't a ghost, who or what do you think it was?"

"It was a young woman," Anne said firmly, "but otherwise, I cannot even guess—I don't know the people around Seaford the way you would. A most mysterious affair. Someone has to know the young woman is missing. Can you think of a local girl with long, black hair?"

Mrs. Mead's eyes gleamed with interest, and she tilted her head. "Hmm, black curls, you say. How young?"

"Seventeen, a bit older or younger. She was gently dressed."

"There is the postmaster's daughter, Adeline, but I saw her this morning, so it isn't her. No one else comes to mind, but I shall think on it and maybe ask around, discreetly, of course. If I learn anything, I hope I may call on you."

Although the woman was angling for an invitation that she would not otherwise have gotten, given Anne's mourning status, Anne did not hesitate. She would take any allies she could get.

"Of course, you may. We shall have a nice chat over tea."

They parted only minutes later, Mrs. Mead rushing off to no doubt tell everyone about their conversation. Anne did not care. After all, Mrs. Colby was already bandying her name around town, and Mrs. Mead's blunt inquiries might actually discover something useful.

• • •

Anne was composing a letter the following morning when Mrs. Mead's name was announced. She straightened with quick interest and set down her quill pen. Had the woman already discovered the identity of the missing woman? Anne rose to greet her guest. "Mrs. Mead, how lovely to see you."

"You did say I might call."

"Yes, of course. Come sit with me. I shall ring for tea." Once they were settled with a more-than-adequate tea tray—Cook had outdone herself—Anne asked, "Have you come with news?"

"Not exactly, but I have made a list of all the young ladies around Seaford of the proper age, and I am sorry to say, well, no, that's not right," she stopped, flustered. "What I mean is I am *happy* to say, no one is missing. We get visitors from Brighton, so I wonder if she could have been from there. The butcher's wife thought she saw a young lady with dark hair come through town about three weeks ago, but the carriage didn't stop but a few minutes in front of the inn. She may be of no interest."

"Doubtful, I agree. This woman I saw had not been dead very long."

Mrs. Mead looked shocked. "Are you saying the murder had just occurred? Might her killer have been close by?"

"I certainly hope not. I believe it had been a few hours, and I cannot say exactly it was murder. It could have been an accident, I suppose. I had assumed the constable would sort it all out, but… well, you know what happened. I truly am at a loss."

When Mrs. Mead had finished her tea and three biscuits, she rose to go. "One last thought I had," she said as she gathered her reticule. "Smugglers. They once used that cave, you know, and some say they still do. Maybe she was a lady pirate or the ladybird of a dastardly smuggler."

"I had not considered those possibilities, but I shall give them proper thought." Anne choked back a laugh. Mrs. Mead was a pleasant and an entertaining guest, and Anne had no wish to offend her, but the woman brought up topics that women rarely discussed—such as references to kept women—not unless they were well-acquainted, which Anne and Mrs. Mead were not. When she heard the front door close, Anne could hold it in no longer and laughed aloud. She hadn't heard the sound of her own laughter in many months. If for no other reason, she was grateful to Mrs. Mead for that.

• • •

Anne smiled at the sparkling eyes that stared back at her from her looking-glass. She truly was excited about the vicar's dinner party. Just the idea of getting out felt good, and the thought she might learn something about the missing girl was intriguing. If the butcher's wife remembered some girl from three weeks ago, others might recall a more recent visitor. She ran a final comb through an unruly curl and stood. She was ready.

The moment she was shown into the vicar's drawing room, her hopes plummeted. Mr. and Mrs. Colby were included among the guests. She put on a polite smile but knew this would be a difficult evening.

And she was right. Although the body in the cave—or lack thereof—was never directly mentioned during dinner or afterwards, the Justice of the Peace shot Anne several glances of disapproval, and his wife made a pointed comment about young people telling fanciful stories for attention. The fact that the vicar looked embarrassed at the remark told Anne he understood the implication—as doubtless did everyone present.

Well, she would show them, she thought, raising her chin. If they hoped to dissuade her by their not-so-subtle attitude, they were much mistaken. Long before the final custard was served, she had made up her mind to continue with an inquiry she had been wavering on just that afternoon.

Colby had clearly set out to quash the story, and she had to wonder why. Was it a matter of male arrogance—having taken a stand against her, he was determined to be correct? Or did he have other, more sinister, reasons to conceal the woman's death? Either way, Anne was going to find out.

And she knew just what to do. She had feared there would be no suitable occasion for contact again, but she needed expert help from an old friend. A smile spread across her lips as she sat down to write to a certain aristocratic secret agent of her acquaintance.

Chapter Four

London, 17 June 1813

Lucien stood on the side of the road with a group of gentlemen acquaintances, watching the approaching curricles driven by two young bucks. The fast-turning wheels were throwing up clouds of dust. Lucien wasn't cheering the racers on as avidly as others were doing, because he hadn't registered a bet. Swinton should be the winner—he had the superior horses—but he was too heavy handed on the reins. As far as Lucien was concerned, the race's outcome was never in doubt, and a sure wager was hardly sporting. As the curricles swept by the finish line, he bushed the dust from his hat and shook his head. Swinton was behind by two lengths.

"How could he lose?" Lord Buxton nudged Lucien. "I have half a mind to buy those chestnuts from him."

"I wouldn't," Lucien said. "He has likely ruined their mouths with his clumsy handling. Swinton is a fine fellow, but he is no horseman."

"I suppose you're right. Devilish shame." Buxton shrugged, the heat of the day causing him to tug at the cravat around his neck. "Shall we repair to Tattersall's for a pint or two?" he asked, including the entire group.

"Or three or four?" another man said with a half-hearted groan. "I lost forty quid."

"Count me out," Lucien said. "I have someplace I have to be."

"Just one round?" Buxton coaxed.

"Enjoy yourselves. Sorry, but it will have to be another day for me."

He walked away as his companions headed down the street looking for their grooms tending riding horses or carriages and lamenting lost bets or reveling in their wins. In truth, no one took either win or loss seriously, as such bets were common among the sporting crowd. Lucien used to be among them. He continued to enjoy a good horse race, of course, and other sporting events, but the betting held little interest—not since his years of spying on the Continent. War had changed him. He took a harder, more serious look at the world than he once had.

He found his red-headed groom Finn waiting with his team of grays, leapt into the curricle, and turned the small, open carriage toward Whitehall. Lord Rothe had sent a message that he needed to see him. Since Sherbourne was in the country visiting his family and Emily Selkirk, whatever Rothe wanted, Lucien would be on his own with this assignment for the next few days.

He glanced at his pocket watch as he climbed the stairs of Whitehall. It was nearly two, the appointed time. He nodded at Mr. Sloane, and the Marquess's secretary gestured for him to go through into Rothe's private office.

Rothe sat behind his desk and motioned Lucien to a seat. "Would you close the door first? What I am going to tell you must remain within these walls."

"Certainly." After closing the door, Lucien turned back with an eyebrow quirked, wondering what required such extra precaution in an office that rarely dealt with anything but secrets. "Something gone awry, sir?"

"Sit, sit." The head of the Prince Regent's private spy unit tapped his fingers on the desk. "It's this Spanish problem again. Not as simple as we hoped. Envoy de Leon wasted no time in finding the traitor in his household. Indeed, his secretary broke down in tears under questioning and confessed all."

"Surely that is a good thing," Lucien said, when Rothe paused.

"Yes, of course, but Pasqual Hidalgo was not a willing participant in passing secrets to Hensley. He was forced to comply. His only child, a daughter, Rosa Maria Hidalgo—only seventeen—was abducted a month ago to compel his obedience."

"Good lord." Lucien leaned forward. "Does he know where she is being held?"

"No, nor does he know by whom. Hensley is an intermediary to other traitors that Hidalgo has never met."

"And if we arrest Hensley, she might be killed…if she is alive even now," Lucien said, stating the logical conclusion.

"Precisely." Rothe ran a hand through his silver-streaked hair, an unaccustomed sign of stress.

"Has he demanded proof she is alive?"

Rothe shook his head. "He is terrified—afraid to ask for anything. I don't believe he will do so, even if we pressure him."

"What are the conditions for her safe return?"

"Keep spying. Hensley has only told him what will happen if he does not do as they say or if he tells anyone."

"A tough situation," Lucien mused. "If we cannot question Hensley, and Hidalgo is afraid to ask him anything, where the devil do we start?"

Rothe looked at him from lowered brows. "*You* shall have to sort that out. We are replacing Hidalgo's footman with one of our men, whom we are calling Jose. He may turn up something, but his presence is more for Hidalgo's safety than a genuine expectation he'll gain useful information. He has been instructed to keep his ears open and that you may reach out to him from time to time."

"I shall not hesitate to do so."

"When does Sherbourne return to town?"

"Late on Sunday or Monday."

"He is at his family's country house?" When Lucien nodded, Rothe said, "I shall send a courier, informing him he is needed. I want both of you on this."

"Could you belay that a day? He hasn't been home in weeks, and family wasn't the only reason for this trip. He planned to visit Miss Emily Selkirk."

"Tomorrow then." Rothe's expression lightened for a moment. "Why does he not just marry the girl?"

"If I'm not mistaken, his work for this office holds him back. It allows scant time for family life."

"You need not tell me. I have a most indulgent wife."

"You do, sir," Lucien said with a smile, picturing the gentle and very wise lady with warm hazel eyes. "I should be off. As Oscar Hensley is the only name we have, I intend to examine his circle of friends and associates. Perhaps one of them has an obvious reason for espionage or kidnapping. The fastest path to finding Señorita Hidalgo is to identify those who have taken her."

• • •

For the next twenty-four hours, Lucien haunted Hensley's footsteps and made discreet inquires at the gentlemen's clubs regarding his acquaintances. He even sent a note to Sophia Castlebridge—his friend and former mistress—seeking any gossip she might have heard about Hensley. Prior to her marriage, she had been his best source for the latest on-dits, and he assumed her nuptials had not changed her entirely. Mindful of Sherry's warning, he had considered whether Castlebridge might object to his wife receiving notes from a bachelor, but it was not unheard of and surely better than a visit to the house. He kept the letter brief and quite circumspect.

Although his other efforts had not yet revealed Hensley's conspirators, Lucien had forwarded the names of three associates, two of them Hensley's brothers-in-law, to the War Office for further scrutiny. So far Rothe's clerks had turned up nothing suspicious in their backgrounds.

Lucien had a very different plan in mind for today. In order to question Hensley's neighbors and keep watch on the house, he could move around more effectively—and discreetly—if we wasn't Viscount Ware.

He stepped before the looking-glass and studied his image—ragged brown laborer's jacket, long baggy trousers, and scuffed shoes. "What do you think, Talbot? Can I pass as a peddler?" He tousled his hair as though it had not been brushed in days, and rubbed a hand across the stubble on his unshaven chin.

"I think you will do, my lord. At least these garments do not have an odor like others you have worn on similar occasions."

"Are they too fresh? That could be a drawback," Lucien said, smelling one sleeve. "Perhaps a bit of dirt or dung might be appropriate."

"Certainly not dung, my lord. Not if you expect to sell that cartload of fruit. What Cook will do with it if you bring it all home, I cannot imagine. I dare say Robert must have emptied the market."

"He did just as instructed. In order to hang around Hensley's street long enough to see who comes and goes, I need to have sufficient produce in the event his neighbors are in a buying mood." While house-to-house peddlers were not as prevalent in London as in the country, they appeared from time to time in all parts of town. He was confident his presence would not raise unusual concern or suspicion.

Lucien completed his disguise with a floppy cap, not unlike the one Finn habitually wore. He smiled at himself in the mirror. If his tailor was correct that apparel made the man, he had become a rather roguish-looking fellow.

With Finn's help, he transported the pushcart by wagon, and they unloaded it several streets from Hensley's residence.

"Wish me good fortune," Lucien said, as he took the handles of the overladen cart. "If you fail to hear from me before four, meet me here around that time."

"Aye, milord. I be here." Finn looked his master over again, shook his head, and grinned. "Have a good day, gov. Don't get picked up by the watch."

Lucien returned a smile. "I shall hope to avoid that. Well, I'm off." He pushed the cart down the street, its wheels squeaking in time with his steps. To his surprise, he was hailed twice and had made his first sales before he reached the street where Hensley lived. At this rate, he might be out of goods too soon.

But Meadow Lane residents proved to be more resistant to peddlers knocking on their door. He sold nothing in the first half hour on the street, then some children ran up to the cart, wanting to buy apples. His business picked up after that, and half his load was gone an hour later.

While he was having some success as a hawker, he was having none with his surveillance of Hensley's home or with his subtle questions. Hensley appeared to keep to himself. He was unmarried, his wife having died some years ago, and his only daughter was staying with an aunt who was introducing her to society. As a consequence, the house received none of the morning calls one might otherwise expect. Lucien saw two food deliveries to the rear entrance, but neither fellow remained long. If they were bringing messages hidden among the vegetables, Lucien had no way of knowing, but no one acted the least bit stealthy or ill-at-ease.

Three o'clock came and went. By half three Lucien's cart was out of fruit. He walked slowly, allowing his body to slump as though tired from a long day. He turned at the end of the street and made his way back for one last sweep of the area...and his eyes sharpened as a closed carriage pulled up and stopped in front of the Hensley residence.

A footman in dark gray livery climbed down from beside the coachman and knocked. The door was opened; the footman spoke briefly to someone inside and then returned to the carriage. Lucien watched every movement carefully, but he saw no letter or package. Whatever information had been exchanged, it had been during that conversation.

As the carriage pulled away, Lucien peered at it from under his lowered cap in hopes of glimpsing the person inside, but the curtain was pulled. He was fairly sure he saw a man's hand and shirt cuff brush the curtain but nothing more. The carriage had no crest or shield, only a small symbol—that resembled a bird with large wings—on the lower corner of the door.

Lucien frowned. No carriage makers known to him used such a mark. If it was part of a coat of arms, it would typically not be shown alone—an oddity, but unlikely to be traceable to a particular person or family. A closer look at the symbol would have been nice, but he thought he would recognize it again. He sighed and kept his fruit cart moving.

Small pickings for the time he'd spent, but surveillance was like that—sometimes you got little or nothing at all.

• • •

Lucien leapt down from the wagon used to transport the produce cart and watched Finn drive away to return the borrowed conveyances. He used the rear entrance of his Hays Mews residence to avoid arousing neighborhood gossip. Such a figure as he presented would never be allowed in the front entrance, and a man with his "hobbies" would be unwise to draw attention to any of his activities.

He went up the back servants' stairs and slipped into his bedchamber, submitting himself to Talbot's skills. He had barely been transformed into a clean-shaven gentleman again when his butler tapped on the door and entered.

"Yes, Hughes?"

"A message, my lord. It just arrived."

"Thank you." Recognizing Sophia's writing, Lucien opened the letter immediately. Reading quickly, he smiled at her mild rebuke that he had chosen to send a message rather than pay a call.

Castlebridge is not a jealous man, she wrote. *He knows of our friendship, and it was he who insisted you should be invited to dinner the other night. I do not fear that occasional visits would cause him worry.*

A very understanding man, Lucien thought. He would be sure not to test that understanding too often.

He returned to the letter. According to Sophy, Hensley was a private man—which Lucien already knew—and being of the middle class, he rarely mingled with High Society. Consequently, Sophy had heard nothing of unpaid debts, ungentlemanly behavior, or illicit affaires. He turned up at an occasional political event—although he kept his opinions to himself—and seldom attended public musicals or balls.

Sorry, Lucien, I wish I could be more help. I assume this is another of your clandestine inquires. I wish you the best of fortune.

Yours in friendship, Sophia Castlebridge

By the by, I am truly happy in my marriage. Only one thing would make me more so, and I hope to have news on that soon.

A child. She had spoken often of her desire for children, and he very much hoped her wishes would be granted. He dashed off a brief thank you, expressing his pleasure in hearing the marriage suited her, and gave it to Hughes.

Returning to his desk, he pondered if he had learned anything of value that day. According to Sophy, looking for Hensley or his friends at social events where gentlemen of titled families gathered would be wasted time. So, what did the middle class do if they had no socially upward aspirations? Many were business owners, which accounted for the daytime, but what about their evenings? Surely Hensley did not stay home all the time. Did he frequent a favored pub? Was there a lady friend?

Lucien rubbed his chin in thought. Sophy had said there was one place Hensley crossed paths with the upper class—political events. Attending those might be worthwhile, or better yet, talking with Salcott. His father, the Earl of Salcott, was active and highly respected in the House of Lords, consulted by and with both the Prime Minister and the Prince Regent, and he rarely missed a political event.

Rising with a smile, Lucien wondered if the earl was dining at home that night. Perhaps he might invite his heir for dinner. Salcott's chef was amazingly skilled.

• • •

The Earl of Salcott expressed his delight in Lucien's arrival and, not needing the slightest hint, invited him to stay and dine.

"My butler tells me we are to have pigeon, venison, and most importantly, cherry tarts, which I believe are a favorite of yours."

"How could I resist?" Lucien said. "I confess I hoped you would ask."

"Never doubt it." Salcott gave him a questioning look. "Is this a social call?"

"Not entirely. I am working on a matter that involves a political hanger-on named Oscar Hensley. That discussion can wait, however. I am eager for the latest word from Sussex—and from Parliament. Is this session ever going to end?"

That launched them into a discussion of the current political climate that lasted throughout a very pleasant meal. Salcott offered his opinion that the disagreements in Parliament over a handful of proposed laws might keep it in session well into August.

It wasn't until they were lingering over a last glass of wine, that Salcott brought up Hensley's name again. "Now, tell me, what is this about Oscar Hensley? A rather dull fellow by all accounts."

"Not as dull as he seems. Not to mince words, the man is a traitor and involved in the abduction of a young woman. Rothe has tried to keep the situation quiet—"

"Is this about Rosa Hidalgo?"

"How did you know?" Lucien asked, rather alarmed that word of the abduction had spread.

"From the Prime Minister. These things have a way of getting around, although I doubt it is common gossip. Hidalgo does not often mingle in society, and I have heard no mention elsewhere."

Lucien frowned in concern. "Nonetheless, any spread of information could alert the kidnappers and lessen our chances of recovering her alive." He sighed heavily. "It cannot be helped. I shall have to work swiftly in hopes of staying ahead of the gossip. Have you met Hensley at political events? Does he have particular friends or associates?"

"Frankly, I have barely noticed him. The Prime Minister did not know the other names involved in the abduction, so I have had no reason to give him any thought. Now that I do, I can say with surety I have never been introduced to him. He has been pointed out as a man of letters, all rather vague, as I recall."

"Hanging about for bits of information as any good spy might do," Lucien muttered. "He doesn't sound like a mere intermediary.

Unless he was there to meet his contact, to pass on information or receive instructions. Please think, sir, can you name *anyone* with whom he has been seen talking?"

Salcott slowly shook his head. "I recall no one. I shall pay greater attention in the future. In fact, there is such an event tomorrow night. If Hensley makes an appearance, I shall take note and send word of my observations."

"Greatly appreciated, sir. Oh, one other thing before we leave the topic—have you seen a carriage with a bird with large wings on the door, an eagle, perhaps? A very small symbol in the bottom right corner."

Salcott's brows narrowed in thought. "Not a family crest?"

"No, and nothing else identified the carriage's owner. The coach stopped at Hensley's row house. A footman in gray livery went to the door, spoke briefly, and they left without the passenger descending. It may be unimportant, but I am interested in who it was."

"Gray livery is common among those hired by the day or hour," Salcott mused. "But not often used by the upper class unless combined with another color. Could be foreigners or landed gentry, I suppose. The eagle symbol sounds like a mere affectation."

"Well, no mind," Lucien said. "What have you heard from the Dowager? Does she remain happy with Cousin Cora?"

Salcott chuckled. "They have become quite good companions. With them and Mother's lady's maid Hester, they are a formidable threesome. If I had good sense, I might dread to go home."

"Then grandmama is going into society again?"

"They are so busy I rarely see them when I am home except at dinner, but rest easy, she is her old self again."

As it had been several weeks since Lucien and his father had spent an evening together, they talked for another hour over a good port before Lucien excused himself.

"I have inquiries I must do tomorrow, so I should get home," he said rising from his seat at the table. "Sherry should be back after his visit to the country, and I shall be glad to have his help. Thank you for the fine dinner and conversation."

Salcott stood and laid a hand on his son's shoulder. "We should do this more often."

"That would be a pleasure, sir." Lucien smiled to himself when he realized that after all their years of estrangement, he meant it.

Chapter Five

London, evening 18 June 1813

"Any messages?" Lucien asked when he arrived home and handed Hughes his hat.

"Nothing that will not wait, my lord. Sherbourne is in the study."

"I had not thought to hear from him until morning."

Lucien bounded up the stairs and found his fellow agent dozing in a chair before an open window. "Wake up, sluggard. I am the one who has been doing all the work."

"I was told you were at dinner," Sherry muttered, straightening with a yawn.

"Can I not eat and work too? As a matter of fact, I was probing Salcott's memory."

"So, what's going on? Emily was not best pleased with my leaving so soon."

Lucien raised a brow. "She will have to get used to it."

"Yes, I know. We have discussed it. It remains an issue." Sherry twisted his head from side to side, loosening the tense muscles, and stood, going to the sideboard. "May I?" he asked, picking up the brandy decanter.

"Since when do you need to ask? Pour two." Lucien collected one of the drinks, and the two men returned to the chairs near the window, taking advantage of a slight breeze.

"Well, what is it this time?" Sherry asked. "Rothe's note said it was urgent."

"The Spanish traitor working with Hensley was a clerk in the embassy, a father whose daughter was abducted over a month ago to force him to work for the French."

Sherry's brows shot up. "The devil you say. And Hensley won't give her up?"

"He is only a lackey. We can't go near him, for fear of getting her killed. Hidalgo—the clerk involved—was ordered to tell no one."

"Are you certain she is alive?"

Lucien shook his head. "The kidnappers have given up nothing."

Sherry swore under his breath. "I don't like that."

"Nor do I, but we must guide our actions as though she is alive." Lucien went over what little they knew and the results of his surveillance.

"Why doesn't Whitehall have more on this fellow's background?"

Lucien shrugged. "He is reclusive. Maybe naturally so and recruited for that very reason, or he is exceptionally good at hiding his secret life. My wager is on the former."

"Are you certain he is not the French agent behind it all?"

"Doubtful. He does not appear to have the wits for it."

"Or he is too clever by far."

Lucien shrugged again. "Yes. I concede the possibility."

"Well..." Sherry stood and set his empty glass on the sideboard before giving Lucien a cocky grin. "It is a good thing I have returned to sort this out for you, but even a man of genius needs sleep. I'll see you in the morning."

"If you can make it by nine, we shall feed you breakfast."

"Capital. I love your cook's plum cake."

• • •

19 June 1813

While Lucien was tying his cravat the following morning, Hughes tapped on his bedchamber door, and at Lucien's bidding, he stepped inside.

"A letter for you, my lord."

Lucien frowned. "Is it from Whitehall?"

"No, my lord."

"Just put it in the hall then. I shall see to it later."

"Beg pardon, sir, but I thought you might want to read it now."

Lucien turned away from the looking glass to gaze at his butler. "What is it, Hughes?"

Hughes held out the letter so that Lucien could see the handwriting.

Lady Anne.

Lucien took it without comment then dismissed both Hughes and Talbot. "Thank you, Hughes. Talbot, I believe I can handle it from here."

"Very good, my lord." Both men exited into the hallway, and Lucien pictured them exchanging pointed looks or even whispered words. Servants were all too inquisitive…and perceptive.

His own curiosity was certainly piqued. He had not anticipated hearing from her again. It was not the custom for unmarried ladies to correspond with bachelors, so it must be something important that had prompted her to write. Or something was very wrong.

He broke the seal and unfolded the letter.

Dear Lord Ware,

I beg pardon for my forwardness in writing to you, but I have a most perplexing problem and need your guidance.

His brows shot up, and he read on. She explained her presence in Seaford, the discovery of a young woman's body in a cave, its disappearance, and that the local authorities did not believe she (and Jenny) had seen anything or were somehow mistaken.

I am dismayed by their dismissal of my concerns, attributed to female hysteria, no doubt, but more so for the woman's loved ones who must wonder where she is. I cannot but be reminded of Lucy Drayton's family going so long without knowing her fate. I have attempted to discover the young lady's name on my own, but without success. The local Justice of the Peace has put it about that there was no body, and so, my inquiry is not well received. I cannot fathom what to do next, but I know something must be done. I am hopeful you can advise me.

As ever, your friend,

Anne Elizabeth Ashburn

Lucien read the letter twice before putting it down. What a strange series of events. He did not consider for a moment that Lady Anne had mistaken what she saw, but why would the body disappear? Only one explanation came to mind—someone did not want her identified. Of course, there could be a dozen reasons for that, but it was an uncanny coincidence that Anne should find a young woman when he was looking for one.

He smoothed the perpetually errant lock of hair off his forehead, and frowned at the open letter on his desk. He wished she had described the body, then he might dispel this nagging feeling he had.

"Hey, Lucien. Have you forgotten you promised me breakfast?" Sherry's voice was accompanied by his footsteps clearly taking the stairs two at a time.

Lucien stuck his head out the door. "In a moment. Something has come up."

"What could be more important at this early hour than eating?"

"This." Lucien retrieved the letter and shoved it in Sherry's hands. "Read it, and tell me what you think."

Sherry looked perplexed, then his brow cleared. "Ah, Lady Anne. Leave it to a woman to disrupt a fellow's day. What has she said to trouble you?"

"I am not troubled, not exactly. Just read it."

Sherry lifted a shoulder. "Yes, my lord. Anything to get you down to breakfast." A few seconds later, he muttered, "Egad, she has found another body?" He continued reading, his expression changing the farther he went, from a frown to a grin—which Lucien assumed was in response to Lady Anne's inquires—and then becoming thoughtful. He looked up, his gaze meeting Lucien's. "You're wondering if it could be Rosa Hidalgo?"

"Too far-fetched? It is four hours away."

Sherry nodded. "It seems a poor wager to think so, and yet an unsettling coincidence. Maybe it is because we know Lady Anne. It is not inconceivable she would stumble into another of our inquires." He peered at Lucien, expectantly. "*Someone* should go and find out for sure."

Lucien pulled out his pocket watch. "I could be there by early afternoon and back here sometime tomorrow—unless our suspicions are founded. If I'm delayed longer, I shall send word."

"Tell me you are not leaving before they serve breakfast."

"Of course not." Lucien clapped Sherry on the back. "I hear Cook has made her plum cake just for you."

Chapter Six

Seaford, 19 June 1813

An hour later, Lucien was on the Brighton Road, while Sherry took over the search for a coach with an eagle on the door and a driver wearing gray livery. The weather was good, the road dry, and Lucien sprang his team of bays, his fastest and strongest distance-goers. With luck, he would make Brighton in four hours or less, and Seaford in five, beating the fast-moving mail coaches by nearly an hour.

Refusing to dwell on the pleasure of seeing Lady Anne again, he kept running her letter over in his head. Dealing with the constabulary and local authorities in Seaford could prove a problem. They had already discounted the word of the daughter of an earl… although he suspected a son would have received more deference. Whatever the situation, he would have to be circumspect and not use Whitehall for leverage, not unless the body had nothing to do with Rosa Hidalgo.

Less than five hours later, he arrived at the Clifftop Inn in Seaford, bespoke a room for the night, and sent Finn to stable his bays. After hiring a fresh team for the curricle, he asked the proprietor where he might find Lady Anne Ashburn, and as expected, the proprietor knew her and supplied directions to the manor just outside the village.

Within minutes, the butler at a modest-sized but elegant home announced Lucien's arrival to the mistress of the house. Lucien entered the front parlor to find Lady Anne, demure in a dark gray-blue gown denoting her half-mourning. It did not diminish her beauty. Indeed, the dark gown set off her fair hair and cornflower blue eyes.

"My lord." Blushing in evident surprise, Lady Anne rose, setting her sewing basket aside. "An unexpected pleasure." She came toward him with a warm smile. "I beg your pardon if my letter has caused you to make what I am convinced is an inconvenient journey. Nonetheless, I am delighted to see you."

"It is my pleasure, and no inconvenience at all, my lady. I would have come if only to see you, and how could I ignore such an intriguing story?" He gave her an amused look. "I do believe this is my first inquiry of a vanishing corpse."

"You may find it amusing, my lord, but I assure you it has not been so for me." Despite her chastising words, she smiled at him, a sure sign he was not the source of her annoyance. Her smile faded as she went on. "The local authorities have been most disobliging."

"I gathered as much from your letter. Shall we be seated, and you can tell me all about it?"

"Yes, of course, but first I shall order tea. You must be peckish after the long drive."

"Hardly that," he laughed. "But tea would be most welcome. My journey was not as lengthy as you might think. The bays made very good time."

"Tell me," she said, turning with a playful smile that showed her dimple. "I have heard the record to Brighton is three forty-five. Did you do better?"

"By five minutes. The jaunt to Seaford was another fifty minutes. The Brighton run was not a wager, however, and will not be recorded in the betting books."

"Nonetheless, worthy of remark. It is good to speak of something to lift the spirits." She stepped into the hall to order tea and was back in a moment. She crossed the room to a seat by the window, and Lucien took a chair near her.

"I am sorry, my lady, for your recent loss. The last few days can only have added to your distress," he said gently.

"Thank you. I received your lovely note last November. I am doing better every day, and the situation with the Seaford authorities is more frustrating than distressful. But let us not dwell on all that. Have you come to counsel me on how I should proceed with my inquiry?"

"Tell me more about it first, and perhaps we could visit the cave."

"As you like. Is there something in particular you wish to know, or should I start from the beginning?"

"From the beginning, if you do not mind."

"Oh, not at all. Jenny and I had gone for a walk on the beach. She had heard stories of the ghost of the Singing Cave, and I was curious to go there."

"What stories?" he interrupted.

She told him both versions, but as they were long-standing local legends, Lucien dismissed them as unlikely to be related to the body in the cave.

"It is amazing how these stories persist," he said.

"And are believed," Anne added. "I was much intrigued to hear a singing cave for myself."

"And did it sing for you?"

"It did. That is what frightened Jenny so, but we have jumped ahead in the story."

"My fault entirely. Please go on."

Her tale was delayed further when Jenny entered with the tea tray and set it on the table next to Lady Anne.

"Shall I stay, my lady?" she asked, giving a pointed look at Lucien.

"Never you mind, Jenny. The door is open, and you may sit in the hallway."

"Yes, my lady. I shall be close by." She gave Lucien a last look as though to remind him of his manners. He gave her an inscrutable smile in return.

Giving no sign she heard the loud and distinct noises of Jenny placing a chair just outside the parlor door, Lady Anne filled their cups and offered him the plate of biscuits. She finally settled back to continue her story. "When we got to the cave entrance, a dark hole in the cliff, we couldn't hear any sounds from it. I noticed an oil lantern and flint box beside the opening, suggesting the cave was used by someone. I assumed it was local children, although Jenny spoke of smugglers and pirates. In any event, we lit the lantern, found a small empty chamber and then a second chamber. That is where we saw the woman, a girl really, in the middle of the floor." Anne paused as though gathering her thoughts. "I saw her bare ankles first, and then… and then I knew it was a dead body."

Lucien leaned forward, speaking gently. "I know this is not easy, my lady. Take your time, and if you can, describe her for me."

She gave a faint smile. "Of course, I can. You know I forget nothing. Not such a blessing this time when I cannot get her out of my mind." She sighed and began. "She was young and pretty, sixteen, seventeen. I could not see all of her face—it was partially covered by her black hair, but she was fair-skinned with fine features. Her eyes were closed. The blue gown was well-made but not the most expensive. I judged her to be gently bred to the gentry or upper middle class."

Lucien's heart sank at the description. Nothing he'd heard ruled out the possibility it was Rosa Hidalgo—and there was a very good reason the spies behind this would want her death concealed. The father's continued cooperation would depend on his belief his daughter was alive.

"As for her injuries," Lady Anne went on, clearly anxious to finish, "I saw blood on her lower chest, and bruises on her cheek and neck."

"Are you certain she was dead? Could she have been unconscious and recovered enough—"

Anne shook her head. "I touched her to be sure. She was cold." She spoke dispassionately, but he could see the effort it took. "That is when I saw the blood on the front of her gown…and we left to fetch the constable."

"Had she been stabbed or shot?"

Anne gave a barely perceptible wince. "I cannot say. I saw no weapon, nor the actual wound, just the blood. I could not bring myself to touch her again."

"I understand." Lucien wanted to take her hands and reassure her but such liberty would be inappropriate. Instead, he distracted her by asking for more tea.

"Forgive me, my lord. I fear I am not being a very good hostess."

"Nonsense, my dear. I am the one who should apologize. I merely asked for tea in hopes of removing the sadness from your face. It was unkind of me to ask you to relive those dreadful minutes in the cave."

"Oh, no, sir. I do not mean to be missish—it is just...she was so very young. And alone."

He did take her hands this time. "Never missish, my lady. You are the most intrepid woman I know, and we shall sort this out together." He debated whether to tell her about Señorita Hidalgo, but decided it was too soon. There was no evidence of the body's identity, only his suspicion. He released her hands and stood, going to the window. "I need to see the cave, but I won't ask you to go again. Is there someone who can show me the way?"

"I suppose there are many, but no one can show you where she was or describe exactly what I saw that day. Well, Jenny could, but she does not have my eye for details, and the ghost stories have upset her. I doubt if she would go back—and certainly not without me, so what would be the purpose of distressing her? I shall go with you."

He turned with a frown. "Are you certain? It may be difficult to see it again."

"That is for me to manage, my lord. Jenny can accompany us to the cave entrance, and I shall rely on you to keep us safe. It has to be done, and I am the best person to do it."

"Much as I would like to deny what you say, I cannot, so let us go without delay. I do not wish to lose the daylight."

Lady Anne stood. "Allow me to change into more suitable attire. I shall do so with haste."

True to her words, no more than fifteen minutes passed before Lady Anne returned with Jenny. Both women wore unadorned gowns and sturdy boots. Even such plain attire could not hide Lady

Anne's charm, and Lucien realized his earlier attraction to her had not played out. That did not mean she felt the same, and he tried not to look overly pleased at the sight of her.

"I drove my curricle, but I left Finn at the inn with my horses. We should all be able to squeeze on board for such a short trip...if you do not object."

Anne eyed the small carriage as they stepped outside. "There is sufficient room for three of us, do you not agree, Jenny?"

"Yes, ma'am," her maid replied with a grin. "I have wanted to ride in a curricle for the longest time—so sporting."

Lady Anne and Lucien exchanged an amused look, and he handed the two women into the carriage. It was a bit crowded with their skirts and Lady Anne's parasol, but they weren't going far, and he did not object to having Lady Anne so close.

• • •

Lucien had never been on the beaches below this region of the cliffs before, and he was surprised they were covered with rock. Walking across it required care, and he offered an arm to both women to avoid anyone twisting an ankle. Once around the cliff point, Lady Anne pointed out the faint path, and they climbed it single file, with Lucien bringing up the rear.

"Oh, dear," Anne called back when she reached the entrance. "The lantern is gone."

Since Lucien had brought a candle and his pocket tinderbox from London in anticipation of visiting the cave, he was not particularly bothered by the news. A lantern would have been more convenient, but its absence was not critical.

"The constable must have taken it," Lady Anne said, as he reached her. "I should have thought to bring one." When he produced the candle and tinderbox, she smiled. "Ah, the tiny tinderbox again." She shot him an amused look, clearly remembering the first time she'd seen it, when she, Lucien, and Sherry were searching a dead man's lodgings in London. "Are you always prepared, my lord?"

"I try to be."

Jenny snickered, and Anne gave her a reproving look. Lucien lit the candle, paying no mind to this exchange between the women.

"Whoever is coming with me, we should go."

Jenny's face paled. "You don't expect me…?"

"No," Lady Anne said. "I already told him you would not be coming."

"I will if you think I should." Jenny straightened. "I am not *that* afraid," she added determinedly.

"Of course not," Anne agreed, "but it is not necessary. We shall return shortly. I shall feel better knowing you are out here to warn us if anyone else should arrive."

"I can do that," Jenny readily agreed. "Take care, my lady."

Lucien smiled at Lady Anne. "Now that is settled, shall we?"

They entered the cave, the first chamber offering nothing of interest, nor did the short tunnel. When they reached the second chamber, he held the candle high where he could see much of the rocky room. It appeared the chamber had been widened by human tools. Stories of smugglers might well be true. He saw a tunnel at the back, which he would explore later.

He turned his gaze to the floor. Scuff marks from boots were obvious, but those were likely left by the constable and others who had come in response to Lady Anne's report.

"Show me where the body was and its position."

Lady gestured to the spot. "She was sort of on her side with her head here and her legs twisted to the right side, her feet pointed toward the cave entrance. Her ankles were showing, and she wore walking shoes."

Lucien studied the floor, crouching to get a closer look. He stood and circled the area, still looking down. What he had expected but didn't see were stains from blood or evidence the floor had been cleaned. He simply could not accept that Lady Anne had been mistaken, therefore, the young victim had been killed elsewhere, bought here until the body was discovered, and then moved again.

Lucien stiffened, realizing what that meant. The murderer had seen Lady Anne and Jenny enter or leave the cave. Perhaps it was fortunate no one had believed them. The killer might try to get rid of witnesses who could attest to the woman's death. Were they still in danger? He would have to deal with that question before he could return to London.

For now, he would stay close to Lady Anne whenever possible and hope that his presence drew the killer's attention to him. In any event, he had to stay until he determined if the dead woman was Rosa Hidalgo.

He frowned looking down at the empty spot on the floor. How long did she lay there before Lady Anne and Jenny came along? The cave's cool temperature would have kept the body fresh longer than usual. Anne had not mentioned noticeable signs of decay, but time of death was important. He had to ask no matter how unpleasant.

"My apologies in advance, my lady. I do not wish to be indelicate, but were there indications the body had been there longer than… say a day?"

Anne hesitated. "She looked fairly normal, except her skin was pale and cold. I have seen dead farm animals and know what you are asking. I did not notice an odor or other changes in the body. Less than a day, I believe."

"Thank you. I am sorry I had to ask."

She gave a single nod. "I know, but I am pleased to help."

If the body was Señorita Hidalgo, she had been kept alive a month before being killed. What would have brought about her death? Did they no longer need her father to spy for them? Had she been a difficult captive, done something to anger them, or was she just too much trouble? Lucien's jaw clenched at the thought of them treating a young life so callously.

"Is the cave different than you first saw it?" he asked. "Anything else missing?"

"No. I have been looking. It is just the same, except the body is gone and there are more scuff marks on the floor. It was otherwise as empty then as it is now."

"Then let us go. Your maid will be wondering what is taking so long."

"Did you not want to see where the tunnels lead?"

"I do, but I would rather get you away from here."

"Why can I not go with you?"

Lucien frowned at her. "Has it occurred to you that whoever removed the body had been watching the cave? He may be watching even now. I don't wish to leave Jenny alone, nor do I fancy having you here if he decides to pay the cave another visit."

"He would not dare with you present." Despite this assertion, her eyes darted to the darkness behind them. "You have your pistol, do you not?"

"I do. Are you getting nervous?"

"Maybe a little bit," she admitted. She didn't mention her own pistol was in her reticule and had been since she'd discovered the body. "I would still like to see the rest of the cave and its tunnels. After all, this is my inquiry. You would know nothing about the body if I had not written to you."

He shook his head. "While I concede your point, my lady, it is not relevant at the moment. I am taking you home and will come back later. Do not bother arguing," he said forestalling the protest that she was barely holding back. "I promise to tell you everything I find."

"You would allow me to come if I were a man."

Lucien sighed. "I believe we have had this argument before. I hope you are not so foolish or stubborn as to go into the caves on your own."

"No, I will not do that, but I dislike being excluded." She turned and marched back toward the entrance but stopped at the edge of the candlelight and looked back. "Well, are we going to leave or not?"

Lucien suppressed a laugh. Despite her annoyance, he was not giving in on this one. It was bad enough she was there now. He could not imagine explaining to her father why he had taken her with him while exploring tunnels and caves used by killers and smugglers.

Chapter Seven

Seaford, 19 June 1813

Lady Anne knew it would be foolhardy for her to be traipsing around an unexplored cave—with or without Lord Ware—but she had no desire to tell him so. On the carriage ride home, she remained silent, and when he left, stating he would be back sometime tomorrow, her response was cool. He could at least have acted as though he had *considered* taking her along.

"It really was too bad of him," she said to Jenny.

"Oh, my lady. He was only thinking of your safety, I'm sure. What if the murderer had come back? Both of you might have been killed."

"Exactly why he should not be going alone," Anne said, her annoyance abruptly turning to concern. "I wish Sherbourne was here. Oh, he could take Constable Harrison." She bit her lip. "Mayhap I should write and suggest it."

"If it makes you feel better, my lady," Jenny said.

"I believe it would. I am rather embarrassed to have taken him from his duties in London. I could not bear it if something happened… Yes, I shall write immediately. Tell Timothy I wish to have a message delivered to the Clifftop Inn."

"I shall tell him," Jenny said. "But I am sure Lord Ware would not have come to Seaford if he did not wish it. I believe he came to see you." With a toss of her head, Jenny walked out of the parlor and closed the door.

Anne stared after her for a moment, then shook her head and went to the desk to write a note. It would not do to harp on the danger, she mused, so she suggested it would be wise for him to enlist someone local, someone who might know his way through the tunnels.

Constable Harrison is at heart a good person, she wrote, *and I am certain he would listen to you. He must know all about the caves, and I beg you will seek his assistance before returning there alone.*

She paused but couldn't resist adding, *Take care, my lord. As you advised me, the murderer may be watching the cave.*

As ever,
Anne Ashburn

• • •

Anne woke early the following day hoping to find a response from Lucien. There was none, and when she had heard nothing by late morning, she sent for Timothy.

"Did Lord Ware say anything when you delivered my note?'

"He wasn't there, my lady. I left it with the innkeeper. He promised to give it to his lordship when he returned."

"Very well. Thank you."

Where could he be? Even if the publican missed him last night, Ware would surely have received her note this morning. She tilted her head with a slight frown. Oh, bother. She had neglected to ask for a reply. Perhaps he recruited the constable, and they were exploring the tunnels at this very moment. She was being impatient—and it would not be the first time.

Determinedly setting her worry aside, she went about her daily activities. Nonetheless, she kept an eye on the time, and by mid-afternoon her fears had resurfaced. If she had not made a promise to Lucien, she might have set out for the cave. Instead, she did the next best thing—she sent Timothy to the inn again.

"If you cannot speak to his lordship directly, look for Finn, his groom, a small man with red hair. He usually knows what his master is about."

"Yes, my lady. I won't come home until I have something to tell you." His emphatic promise made her realize the servants were aware of her growing alarm. She hoped they were not making too much of it. It was only natural for her to feel responsible after bringing him to Seaford.

"Thank you, Timothy. I am sure his lordship has merely been busy."

A half hour passed before she heard voices at the door. Her butler, Timothy, and Finn arrived with everyone trying to talk to her all at once.

"Please, one at a time," she interrupted them. "What has taken place?"

"Master Lucien has gone missin'," Finn blurted. "Sometime last night, and he dint come home yet."

"Are you saying he has been gone all night?"

Finn remembered his cap and snatched it off his head. "Caint say for sure, ma'am. Last saw 'im 'bout ten last night."

"What about his horses?"

"He musta left on foot," Finn said, wringing the cap in his hands. "The horses, they still be in the stables, an' he returned the hires."

Anne tried not to show her growing apprehension. Finn was upset enough for both of them. Had Lucien gone back to Singing Cave? Surely not at night, but where else could he be all these hours? It was in easy walking distance of Seaford.

Merciful heavens. Had something befallen him there? An accident, an attack?

"Somethin' terrible has happened to 'im, my lady."

"We must not think the worst, Finn, but we certainly need to find him," she said maintaining a steady voice much calmer than she felt. "If he has worried us needlessly, I shall be sure to give him a severe scold."

Finn looked doubtful. "Yes, ma'am, but wot kin we do?"

She was relieved his voice had dropped an octave. "We shall start by looking for him at Singing Cave. He wanted to explore the tunnels and may have lost his way."

Having made a decision that was sure to anger Lord Ware if nothing was amiss, she sighed and sent them off to harness the horses to the large coach, then fetch Constable Harrison—and to do it with all haste. She hurried upstairs to change clothes, and sent Jenny to collect lanterns. While she would not break her promise to his lordship, she intended to be waiting in the coach—while others searched Singing Cave and its tunnels.

Nearly an hour passed with Anne fretting and pacing the drawing room before Constable Harrison arrived, an anxious look on his face. "What's this about some London lord being lost or murdered?"

"Viscount Ware," she clarified. "I certainly hope he has not been murdered, but he does appear to be missing, and it is all my fault."

As swiftly as she could, she explained having written to Lord Ware asking for help, his unexpected arrival, and their trip to the cave.

Harrison frowned at her. "You think he might have been in the caves all night looking for the body? He must be lost."

Although she had suggested it herself to calm Finn, she was positive Lucien was not lost. "You would not say that, if you knew his lordship," she said. "I am concerned something worse has happened. And…I would appreciate it if you took me seriously this time."

Harrison seemed taken aback. "What is it you think I should be doing?"

"Go look for him." She took a deep breath to quell her rising temper. "Lord Ware is not one of the idle rich, sir. He served in intelligence for Wellington and would not *get lost*. He has not been seen since last night, and I very much fear he went to Singing Cave to locate the missing body that you do not believe exists. He believed my story, of course, and expressed concern the killer was watching the cave. He may have met up with him."

"I don't know about that," Harrison said, doubtfully. "But the caves can be dangerous, the tunnel path is wet and slippery in places, and there are deep cracks in the floor. Anything might happen…" He rubbed his chin. "I should go back to town, round up some men and lanterns."

"No," Anne insisted, bringing him up short. "We have delayed long enough. I have all the lanterns you need, the use of my coach, and Finn and Timothy will help you search. I shall wait in the carriage if I must, but I do not believe the viscount would want the town involved."

"Why not?"

Lady Anne knew she must be careful what she said, but she had to tell him something. "It is possible somebody local murdered that young woman, and Lord Ware does not wish for the village to know he is investigating. I trust you can hold your tongue."

Harrison stared at her as though absorbing what she'd said. "All right, my lady. I guess I can do that…for now, but if we cannot find him…"

• • •

Anne peered out the carriage window. The men had been gone forever. High on the clifftop, she and Jenny sat in the carriage waiting anxiously for their return. Anne had her pistol in her lap. It made her feel better but only marginally. She stiffened at every strange sound, and she could sense how nervous Jenny was beside her.

The sun had not yet gone down, but it would be dark in another couple of hours, and the cliffs were bound to feel more isolated, more threatening then. Anne stifled a shiver of apprehension and prayed this was over soon.

"Do you think they'll find him, my lady?"

"I hope so, Jenny, because I do not know where else to look."

"Maybe he is back at the inn," Jenny said hopefully.

"He would have let us know. I sent the butler with another message telling him where we were and why."

Jenny wriggled in her seat and sighed. "I guess we just wait some more, my lady."

"Yes, Jenny. There is little else we can do. I'm going to get out and stretch my legs, if you wish to join me." She opened the carriage door and hopped down. Jenny followed, looking warily around.

Anne turned to gaze toward the empty path that led downward. "I am certain they shall return within the hour."

But what news would they bring? As the minutes ticked past, her throat tightened, and she began to pace. Where could he be?

Chapter Eight

Seaford, 20 June 1813

Lucien groaned and opened his eyes. Bloody hell, where was he? His head throbbed, there was a great weight holding him down, and he couldn't see a thing. Was he blind? He furrowed his brow in his efforts to clear his thoughts and suddenly everything flooded back—the shots fired, the rumbling of moving earth, and the cave-in. The tunnels behind Singing Cave had collapsed, burying him in limestone.

How long had he been there. Minutes? Hours? He cautiously freed a hand and brushed the powdered chalk dust from his face, otherwise he lay unmoving, listening for the voices or activities of his attackers. The tunnel was eerily quiet. Had they left, or were they waiting to see if he was alive? And, who were *they*? Had he run afoul of the murderer or stumbled upon something else?

Lucien wiggled his toes, then shifted his legs slightly. Everything seemed to work, and the rocky layer was much lighter than he had first thought. He moved his shoulders and arms, freeing his other hand, and began to shove off the restricting debris. Within minutes, he sat up, shifting and pushing. Bracing himself with one free leg, he toppled the last large chunk and rolled free. He did another quick assessment—no limbs appeared to be fractured, although his chest hurt like the devil.

He rose to a crouch and stopped to listen again. If his assailants were around, they had surely heard him by now. Would they come to finish him off? He waited but heard nothing. He appeared to be alone—suggesting his attackers had not murdered the woman. Such a person or gang would not have left a potential witness behind without being certain he was dead.

Lucien rubbed his head with one hand. It was wet, bloody, he assumed. His head continued to pound, but blood wasn't running down his face. Had he been shot or struck by falling rock? Did it matter? He pulled off his cravat, used it to wipe off the blood, and tossed it aside.

What now? How was he to move around when he could not see? The natural parts of the cave tunnels held obstacles—stalactites, stalagmites, and deep fissure drop-offs. Fortunately, most of the tunnel system was man-made. Those areas he should be able to feel his way through. His greatest threats would be the natural fissures—and whoever had shot at him. He suspected a band of smugglers or shags who looted disabled ships were using the caves. If they were still moving their goods in or out of the tunnels, they'd be back.

He felt around him, first establishing where the nearest wall was, then branching out, searching the ground for his missing lantern and his pistol. The pistol was out of bullets, but he could use it as a bludgeon, if it came to that. The lantern was vital. He had the pocket flint box, and light could get him out of here—unless the head blow had left him truly blind.

He renewed his efforts, moving rock after rock, most of them much larger than what had fallen on him. After an hour or more, he realized the tunnel had collapsed to his right, that he'd been fortunate enough to be at one edge of the cave-in. If he had his directions correct, to returned the way he had come—through Singing Cave—he needed to open enough of the blockage to crawl through or over it.

Lucien leaned against the wall, taking pressure off his ribs and rubbing his right arm that had started to ache. Where was the lantern when the cave-in started? Ah, yes. He had blown the light out when the first shots were fired and set it next to the wall. But which wall? This one or the one across the way? He got up and felt his way ten steps to the left, then counted twenty to the right. To return to his original spot took another ten to the left. No lantern. He squared his back against the wall and walked forward, doing his best to stay in a straight line.

When he reached the far side of the tunnel, he performed the same search counting steps, and, unfortunately, with the same results. The lantern must have been hit by falling rocks and knocked away. Hard to say whether it would work, even if he found it, but Lucien was not one to give up. Keeping one boot touching the wall, he stretched out to search the middle of the passage. It was a slow, tedious job as he moved up and down the wall.

His fingers unexpectedly touched metal, and he shifted closer to get a grip on it—the pistol. Not what he was hoping for, but he tucked it in his pocket and continued to search. When he came up empty over and over, he returned to the large pile blocking the tunnel. The lantern must be underneath.

Lucien sighed and began to move rocks, one at a time, for these were much larger. His ribs and right arm were throbbing constantly now. He flexed his shoulder to ease the pain, only to realize it was stiffening, If he had to move the blockage with one arm, it might take days to get out of here.

So be it. He got back to work, and his persistence was eventually rewarded. He found another metal piece, and this time it was the edge of the oil lantern. He tugged it out, but it felt wet and slippery, and one side was dented. *Devil take it!* Had all the oil drained out?

He retrieved the tinderbox from his pocket and was ready to have a try at lighting the lantern, when he heard a sound and froze. Were those distant voices? He strained to hear and this time he was certain it was voices from the tunnels that went deeper into the cliffs. Had his attackers returned?

He had no ammunition for the pistol and no place to hide. When they reached his location, he'd be caught in the light of their lanterns.

Scrambling to the side of the tunnel, Lucien stacked fist-size rocks beside him. If he could throw even reasonably well with his left arm, he might knock out the lantern or torch they were using, leaving them in the dark. It would at least temporarily even the odds.

He crouched and waited, gripping the first rock, ready to take aim. The voices grew closer, and Lucien frowned. He could have sworn someone had said his name. But no one knew he was in the tunnels, except his attackers. How would they know his name?

A moment later, he was certain he heard his name—and a familiar voice. Was it possible? Was he hallucinating?

When he saw a distant glow of lantern light, he heaved a sigh of relief. He wasn't blind. Then the voice called again, and he was certain it was Finn.

He grinned and called, "Finn? Over here. Just ahead of you."

"By 'gor, gov! We's acomin'."

Lucien heard running feet and seconds later, three bobbing glows of light appeared. Finn arrived out of breath, following by two men Lucien didn't know.

"Milady said you'd be here," Finn gasped. "I feared we wouldna find you."

"I am delighted you did."

"Lord Ware, I'm Constable Harrison," the younger of the other men said sticking out his hand. "What caused this? I've never heard of a cave-in down here."

"It wasn't a natural cave-in. I believe the rock fall was caused by an exchange of pistol shots with a band of smugglers or shags."

Harrison swore under his breath. "Could you identify anyone?"

Before Lucien had a chance to answer, Finn interrupted. "Milord! Are ye bleedin'?" He raised his lantern, shining it in Lucien eyes."

"For Lord's sake, lower that thing," Lucien growled. "My head is already thumping like a drum."

"Sorry, but you *is* bleedin'." Finn's disapproving tone rivaled Talbot's.

"Not much." Lucien turned to the constable. "I stumbled upon a group of men moving boxes and barrels. Looked like smugglers or shags to me, but I did not get a close look at anyone. They obviously didn't welcome the company. I tried to back out, and then the shooting started. The rocks began to fall, and the next thing I knew, I woke to find myself trapped and without a light.

How did you find me? And how did you know there had been a cave-in?"

"Lady Anne sent us to look for you. We came through Singing Cave but had to stop when we ran into a wall of rocks. We knew Lady Anne would insist we try again from the other end, and growing up around here, I just happened to know the location of the other entrance."

Just happened? Not likely. The constable was at least turning a blind eye on the local smuggling, if not actively involved. Since Lucien wasn't there to catch smugglers, he was simply grateful Harrison had known the way.

"Indeed, fortunate." He brushed at the limestone on his jacket and coughed from the fine powder he raised. Stabbing pain shot across his chest. "Can we set aside further discussion until later? I'd like to get the bloody hell out of here."

On the way, Lucien was introduced to Timothy, Lady Anne's groom and temporary footman for the summer. "Most of his lordship's servants went to London with Lord Chadley to set up his residence there," Timothy explained. "Her ladyship will be glad to see you," he added candidly. "She has been mightily worried."

Lucien didn't know what to say to that, but Harrison rescued him by asking, "Did you find any evidence of the dead body?"

"No, but I don't doubt it had been there. I have the advantage of knowing Lady Anne, constable. If she said there was a body, there was a body. I assume she gave you a precise description. Did you honestly think she had imagined it in such detail?"

"Well, I wondered, but Justice Colby was so certain..."

"Yes, I see." Harrison's judgement had been influenced by a man in a position of authority. But why was Colby so disparaging? Had he simply discounted Lady Anne because she was a woman, or for a more sinister reason—covering up a murder or protecting the smuggling trade? At any event, Colby had willingly increased the chances that a young woman's murder would go unsolved. "Your justice of the peace has an odd take on justice."

An awkward silence fell, and the four men walked without speaking for several minutes. As they neared the entrance and Lucien could see the evening sky outside, Harrison muttered. "I guess I didn't do any better, my lord. I let Colby convince me it was nothing, but I knew Lady Anne wasn't a frivolous woman."

"How old are you, constable?"

"Twenty-four, sir. Why do you ask?"

"It's hard to stand against someone older and in authority. You will learn to follow your own instincts."

"I suppose. I appreciate your understanding," Harrison said doubtfully.

"Lady Anne may not be as forgiving."

"I expect not." The young constable's voice was glum.

They had to take the narrow exit one at a time, and this time it was Timothy who followed Ware. "Sir, your jacket is soaked with blood."

"Surely not. I doubt if my head bled that much."

Finn dropped back to take a look. "It's blood fer sure, milord."

"It will have to wait. I am keen to get back to my lodgings," Lucien said, seeing the coach waiting for them. The carriage lanterns were lit, giving off a welcoming glow. It was the best sight he'd seen in a long time.

Then it dawned on him what he was seeing. Lights—at twilight. Egad, he must have been unconscious for hours. Unable to sleep after he'd visited the cave with Lady Anne, he had gotten up and arrived at Singing Cave to explore the tunnels around five, at the very first light of dawn. Judging by the growing darkness, that was a good sixteen or seventeen hours ago.

Then the carriage door swung open, and Lucien forgot all about the passage of time, as Lady Anne emerged.

Blood hell. What was she doing there? And left all alone? He had assumed she was waiting at the manor, not out on the lonely cliffs of the Seven Sisters, so named for the number of remote rolling hills.

Timothy ran forward to give her an assist in getting down, but she did not wait for him.

"My lord, thank heavens, they have found you," she said sweeping across the clifftop. She stopped, took a long look at him, and called over her shoulder, "Jenny, bring me a blanket, please. We would not wish for his lordship to bleed all over the carriage seats."

Chapter Nine

Seaford, 20 June 1813

Although Lord Ware requested to be taken to the inn, Lady Anne was having none of his nonsense. She ignored his protests, stopping in town just long enough to send a street boy for the doctor. When the carriage arrived at her manor, she abided by society's demands and sent Finn and Timothy upstairs with Lord Ware to assist him in stripping off his bloody shirt and jacket, wash the blood out of his hair, and clean the long cut they had discovered on the back of his right shoulder. She tasked Jenny with supplying them with suitable garments from her father's wardrobe, so that his lordship would be sufficiently attired to join them in the front parlor once the doctor had come and gone.

Satisfied she had done all she could for his comfort, Anne ordered a tea tray and sandwiches to be brought to the drawing room, then she entered the room to find Constable Harrison standing at the window with his back to her.

He turned immediately. "My lady, I, um, well, I must beg your pardon. Lord Ware has stated plainly that I have treated you poorly, and I must confess he is not wrong."

Anne arched a brow in surprise. "Very prettily said, constable. Do sit and quit looking as though I might ring a peal over your head. I shall not." As soon as she seated herself, he sat across from her.

"I am most grateful, my lady. While we are waiting, would you mind going over what you saw that first day in the cave? I fear I was not as attentive as I should have been, expecting to view the scene for myself. And, um, as things transpired, I failed to do my duty by following up. I promise to do better this time."

Now that Lord Ware has arrived, she thought with some asperity. But it was the way of things, and she would not hold Harrison to account for all of society's faults—not now that he had made his apology.

Anne went over her discovery of the body again, only interrupting herself when the doctor arrived. After sending him upstairs, she continued talking with Harrison and was gratified to observe he truly was listening with care, even asking her to clarify a few details.

When she finished, he looked amazed. "How can you recall in such detail, my lady? You have a remarkable memory. Have you had any thoughts on who might have done this? Or where and why the body was taken?"

Anne smiled. "Thank you for the compliment. I grant you my ability of recall is somewhat unusual, but it does not lend itself to answering your other questions. Hence my appeal to Lord Ware, who has extensive experience in these matters."

"How did you say he came by such knowledge?"

"The war, I believe," she answered vaguely, afraid she had already said too much.

"Ah, yes, I see. Has *he* come to any conclusions?"

"If so, he has not mentioned them to me. I am hopeful he will join us after the doctor is done with him."

Since the constable appeared serious about pursuing an inquiry this time, Anne shared what little she had learned on her own. Harrison confirmed that none of the local young ladies he knew fit her description of the body. Nor had he received any reports of missing locals. They were speculating on why the murderer had hidden the victim in the cave when they heard the doctor's footsteps on the stairs.

"His lordship will be fine," the doctor declared upon entering the drawing room. "He is a healthy young man, nonetheless, he should rest for a day or two. He is bruised and battered, and the shoulder cut will need to be kept clean. I suspect he has broken ribs, and those bandages should be kept tight. He may be stiff enough to limit his activity, but having had the measure of him, I am doubtful. You need not worry, my lady, he will soon be himself even if he ignores my instructions. If he should take a turn—which I don't expect—or you have other concerns, send for me at any time."

He declined tea or other refreshments, stating he had other calls to make, tipped his hat to Lady Anne, and was out the door.

She looked at Harrison in amusement. "Is he always that brisk?"

"'Fraid so. He's the only doc for miles around. It keeps him too busy to be social 'cept for a pint every now and then."

It wasn't long before Finn and Timothy came downstairs, waved, and left by the back door. Moments later, Lord Ware joined Lady Anne and Harrison in the drawing room.

"I apologize, my lady, for appearing in shirt sleeves and waistcoat. I am somewhat larger than your father, and his jackets do not fit. I would have waited until I retrieved my own garments and was properly attired, but I knew you were eager to hear what landed me in such trouble."

"Indeed, sir. I would have been exceedingly annoyed if you had left without telling us." She smiled and gestured toward the chairs. "Please join us. The constable and I have been discussing the young woman's death. Ah, here is Jenny with a fresh tea tray and more sandwiches."

Lucien's eyes lit up. "Excellent. I am rather famished. It has been a very long day."

"For all of us, my lord. I promised myself I would not scold, but why on earth did you go off to the cave without telling someone?"

"Who was I to tell at five in the morning?" His report of events was rather disjointed until he had devoured three sandwiches and two cups of tea, but he managed to convey his night of broken sleep and his decision to explore the cave tunnels. He finally set his teacup down and sighed.

"Are you perhaps ready for a bit of port or brandy," she asked.

Lucien grinned. "I would not turn down a finger or two of brandy, my lady."

"And you, constable?"

"I'd be most grateful, ma'am. Thank you."

Anne poured their drinks and her own glass of madeira. "Now, that we are properly fortified, please continue, Lord Ware, I believe you had just arrived at the tunnels behind Singing Cave."

"I had been inside no more than a half hour when I heard voices. Although I used greater caution in going forward, the path abruptly turned into a large chamber where two men were moving barrels. There were at least four or five other barrels, several boxes, and the way they were arranged, I am certain there had been more." He took a quick sip of brandy. "I pulled back, but I'd already been spotted, and they fired their pistols at me. As bullets ricocheted off the walls, I scrambled away from the turn. When I heard shouts from the rest of the gang coming, I retreated back down the tunnel, doused my lantern, and returned fire to prove I was armed. I hoped that would be the end of it, but then I heard footsteps coming toward me, and they fired several more shots."

"It is a wonder you were not..." Anne could not say the word and started over. "You were fortunate they were such bad shots."

"Well, it was dark, after all. That's when the tunnel ceiling cracked above me. Rocks started to fall, and I dove backward, and then something heavy—a large chunk, I assume—hit me."

Lucien shrugged, then frowned as though the movement had been painful. Anne was tempted to suggest he lay down and delay further discussion, but she doubted he would welcome her concern. She decided to keep an eye on him and remain silent for the moment.

He picked up the story again. "I woke sometime later...I had no idea how long...covered in rocks and a fine chalk powder. My lantern was gone, so was my pistol. Fortunately, so were the smugglers—or whoever they were."

"Pardon me for asking, but why did they not murder you?" Lady Anne said, clasping her hands tightly in her lap.

"They certainly had plenty of opportunity while I was unconscious. I don't believe that was their intent. I think my sudden appearance startled them and someone panicked. The shots all sounded as though they went into the rock ceiling, leading me to conclude they were extraordinarily poor marksmen, as you suggested, or they were not aiming to kill me."

Constable Harrison had been quiet while Lucien was talking, but he nodded at this last remark. "So, the cave collapse was an accident?" he asked anxiously.

"Let us say it was an unintended consequence."

The constable's face was easy to read, Anne thought. He knows the smugglers. More than likely, they are friends who see this as a harmless activity. If I am right, it puts Harrison in a very awkward position. She shot a glance at Lord Ware. From the speculative look he was giving the constable, she was certain he had drawn the same conclusion. She waited to see what both men would do.

"I have an idea of who might be involved," Harrison said reluctantly. "If you are lodging a formal complaint, Lord Ware, I will bring them before Justice Colby."

Lucien took a moment. "My interest is in a young woman's murder, not local smugglers. I shall not lay formal charges, however, I would like to know if they can shed any light on the murder."

"I'll ask around," Harrison said, obvious relief in his voice. "I believe they will tell me if they know anything."

"While you're chatting with them," Lucien added with a stern look, "it would be wise to warn your friends to take care who they are shooting at in the future."

The constable nodded. "Absolutely, sir."

Thus, it was settled, Anne thought, but they were no closer to identifying the body she'd found or the killer, not unless Harrison was mistaken in his friends. She was keen for the constable to leave now, because she wanted to discuss the inquiry with Lord Ware. When Harrison rose to go, however, Lord Ware stood to follow him.

"I too must take my leave. It is getting late. Thank you for raising the alarm, Lady Anne." Lord Ware bowed over her hand. "I shall return tomorrow, but tonight I am in need of rest. What time may I call upon you?"

"I shall leave that to you, my lord. I am not the one who will be suffering from the bumps and bruises of a rock fall."

"I shall plan on mid-morning." He smiled. "If I am unable to attend you for whatever reason, I shall send word."

• • •

21 June 1813

While Lady Anne awaited his lordship the following morning, she received a letter from her father, posted from London. She wrote to him weekly and was in the habit of telling him everything of interest. Consequently, she had mentioned finding the woman's body, knowing that he would over-react if he heard it from anyone else. She had done her best to reassure him, but the letter in her hands proved she had only been partially successful.

My dearest daughter, I cannot rest easy with you so far away—and on your own—with a murderer free in the community. We had planned for you to come to London in another month, but I am convinced you should come now. I shall be hiring a full staff immediately, and I hope to see you by the end of the week.

Oh, dear, no, she silently protested. Not so soon. Two weeks ago, she would have scurried to pack, eager to get to the city, but now there was a murder to be solved. She simply could not leave yet. Anne pursed her lips in thought. She would have to think of a good reason to delay her departure—the megrims, a sore throat? Either might gain her a few days, but she was not in the habit of lying to her father…omitting things, maybe… well, definitely, but not true lies, particularly over something important. She would write tomorrow, protesting she needed more time, and then hope a good excuse presented itself before he wrote back asking why.

Having settled that in her mind, she smiled when she heard an arrival at the front entrance. His lordship was earlier than expected, she thought, and was surprised when Constable Harrison was announced a moment later.

"I pray I have not come too early, your ladyship," he began, "but I had hoped to give you a report in time to pass it on to Lord Ware."

"Of course, constable. Please sit down and tell me what has occurred."

"Oh, it's nothing, well, it is, but..." He stopped and started over. "I was able to talk with...um, a few villagers this morning, and I am assured no harm was intended to his lordship. They were surprised, was all, and as Lord Ware thought, they were moving a few objects of a somewhat illegal nature."

How can anything be *somewhat* illegal, she wondered. But she nodded and encouraged him to go on.

"I gave them a stern warning, and such an incident won't happen again—at least I hope not. They wanted me to make their apologies."

The *incident* being the pistol shots, not the smuggling, she assumed, but hopefully they would go about their future endeavors with greater care.

"What about the murder?" she asked.

He shrugged. "Nothing. They hadn't been in the tunnels for a couple of weeks, so no one saw the body or anyone hanging 'round Singing Cave. Without the slightest rumor in the village of who she might be, I'm pretty sure she was a stranger to Seaford."

Anne sighed. "That will make it most difficult to identify her. Let us hope Lord Ware has an idea how we may proceed."

"We?" Harrison questioned. "I have agreed to investigate, my lady. You need have no further concern."

"I cannot agree," Anne said as gently as she could. "I hope you will not attempt to exclude me when I have already invested so much time and effort."

Perhaps fortunately for both of them, Viscount Ware was announced at that moment. He entered with a brisk walk and a grin. "Good morning, my lady. Constable Harrison, I had not expected to see you again so soon." He turned back to Anne. "You are indeed keeping country hours. The ladies in town would not yet have shown their faces downstairs." He bowed over her hand, his eyes alight with amusement.

"We country folk do not get home at four in the morning from partying all night," she countered with a laugh. "When I return to London, I too shall become a slugabed."

"Are you returning soon?"

"I had planned to join my father toward the end of summer, but he is alarmed by the murder and has suggested I come right away. We shall see."

He gave her a skeptical look as though he knew full well her father had not merely *suggested* she remove to London, but he did not comment, instead turning to Harrison.

"Have you brought news, constable?"

Harrison repeated what he had told Lady Anne. "Since it is doubtful the woman was from Seaford, we were discussing how difficult it will be to identify her. I confess I have not had a matter such as this before." He gave Lord Ware a hopeful look."

"You may need help from Brighton or London, and I could assist you in expanding the inquiry, but locating the body is the place to start."

"I can gather mates and neighbors for a search."

"Can you?" Anne asked skeptically. "Or will Justice Colby continue to object?"

Harrison hesitated. "He has changed his mind."

"Excellent," Lord Ware said quickly as though to forestall her from probing deeper.

She would not have done so. It was obvious the community had decided to cooperate as a result of Lord Ware's decision to disregard the shooting incident in the tunnels. No doubt the smugglers would be a large part of the search party.

"Someone needs to walk the beaches," Ware said. "They may have disposed of the body in the water or hidden it among the rocks. If there are other caves, even small ones, they should be inspected. Beyond that, you know the area better than I, constable. The murderer is clearly desirous of keeping her body hidden as long as possible. Look for remote places or those with difficult access."

"I have a few places in mind, and I'm sure some of our frequent hunters will think of others. I'll go now and arrange the search parties. By midday, I should have a couple of dozen men out looking."

"Excellent." Ware's voice held genuine approval. "I leave for Brighton from here to speak with authorities there. Perhaps they have a missing woman or have found a body washed up on their beaches."

"Oh, good idea, sir," Harrison said eagerly.

"Don't count on it," Ware cautioned. "It's unlikely, but we would be foolish not to eliminate that possibility."

Harrison shrugged. "Well, then, sir. I'm off to get the search parties going. I hope good fortune smiles on one of us."

After Harrison left, Lord Ware turned to Lady Anne. "I should go too. Brighton is not far, and I hope to finish my business there in time to help with the searches."

"May I come with you? I have a bit of shopping to do, and it would be impractical to take two carriages."

"I would be delighted, my lady, however, I am driving the curricle, and I need Finn with me. There would not be room for both you and Jenny. In any event, it will be windy in an open carriage."

"Are you trying to fob me off, sir?"

"Not a bit, my lady. But those are the facts."

"I do not see the problem. I have a bonnet to protect against the wind, and Finn will just have to play chaperone."

Lucien's eyes widened in disbelief, and he chuckled. "And escort you into the shops, my lady? He is a good fellow, but I fear he would quit on me if I insisted he take a female shopping."

"Oh," she said, disconcerted. "Yes, of course." She laughed at the image of the small, red-haired groom hanging around the women's shops while she purchased unmentionables. "I would not wish to cost you your groom. My shopping is not so urgent that I cannot go another day."

"Aha, admit it," he said with a grin. "You had not planned to go today. You merely dislike waiting to hear what the Brighton constabulary has to say."

"In truth, that may be part of it," she admitted with a coy look. "But it is a lovely day for a drive."

"So it is. All right, my lady. Perhaps Finn could ride astride, which would make room for Jenny in the curricle."

"I have the perfect mount for him," she offered eagerly. "My mare is wonderfully mannered."

• • •

By half eleven, the foursome set forth for Brighton, the ladies in their bonnets, and Finn riding alongside on Lady Anne's chestnut saddle horse. Although breezy, it was a fine day with a clear sky, and Lord Ware kept the team at an easy pace, covering the thirteen miles in an hour and a quarter.

He delivered Anne and Jenny to the market area, promising to meet them there at 2:30.

"That should be adequate time." Anne waved as Lord Ware drove away with Finn in his usual perch and her mare tied on behind. "Come on, Jenny. We have things to buy if we are to leave for London soon." She had several unmentionables, trimmings, and gloves to replenish, and Seaford simply did not carry the quality of material she would need for London.

After a pleasurable hour, they emerged from the last store with three bags and extra time on their hands. Anne and Jenny strolled along gazing at shop windows and steadily moving toward the agreed meeting place.

"Is that not Mrs. Cummings, the butcher's wife from Seaford?" Jenny asked.

"Yes, I believe you are right," Lady Anne said thoughtfully, remembering that Mrs. Mead had said the butcher's wife had recently seen a young woman with black hair passing through the village. No matter how unlikely this was the missing girl, it would be prudent to ask for the details, particularly when Anne was offered such an opportune moment. "It would be rude not to acknowledge her," she said aloud.

"Would it?" Jenny murmured. "What are you up to, my lady?"

"Just a question or two." Anne looked both ways and then cut across the street when a young whipster halted his phaeton to accommodate her. Upon reaching the other side, she flashed him a quick smile, and he gave an elegant nod before driving on.

Anne turned just in time to intercept the butcher's pretty, plump wife. Picturing the grizzled, gray-haired man, Anne calculated his wife was twenty years his junior, putting her in her late thirties. "It is a glorious day, is it not?"

"Yes, my lady. It truly is."

Mrs. Cummings appeared gratified to have been addressed by the earl's daughter and smiled rather shyly. Anne credited Constable Harrison with gainsaying the hostile gossip in town.

"We could not resist a little shopping." Anne gestured to the bag the woman was carrying. "I gather that was the reason for your trip as well."

"Yes, a few things for my girls. Ribbons, lace, gloves. There is a cotillion in two weeks. Shall we see you there?"

"I fear I shall miss it. My father has requested that I join him in London. He is concerned about the recent unsolved murder as I am staying here alone."

"Oh, my, yes. That poor woman. Mrs. Mead told me about her."

"Mrs. Mead has been helpful in our efforts to identify the woman—not that we know who she is yet—but she has helped us gather information. She said you might have seen the girl a few weeks ago."

Mrs. Cummings hands flew up to her face. "Oh, dear, no. I never said that, only that I had seen a dark-haired girl—a child barely out of the schoolroom—in a carriage at the inn. It was weeks ago, and I probably shouldn't have said anything."

"I am so glad you did," Anne said, linking her arm with the

startled woman. "Every possibility must be followed, no matter how remote. Why, you might be the only person who saw her. Would you tell me about it?"

"Goodness me. Of course, I want to help. If you indeed are interested..."

"I am," Anne said quickly. "What do you recall?"

"Well, it was hot that day, and the coachman was watering the horses at the trough outside the inn. This young woman peeked out the window for a moment before someone jerked the curtains closed."

How odd. Why close them in the heat of day—unless they didn't want to be seen?

"You said 'someone,' does that mean it wasn't the girl?"

"I don't think it was. I was almost sure at the time it was a man's much larger hand on the curtain."

Anne nodded. "Good observation. What else did you notice regarding her, the coach, the horses, the coachman. The smallest detail might help."

Mrs. Cummings stopped and looked at her. "You believe it was her, don't you?"

"I cannot say. Perhaps if you described her a bit more."

"Allow me to think a moment," the woman murmured. They began walking again. "Her hair was dark, black ringlets. Very pretty girl. I remember wondering if she was out in society yet, that she would not lack for suitors. And yet, she looked unhappy. No, that's not the right word. She wasn't upset or frightened—but poorly...as though she wasn't feeling well."

Or afraid to show her fears, Anne wondered. "Do go on. What about the coach?"

"Nothing special. Black or dark brown, pulled by four horses...I believe. I'm not certain, and I barely noticed the coachman. A big man...is my impression."

"Was he wearing livery?"

"No. I'm sure he wasn't. I am sorry to be so uncertain, my lady."

"To the contrary, you have done splendidly," Anne said.

Her praise was received with a smile. "I do hope so."

"My lady," Jenny said quietly, "we will be late if we do not hurry."

"Oh, dear, is it late?" Anne asked, stepping away from Mrs. Cummings. "Lord Ware was kind enough to offer us a ride, and I must not keep him waiting. Thank you for speaking with me, Mrs. Cummings. You have been most obliging."

Chapter Ten

Brighton, 21 June 1813

Lucien had little trouble finding the Brighton constabulary. Because of the Prince Regent's fondness of the seaside resort, the once sleepy town had gone from a populace of 3,000 to 20,000 over the last thirty years. One constable was simply not enough, and during the summer months in particular, the number of constables might be half a dozen or more with two justices of the peace. Although the gaol was in nearby Lewes, and the military camp was a law onto itself, the constabulary was large enough to require its own station house.

As Lucien drove through the congested streets, he wondered how people considered this a place to relax. He knew it was worse when the Prince Regent was in residence and was grateful Prinny was detained in London at least another week. By that time, Lucien should be home. He intended to leave the area in the next day or two—whether or not he could confirm the dead woman's identity. He could not spare more time on what might be an unrelated death.

Living in Prinny's favorite playground and so close to London, the Brighton constables were used to working with both Bow Street and the palace. A simple mention of Whitehall earned Lucien the immediate attention of Constable Evans, the senior officer.

"My lord, I understand you had a few questions?"

Lucien summarized the situation in Seaford, explaining his own presence by citing Lady Anne's request and saying nothing about the London inquiry. If Evans thought his persistent interest in the matter was unusual, he didn't say so. The constabulary of

Brighton was doubtless familiar with the whims of royalty and aristocracy, and no longer took much notice of seemingly odd behavior.

"Young Harrison means well," Evans said. "I'm surprised he failed to reach out to us rather than dismiss Lady Ashburn's report."

"I believe he was influenced by the local Justice of the Peace."

"Eh, yes, that would be Colby. Well, I suppose it doesn't matter, as I have nothing to help you. With the number of people who come and go from Brighton, we wouldn't know if the young lady had been in town or not, but I can guarantee we've had no reports of missing women or unclaimed bodies on the beach. We had a drowning in the spring—an older woman, nothing like you describe."

"What if someone attempted to treat the death as natural? Any doctor, undertaker or the like in the death trade who might be agreeable to a quiet burial if paid enough?"

Evans' brows went up. "I suppose so, but the young lady's family would have to be involved in the conspiracy, and then there would be so many to bribe—those who washed and prepared the body, the coffin maker who would need to measure the corpse. In any respectable death, there are several others, all of whom might question her injuries."

"It does seem doubtful," Lucien agreed, but he knew that enough money offered to one or two of the right persons might dispense with everyone else. "Nonetheless, I would like to speak with those whose reputations are less than impeccable."

Evans shrugged. "I can give you a few names, sir, but I doubt they'll talk."

"Perhaps not, but I'd like to try." Lucien didn't argue with him, but those who can be bribed into silence might just as easily talk to a higher bidder. And Lucien traveled with a fat purse.

• • •

As he exited the shabby establishment of the fourth and last name Evans had given him, Lucien frowned. He'd flashed a large roll of bank notes, seen the greed in their eyes, but none of the four men he'd questioned had any information to give. Two of them had tried, pretending to know about an irregular burial, but not a single detail matched the missing woman. Lucien returned to his curricle, disgusted that he'd wasted the day. It was time to meet the ladies and return to Seaford.

Climbing aboard the curricle, he took the reins from Finn and turned the team toward the shops area. Having failed to further his inquiry in Brighton, he was eager to get back to Seaford, hoping Harrison had had better luck and found the body. If not, he had hit a dead end and must leave the inquiry to Harrison while he returned to London. Lady Anne would be disappointed, but he could not linger, not with Rosa's fate unknown. He sighed, realizing he must broach the possibility of returning to London on the ride back.

As he halted the horses at the agreed meeting spot, he saw Lady Anne and Jenny hurrying up the street. He smiled at the sight, as they held their hats and the bags bounced against their skirts. Lucien stood and waved as he stepped down, letting them know he saw them, and Lady Anne waved back.

"I was afraid we would miss you," she said, catching her breath as he took two of her bags and tied them on behind. Jenny held on to the other bag.

"My lady, you could not think I would leave you stranded in Brighton," he said. He handed her and Jenny into the curricle, while Finn mounted the saddle horse.

"No, of course not, but if you had gone looking for us, it might have been some time before we met up. Brighton is quite congested today." Anne settled her skirts around her and took the bag from Jenny, securing it at her feet.

"Ah, but I would not have moved," he replied, flicking the reins. "I am well aware that ladies can lose track of time while shopping."

"Not this time," she said with a satisfied smile. "Did you learn anything from the constables?"

"No missing women or unclaimed bodies. They gave me the names of some very shady fellows who might have disposed of an unwanted body in a private burial, but nothing came of it."

"I assume you offered them money.

"Naturally. It sparked their interest, but they hadn't the desired information to give."

"More's the pity. What now?"

He shook his head. "Unless the search parties were more successful, it is time for me to return to my duties in London."

"I know you cannot stay indefinitely, but I have learned something you may want to pursue. I believe a witness saw the girl in Seaford three or four weeks ago."

His gaze whipped to her face. "Who said so? Are you certain?" They had just left Brighton, and he pulled the horses to the side of the road and stopped.

"No, I'm not certain," she said, giving him an exasperated look, "but the facts seem to fit. While we were shopping, I met up with Mrs. Cummings, the butcher's wife from Seaford. She had told Mrs. Mead she'd seen a girl, a stranger, a few week's go, so I asked her about it. The young woman was in a closed carriage outside the Clifftop Inn, and her description was very similar to the body I saw."

"She had been in Seaford for weeks before she died," Lucien murmured to himself.

"In all that time, others would have seen her, would they not?" Anne asked.

"Not if she was kept hidden," he said, starting the horses moving again. He shot her a sideways glance. "Nice work, my lady. If you would, please tell me everything Mrs. Cummings said."

It took most of the ride home for her to relate the details of the conversation—he asked her to repeat everything twice—and for them to discuss the possibilities it raised.

"Why did you use the words *kept hidden*? Do you think she was held against her will?" Anne asked.

"We cannot rule out anything," he said, keeping his voice noncommittal. Lucien knew from past experience that Lady Anne was far too perceptive, and she was very close to the truth on this one. Rather than have her speculate and inadvertently alert those involved in the London matter, he might soon need to tell her the whole story. She could be trusted to keep a secret if she was aware of the stakes.

Knowing he was getting ahead of himself, he turned the conversation by asking if she was going to London in response to her father's letter.

"I have delayed my departure for a few days, but Father will not accept that for long. I had hoped to be here when the murder was solved, but..." She shrugged. "I should be in London by the middle of next week."

"And when Parliament's session is over, will you and your father return to Warwickshire?"

"I am unsure. Neither of us may be quite ready. I love Chadley Hall dearly, and I am sure Father will never sell it, but it will not be the same for either of us. When we discussed this before we came to Seaford, Father asked what I thought about purchasing a house in London, but he has not raised the idea again. He may have changed his mind."

As they were already pulling up before Lady Anne's house near Seaford, Lucien left the matter there. He would be pleased if Chadley decided to establish a town residence. He suspected the Hidalgo matter would keep him busy for several weeks, and—while justice for Rosa and the security of England must come first—it would be agreeable to know Lady Anne would be in London when Lucien was free to squire her around town.

He helped Lady Anne and Jenny down at the manor and walked them to the front door. When her butler appeared, Anne asked him if she had any messages from Constable Harrison.

"No, my lady. If I might add..." He paused expectantly.

"Yes, of course, please go on."

"Timothy joined in the search of the beaches. He returned a short time ago to report they found nothing."

"But no word on the other searches?" Lucien asked.

"No, my lord."

Lucien turned to Lady Anne. "I shall inquire in the village how the other search parties fared. If there is anything to report, I shall return or send a message."

He turned to leave, but she stopped him with a light hand on his arm. "You will see me before you leave for London, will you not?"

He smiled at her. "I shall, my lady. Until then, thank you for the pleasure of your company today." He leapt back on the curricle, tipped his hat, and set the team at a brisk pace toward the village.

• • •

It was just after five, and the Seaford shops were still open. Many of the able-bodied men had been recruited by Harrison, leaving the village's main road primarily occupied by women, children, the old or infirm. Everyone was talking about the search parties.

As Lucien entered the Clifftop Inn's taproom, he overheard a variety of speculation. The village gossips had outdone themselves, and everyone had a different theory on who the victim was and why she'd been killed. Some of the more lurid guesswork was annoying, and he shut it out.

The publican looked up as Lucien approached the bar. "Lord Ware, what can I get you?"

"A pint of ale and some conversation."

"Reckon I can do that." Mr. Weaver drew a pint and set it on the counter. "You know anything about these searches?"

"If you mean, have they found her, I don't know. I was in Brighton all day."

"I wish them luck. Poor lady deserves a Christian burial."

Lucien nodded and sipped his beer. "I heard she might have stayed at your inn."

"That right? I don't know why anyone would say that. I ain't even been asked."

"I'm asking."

"That so." Weaver stroked his short beard. "A young lady, I heard, with dark hair?"

"Yes. Possibly a foreigner. It would have been three or four weeks ago. The butcher's wife says she saw a girl that fit the description in a coach just outside the inn."

Weaver shook his head. "Not that I recall. We get visitors from Brighton that come for the day. Maybe they left their horses tied out front."

"Could be. The coachman was watering the horses."

"That would explain it. I don't charge for water, so they might come and go without me knowing about it. Sorry, wish I *could* help."

"All right, thanks." Lucien finished his pint and tossed a coin on the counter. "Let me know if you remember anything."

Weaver nodded, and Lucien walked out to the road, wondering where he might find Harrison. If the constable had returned from meeting up with the searchers, where would he go without an official constable's station?

While he was debating the possibilities, Finn came around the inn from the direction of the stables. "Milord," he said, hurrying to join him. "I think the stable lad done seen the coach Lady Anne was talkin' 'bout."

"The one with the young woman?"

"Aye, gov. The boy kin tell ya." Finn turned, heading back around the building, and Lucien strode briskly after him. They entered the stables, and Finn stopped beside a boy of sixteen or so brushing a small chestnut mare. "Tell Lord Ware wot y' tol' me."

"I dint see no lady."

"What did you see, lad?" Lucien asked, casually leaning against one of the stable's support poles. The lad seemed nervous, even defensive, and Lucien hoped to put him at ease by showing only mild interest in his answers.

"A coachman an' coach. He stopped fer to water four nice black geldin', asked me if it were all right." The boy shrugged. "He watered 'em an' left."

"Did he say where he was going? Or where he'd come from?"

"Naw. I reckon it were London, said the road were crowded an' dusty."

"What did he look like?"

Another shrug. "Big. Old."

"How old?"

The lad looked Lucien up and down. "A bit older than you, I guess."

Lucien smiled. It was the first time he'd been called old, but when he was sixteen he must have thought the same about anyone approaching thirty.

"Was he wearing a livery?"

"Naw." He looked down at his own worn shirt and trousers, a nondescript brown. "More like me."

"Tall or short?"

"Tall as you, sir, but rather fleshy."

"What about the coach? Anything unusual?"

"Closed coach. Black. Might a been some kind of mark on the door."

Lucien stiffened. "Did it look like a bird?"

A shrug. "Dint really pay no mind. You know this coach, sir?"

"I may have seen it." Lucien straightened thoughtfully. Yes, indeed. It may have been outside Hensley's residence in London. His stomach tightened at this tentative connection between London and the body in Seaford. "Thank you." He handed the boy a coin and walked back toward the road.

Finn joined him. "Did that help, milord?"

"Indeed, it did, Finn. I fear it confirms exactly what I did *not* want to find."

The small groom looked up at him with a somber face. "It be 'bout the missing lady from London, eh?"

"Yes, Finn, but we must keep this to ourselves. At least for now."

"Aye, gov. Nary a word."

After thanking him and promising to buy him a pint later, Lucien sent Finn back to the stables and stopped in front of the inn, thoughtfully looking at the horse trough where the coach and horses would have been. He was thinking about that small mark on the coach door. Was it the eagle symbol again? If so, it was a strong indication Rosa had been in Seaford and strengthened his growing suspicion that the girl was dead.

The sound of galloping hooves interrupted Lucien's sober thoughts, and he turned to see three men racing toward him. Others on the street stopped to stare, a few of the younger men running after them, clearly hoping to hear what had brought the men into Seaford with such haste. Lucien recognized Harrison in the lead before the constable hailed him, reined his horse to an abrupt halt, and leapt off.

"I think we've found it, the body. Up on the cliffs, in the scrub brush. We didn't try to move it." He made a face. "It's in bad shape.

"Really bad," one of the other men said. "The heat, the foxes… you can imagine."

"Her own mother wouldna recognize her," said the third rider.

"This is Mort and Sam," Harrison said, belatedly introducing his companions. "We left a couple of men guarding it. I reckon this is the body her ladyship saw—'cause we don't get many bodies around here—but I don't know how we'll ever prove it."

"Maybe if Lady Ashburn took a look," Mort suggested.

"Goof grief. Are you dicked in the nob?" Sam exclaimed. "You can't go showing *that* to a lady."

"He has the right of it," Harrison added, nodding at Sam. "One of our lads was sick as a cat. It is no sight fit for a lady."

"Perhaps Lady Anne can tell us something specific about the clothes or jewelry that might assist with identification," Lucien said. "We might even show her a scrap of clothing."

"I hadn't thought of that," Harrison said. "Shall we see her ladyship first? She'll want to know what we've found, and I owe her another apology for not believing her before. If I had, we might have found the body when it was recognizable."

"While you're doing that, Mort and I will find the undertaker and tell him he's going to be needed," Sam said.

"Warn him not to touch anything until we've had a look around," Lucien said. "There may be evidence on the remains or in the area that would help identify her or the murderer."

"We'll tell him."

After the two men left, Lucien collected his team and curricle and set off for Lady Anne's with Harrison riding on horseback.

They found her overseeing the watering of the garden flowers. She immediately abandoned the task and invited her guests to join her in the drawing room. It didn't take long to apprise her of the somber find.

"Thank the lord," she said. "Perhaps we can now identify her and inform her family." She looked at Lucien. "I want to see her… to be certain."

Both men shook their heads.

"She is not fit to be seen, my lady," Harrison said. "But it has to be her. I cannot recall ever before finding an unknown body near Seaford."

"You must be certain before telling her family," Anne insisted.

"Of course, my lady, but looking at the remains won't help with that," Lucien said gently. "Is there a detail about her clothes or jewelry that could assist us in confirming this is the body you saw?"

Lady Ane blanched and looked at him. "It is that bad?"

"Yes, I am afraid so."

She took a deep breath. "Her gown was blue, entirely too dark for a girl her age, with white embroidery around the neck. The sleeves were long, and they were trimmed with white, as was the bodice. The left sleeve had been mended near the shoulder. She wore black boots, both scuffed on the back, and I didn't see a hat or bonnet. No jewelry, but she had a hair comb." She stopped suddenly. "Oh, this will never work. I must look for myself."

"Out of the question," Lucien said firmly.

She looked at him, studying his face. "Constable, I wish to speak privately with Lord Ware. We shall return in a moment." She linked her arm through Lucien's and led him from the drawing room to a small study just steps away. Once inside, she moved away and turned to confront him. "I have known since you first arrived in Seaford that there was something you were not telling me. The longer you stayed, I became convinced I was right. This has something to do with Whitehall, and it is important—beyond normal compassion for the family—that you identify this woman, is it not?"

Lucien hesitated. Everything she said was true, and he knew he could trust her. Why was he so reluctant? Because it went beyond his orders? Or to spare her feelings from a desperately sad sight?

"My lord…Lucien, allow me to help you. I know I can determine whether or not this is the body from Singing Cave."

"I am not sure you can. A local man who saw the remains remarked that her own mother would not recognize her."

"I understand—I do, but there are other details I can look for, and you need not be so concerned about me, I am a country girl. I have seen decaying corpses of animals."

Lucien shook his head. "It is not the same. It feels different when it is a person."

"I imagine so, but I will be concentrating on her attire, her belongings, not her ravaged body." She took a step forward and turned her face up in appeal. "Let me try. You will be there to support me if I am overcome, will you not?"

He took her hands in his. "How can I agree to this, my lady?"

She raised a delicate brow. "Are you going to force me to follow you and drive myself?"

He sighed. "No, I will take you, but we shall bring a piece of her clothing to the carriage for you to inspect. Perhaps that will be sufficient to prove it is the same body."

"As you like."

Nothing about this was as he'd like, but he would do his best to protect her from the worst of it.

They returned to the drawing room, and Lucien gestured to Harrison. "Let us be on our way, Constable. I shall take Lady Anne in my curricle."

"Sir?" Harrison looked shocked.

"She has threatened to follow on her own if I do not take her. Believe me, I am well enough acquainted with the lady to know she would do exactly that." He strode from the house with Lady Anne on his arm.

• • •

Lucien tensed the moment he descended from the curricle. A swarm of flies marked the location of the remains in a dense area of scrub brush at the bottom of a steep slope, and a rancid odor permeated the area. Why the devil had he let Lady Anne convince him to bring her?

The two men left guarding the corpse were keeping their distance from it, and a third man stood beside them with an undertaker's wagon parked nearby.

"You could change your mind," Lucien said softly.

"In a way, I have. I thought about it all the way here, and I cannot make a definite identification from one small piece of clothing. You were thoughtful to try and spare me, but I need to look for myself."

He studied her face, saw the determination in her eyes, and knew she wasn't going to budge, but he had to try. "Do you comprehend how unpleasant it will be? I wish you would not do this."

"I know you do, and maybe you're right, it will be even worse than I think, but I am determined to try." She looped her arm through his. "Let us do what must be done as swiftly as possible."

"I shall stay here, if you don't mind," Harrison said, knowing the argument was over. "One look was enough for me."

"I dare say," Lucien murmured. "We shall not be long."

Lucien led her down the slope, picking his way on a surface littered with rocks and weeds. The terrible odor grew stronger with each step. Lady Anne was using a dainty lace handkerchief over her nose, not nearly sufficient, and he took out his own larger version and handed it to her. "Use this one. It may help." He leaned toward her ear. "You are an impossible woman, you know."

Lady Anne took the handkerchief, covered her nose and mouth, but otherwise did not respond, her eyes already frozen on the gruesome sight in the brush.

"Remember to look at her garments, not the body or face," he said quietly. "Block out the rest of it."

She tightened her grip on his arm. "I shall try."

After staring at the remains for a long moment, she pulled back, closed her eyes, and nodded. "It is the same body."

Lucien stepped between her and the remains, turning her back toward the carriage and moving up the slope as swiftly as possible without risking a twisted ankle or fall. When they reached the top of the hill, he handed her into the curricle beside Jenny and stepped away to speak briefly with Harrison and the undertaker. He arranged for the body to be sent to Dr. Pettigrew in London for examination. If she turned out to be local to Seaford, they could always return the body, but he was convinced that wouldn't be necessary. The age and description fit, and that symbol on the coach—tenuous ties, perhaps, but his instincts told him they'd found Señorita Hidalgo.

On the road to the village, Lucien didn't speak for several minutes, giving Lady Anne time to compose herself. She broke the silence by asking if they could make a stop before returning to her residence.

"At your pleasure. Where do you wish to go?"

"Not far." She directed him to a spot on the coast with a lengthy view of the white cliffs—known as the Seven Sisters—and the sparkling water underneath that stretched to the horizon where it met the blue of a summer sky. "I needed to remind myself how much beauty is in this world," she said quietly, drawing in a deep breath of fresh sea air.

They spent a few minutes in companionable silence before she turned to him and nodded. "Thank you. I'm ready to go."

While they had been standing there, Lucien had done some thinking of his own, and when they reached the manor, he asked if he could talk with her in private.

"Certainly, my lord. A walk in the garden would be lovely."

She sent Jenny into the manor, Lucien left the horses in care of Timothy, and they took a turn around the rear garden. It was not very large, and they made it twice around before Lucien finished telling her about Rosa Hidalgo, Rosa's father's arrest for spying, learning of the abduction, and Lucien's belief that the body was the young señorita.

"Oh, how terrible. Are you going to tell the father what you suspect?"

"Not until I have more confirmation. I intend to follow up on the coach that stopped at Clifftop Inn. If she was brought to this area shortly after the abduction, I find it hard to believe they kept her so well hidden that no one caught a glimpse of her in all that time. If I could discover where she was held, the scene might hold hints to the identity of the kidnappers."

"I wish I had the talent to draw you a picture of her. It might help jog someone's memory," Anne said thoughtfully. "Looking for a pretty girl with dark hair is not going to get you far."

"I fear you are right," he admitted, then he suddenly smiled. "I just happen to know a very skilled artist in London, a lady who dabbles for pleasure. Whether she can work from a description, I do not know. It might be worth asking. When are you leaving for London?"

"I have no reason to linger now the body has been found. Two or three days, I suppose."

"Perhaps I could bring her down here to meet with you before then?"

"You're feeling some urgency, are you not? I suppose I could leave the others to follow on their own with all the trunks." She frowned, looking a bit uncertain. "I cannot think right now how that would work, but I could try to sort it out."

"If you can, we could take the curricle," he offered. "A much faster trip, but it won't carry more than a small bag or two."

"What about Jenny and Finn? Does he want to ride my horse again? I do have to get Lady Fox to London," she mused.

"Lady Fox?"

"My chestnut mare."

"Ah, of course." Lucien was pleased to see the color return to her cheeks as she turned her thoughts to something other than that scene in the gully. He hoped to keep her attention engaged, challenging her to come up with a workable plan for the trip to London.

"I could leave at any hour in the morning," he said. "If we go early enough to do our business and return the same day, we wouldn't have to worry about bags."

"That is the answer," she said brightening. "A swift trip to London and back, and then I can finish packing and leave when everything is ready."

"It would be a long, hard day," he warned. "I shall need to change teams in London."

"Do I truly look that fragile?"

"Not fragile, but it is a demanding trip. I would not consider it except for the urgency of my inquiry."

"Then it is settled…this is the best way. Say eight tomorrow? Or would you prefer seven?"

"My, you do keep early hours," he said with a smile. "Very well, I accept your challenge and shall be here by seven. It would help if your mare was saddled and waiting."

"Never fear, my lord. We shall be ready."

Chapter Eleven

London, 22 June 1813

Lucien glanced over at Lady Anne's face. She appeared to be enjoying the ride in his open curricle, and they were making good time. When he had arrived at her manor house at seven, she and Jenny had been waiting with their bonnets. After tying one travel bag on behind, they were on the road by a quarter past with Finn riding the postillion position on Lady Anne's chestnut mare.

The weather was mild, the road fairly free of congestion, and they reached London by mid-day. At Lady Anne's request for an opportunity to freshen up, Lucien delivered her and Jenny to the lodgings Lord Chadley had rented, but he extracted a promise she would be ready in an hour.

Upon reaching his townhouse, Lucien left Finn to deal with the horses—switching his bays for his gray team—and sent his footman Robert to Lady Julia Castlebridge with a message asking if she would receive him and Lady Anne for the purpose of obtaining a sketch of a missing girl. He promised to explain in greater detail when they arrived.

"Wait for an answer, Robert. It is urgent, as I hope she'll receive us within the hour."

The footman grinned. "Yes, my lord. I guess I'd better hurry."

By the time Lucien had washed up and Talbot had fussed over brushing his garments and taming his windblown hair, Robert was back. He was out of breath but nodding happily.

"She said she was intrigued and would be home all afternoon."

"Excellent. Thank you, Robert." He turned to Talbot who was giving his hat a final brushing. "I must go. After my business is finished, I am off to Seaford again and shall not return for another day or two."

"Very good, my lord."

Retrieving his hat from Talbot's intense inspection, Lucien hurried down the stairs and out the front door. His coachman Gregory was waiting with the grays hitched to the enclosed coach more befitting a social call, particularly when escorting a lady, and Lucien climbed inside, tapping on the frame for Gregory to proceed. The frisky team made short work of the trip, and as Lady Anne—looking as though she had had hours to prepare—and Jenny were ready to go, they reached the Castlebridge residence by half twelve.

Lady Anne turned to him. "How much do we tell Lady Julia?"

"Only what we have to. It is important that the kidnappers do not learn we have made the likely connection between Rosa and the body in Seaford."

She nodded with a sigh.

Lucien introduced the two women and shared an abbreviated version of the situation with Lady Julia, presenting it only as an unidentified body with no mention of spying or smuggling.

"My dear Lady Anne, what a terrible experience for you," Lady Julia said when he finished. "That poor girl, and how her family must wonder where she is. Of course, I am eager to help you or make the attempt. I have not done a portrait sketch without working from a model."

"That leaves it up to me to give you enough detail that you can see her in your mind," Lady Anne said.

"This should be fun." Their hostess rose. "If you hope to return to Seaford by dark, we should get started. "I am rather excited to see if we can do this." She led them to a parlor with an abundance of windows that flooded the room with sunlight. Her sketchbook and watercolors were set up on a table and easel.

"I prefer to work under natural light," she explained. "When we were first married, my husband indulged me by commissioning the changes in this room as a wedding gift."

"It is lovely," Lady Anne said admiringly.

Lucien stood at one side of the room while the two women put their heads together. After a brief discussion, Lady Julia began to draw with Anne watching over her shoulder, supplying details, approving her efforts or suggesting changes.

He was surprised how easily they got along. After several intense minutes of concentration, they were nodding and smiling together. In no time at all, Lady Julia presented him with a finished sketch.

"This is the best I can do."

"It is wonderful," Anne said. "That is an exact likeness of the young woman I saw in the cave."

He studied the drawing of a pretty young woman with long, shiny black curls and dark eyes—and a very Spanish look about her. Anne seemed sure this was the body from Seaford, and he would wager it was Señorita Hidalgo. "Remarkable. Lady Julia, I am not surprised but simply amazed by your work."

"Thank you, my lord, but I could not have done it if Lady Anne had not such a wonderful gift for detail."

"I beg pardon," Anne interrupted indignantly. "This drawing could only be done by the hands of a very talented artist."

Lucien laughed. "Listen to you. Ladies, shall we call this an astonishing joint effort?"

"I believe we can accept that," Anne said, exchanging a smile with the artist.

Lady Julia blushed with pleasure. "You are very kind. I know you eager to return to Seaford, but do you have time for tea? It would not take long."

Lady Anne appealed to Lucien. "You decide. I am happy either way."

"Well, my lord?" Lady Julia already had one hand on the bell rope.

"Perhaps we can compromise. I have someone I must see before we leave town. If I return in three quarters of an hour, that should allow you time to take tea."

Lady Anne approved his suggestion without asking about his errand, and for once Lucien was glad she knew about the delicate work he did for Whitehall.

"I'll take the sketch with me," he said, "and safely pack it away in the coach."

Julia pulled the rope to summon a maid. "I wish you could stay, my lord, but I welcome the chance to become better acquainted with Lady Anne. Before you go, allow me to find you something to protect the sketch from damage."

• • •

While Lady Julia was wrapping the sketch, Lucien sent her footman with a message for Sherry to meet him at Whitehall, and he was delighted to find his partner waiting when he walked into Rothe's office a quarter of an hour later.

"I think I have found Rosa Hidalgo, but the news is not good." Lucien showed them the sketch, and related the recent events in Seaford. "I need someone to confirm this sketch is Rosa," he said, "but I was reluctant to approach the father until I had spoken with you."

"Bloody hell," Rothe swore. "They murdered her."

"The woman in this sketch is dead," Lucien hedged.

"She died just a few days ago?" Sherry asked with a puzzled frown. "If it is Señorita Hidalgo, where has she been all that time? Why wait until now to kill her?"

Lucien shrugged. "Nary a clue. Once I've confirmed this is Rosa, I plan to show the sketch around London and Seaford, hoping to track her movements since May 14th and follow that trail back to the killers."

"I cannot allow you to do that," Rothe interrupted. "If Hidalgo learns his daughter has been murdered, he will not be able to keep up the pretense of working with Hensley. It would be hard for any man, and Hidalgo…he is a doting father. We can certainly confirm her identity, however. The Envoy's wife, Carmen de Leon, was somewhat acquainted with the young lady and should be able to tell us yes or no."

Lucien frowned. Keeping the truth from the father did not sit well with him, but he had to concede Rothe's point. They might never catch those responsible if the conspirators grew suspicious—they would vanish to carry on their nefarious activities somewhere else.

Thus, Lucien kept his own counsel and accompanied Lord Rothe and Sherry to the Spanish Embassy. While they were talking with the deputy envoy, Pablo Ruiz, Señora de Leon returned from a shopping trip. The round-faced, matronly woman sent her maid off with two pink and white bandboxes of new hats and turned with a smile.

"You wished to see me?"

Rothe explained why they were there, and Lucien produced the wrapped sketch.

"Why, yes, that is Rosa," she said, smiling the moment Lucien removed its cloth covering. "An excellent portrait. Who did it?"

"A friend," Lucien said keeping it vague. "We thought a sketch might help in our search."

The señora's brow wrinkled. "There is still no word of Rosa?"

"No," Rothe said. "But we shall keep looking. It remains imperative that news of her abduction is not talked about."

The señora nodded with a small sigh. "It is so disturbing."

"Very good, gentlemen," Ruiz said ending the visit. "Envoy de Leon is at the Parliament at the moment, but I shall inform him of your visit and the current status of this matter."

As they stepped outside the embassy, Rothe reiterated, "No one must learn of her death—not yet."

"Absolutely." Lucien agreed. "If we cannot tell the father the truth, we must conceal it from everyone. How terrible for him if he heard it through gossip. I wish to use the sketch in Seaford, however, to discover where she was held and by whom. Her name and ties to London are not known, and they can easily remain so."

"Very well. You could give her a false name, if necessary"

Lucien nodded. Sometimes Rothe thought aloud and stated the obvious. He and Sherry had learned not to take it personally. "Yes, sir, if the situation demands."

"Well, then, let us get on with it. Keep me apprised." Rothe walked away in the direction of Whitehall, and Lucien turned to Sherry. "Any progress with Hensley?"

"Nothing to note. I've followed him and watched the house, but he's gone nowhere out of the ordinary, met with no one except family, and the black coach has not appeared again…nor has he tried to arrange a meeting with Hidalgo. I wonder if they are done with him."

"That might explain why they killed the girl," Lucien said. "Or it could be her death came first—perhaps unintended, such as during an escape attempt—and they are trying to sort out what to do now they have lost the means of forcing Hidalgo's cooperation."

"If they are ill-informed of how much we know, they may be bold enough to resume activities," Sherry said. "I'll keep doing what I've been doing, mostly watching Hensley's home. Oh, I also made contact with Jose, the footman Rothe planted in Hidalgo's residence. He has seen nothing unusual, and everyone in the residence appears to be exactly who and what they claim to be."

"All right. Let's keep it up for a couple more days. I'm returning to Seaford. If I can find where Señorita Hidalgo was held or identify her captors, maybe we can get them to talk and lead us back to Hensley. With that kind of information, we could take Hensley into custody and pressure him to give up the entire spy operation."

• • •

After switching to the curricle and leaving Finn behind at Hays Mews, Lucien was only a few minutes late in picking up Lady Anne and Jenny, and they were exiting London by half three with the wrapped sketch on Lady Anne's lap. To Lucien's satisfaction his team of grays delivered them to Seaford well before dark.

"I like your friend Lady Julia very much," Anne said, as he escorted her to the door. "I hope it is acceptable if I call on her when I return to London."

Lucien lifted a brow. "Of course. Why would you think otherwise?"

"I was unsure of your, um, relationship with her. She mentioned she was a cousin-by-marriage with the former Mrs. Stine, whom I believe you know quite well."

Lucien grinned. Her ladyship could certainly be bold at times. "Really, my lady. What are you suggesting? Had you thought it might become awkward? Allow me to ease your mind—I have never had a liaison with an Englishman's wife, nor do I plan to…not even the lovely Lady Julia or the newly wed Sophy Castlebridge." He deliberately used Sophy's Christian name, making no secret of his close friendship with her. If Anne could be so outspoken, so could he.

She cocked her head. "I am delighted to know there will be no unpleasant gossip surrounding Lady Julia."

A subtle set down, he thought, implying her only concern was for Lady Julia's reputation. Nonetheless, he hoped her inquiry meant the months apart had not left her completely indifferent to him.

"I am just as delighted to dispel your fears, my lady." Tipping his hat with a smile, he leapt into his carriage and drove toward the Clifftop Inn. After a moment of smiling reflection, he glanced at the wrapped sketch on the seat beside him and began making plans for tomorrow.

Chapter Twelve

Seaford, 23 June 1813

Early the following morning, Lucien tracked down Mrs. Cummings, the butcher's wife, in her vegetable garden to confirm the sketch resembled the young lady she'd seen in the carriage a few weeks earlier.

"Oh, my. I only had a brief look, mind you, but it does look like her." She nodded at the sketch. "Where did you get her image? Does this mean you have discovered who the poor thing was?"

"I am afraid not. The sketch was made by a friend, using Lady Anne's description."

"That is remarkable."

"I hope it will refresh someone's memory, and we can fill in the missing weeks."

"What a splendid plan. I suppose she *was* staying around here," she added thoughtfully. "It is odd no one has come forward, is it not?"

"I agree, but perhaps they were unsure. The sketch may help." He excused himself before she could ask more questions and went in search of Harrison, showed him the sketch, and continued to flash it all over the village—the shops, the market, and strangers on the main road. No one admitted seeing the young woman—whom locals were calling Lady Blue, due to her blue gown—prior to her death. After a couple hours of this, Lucien returned to the inn for a pint of ale.

He took a long swallow to quench his thirst and continued to ponder where Rosa had spent her last weeks. After the sighting in front of this inn, her trail appeared to vanish again. He might have concluded the village was a stop on a longer journey…if the body had not been left in Singing Cave, less than a mile away, and then moved to the Seaford woods on the edge of the village.

She'd been kept nearby…and like as not, someone he'd spoken to that day had seen her and lied to him. He glanced around the pub, filled with cigar smoke, the smell of ale, and two dozen male drinkers. Might be someone in this very room…but who?

The villagers had been uncooperative in the beginning, but hadn't that been a combination of a missing body and a fear of exposing the local smugglers? Didn't they yet understand the contraband was irrelevant? Indeed, he enjoyed a good bottle of French brandy and was aware his own cellar might have a few bottles of questionable origin.

Attitudes toward his inquiry had changed somewhat as soon as the body was found—except for one man—Justice of the Peace Colby. He hadn't openly opposed anything Lucien was doing; in truth, he had remained conspicuously absent, avoiding the search and recovery of the body. Was that significant? Was he working against them behind the scenes? If so, why? Was it the resentment of a man of local consequence for intrusion by the London aristocracy? Or embarrassment he'd made a mistake? Or worse yet—guilt? Whatever it was, he bore watching.

Lucien finished his pint and ordered another. He would give it one more day in Seaford, then return to London. Perhaps it was time to take the initiative and set up a trap for the French spies with false documents. He'd discuss it with Rothe upon his return.

He sighed and pushed his empty mug away. No help for it, he needed to have a frank discussion with Constable Harrison. Although the young man was basically honest, he was covering for the smugglers, and they were somehow involved in this. If Lucien could get him to open up, it would give him a clearer picture of the situation and whether the locals were part of the chain sending coded messages to and from Boney's forces in France. It would only take one rotten apple in an otherwise blameless crew—at least blameless of espionage.

Lucien was half-way off the bench when the tavern door swung open and Constable Harrison walked in.

"Lord Ware, just the man I hoped to find."

"Well met, then, Harrison. I was coming to see you. Have a seat. May I buy you a pint?" Lucien deliberately avoided calling him Constable Harry as he'd heard others do. He suspected the man had a hard time gaining respect due to his youth, and the nickname didn't help.

"Thank you, sir. I sure am dry." Harrison pulled up a bench and sat. "How is it going with the sketch? Any luck?"

Lucien shrugged. "If anyone recognized her, they weren't telling me."

The publican dropped off two fresh pints, and Harrison took a swallow before nodding. "I could have a go at it, but they're afraid of talking to anyone in authority."

"Because of the smuggling," Lucien said.

Harrison's hand froze with the mug half-way to his mouth, and he set it down with a sigh. "How did you know?"

"It is rather obvious. Lady Anne drew my attention to the French wine in every household, and there were other clues. I'm not here to cause trouble over French lace or wine. I'm only interested in what happened to this woman—where she was killed, by whom, and where she was kept for nearly four weeks before she died."

Harrison sat back in his chair, his eyes narrowed. "How do you know that? I'm certain there is more to this story than you have said. Are you going to tell me?"

Lucien hesitated. "Not all of it. But I know who she is and that she was abducted four weeks ago. The situation is complicated, and I cannot give you all the details. What I do tell you cannot go beyond us. Not to anyone," he said, giving the young man a frank look. "Ongoing events would be adversely effected if word of her death reached the wrong ears."

"I understand…well, I don't, but I can keep quiet."

Lucien leaned forward and locked eyes with him. "Be certain that you do, Harrison. Lives depend on your silence." He paused for that to sink in, then went on, "We must continue to act as though this is a local matter. It is not, and someone in Seaford knows it. We cannot let him or her suspect that *we* know."

The constable's eyes widened, and his head bobbed several times. "You can trust me, my lord. Honestly. I can keep mum when needs be." Harrison's look of earnest innocence made Lucien feel the full weight of the four years of age—and of the war—that separated them.

"Good, lad. If those—such as Colby—press you too hard for answers, refer them to me." Lucien grinned. "I have experience in talking without saying anything."

Harrison grinned back. "I appreciate your confidence, sir, and won't let you down. How can I help?"

"Tell me about the smugglers. Are any of them a bit shady, maybe willing to do almost anything for money, such as spying for France?"

"Wot? *The devil you say.* Is that what this is about? Spying? I don't hold with the Frenchies. Good Lord, I haven't seen anything like that. How would I recognize it, Lord Ware?"

"A note or packet handed to someone in France or hidden somewhere over there would be the most obvious, but private meetings or anyone going off on their own while in France would be highly suspicious. And, well, any contact with the French that doesn't seem necessary."

"Oh, well, I myself haven't been in a position to see those things. I may look the other way, but I've not been on a smuggling run. If I start asking questions now, won't I rouse suspicion?"

"Probably," Lucien said, frowning in thought. "I wonder if they'd allow you to go with them."

Harrison looked worried. "Maybe, but it don't seem right."

"No, I agree," Lucien said hastily. "I was merely thinking aloud. It would not do at all. They'd have no respect for your authority in the future."

The constable nodded, visibly relieved. "I have a friend who might tell us what goes on and what he's seen—because he loathes the Frenchies—but we'd have to tell him why we're asking."

"Do you trust him?"

"Aye, he's been my mate forever."

"Let's set up a meeting…somewhere private. Perhaps at Lady Anne's?"

Harrison's brows shot up. "Does she know about the…" he lowered his voice to a whisper, "the spying?"

Lucien laughed. "Little happens around her that she is not aware of—or at least suspects. A most perceptive lady whom I have had to take into my confidence more than once—to my ultimate benefit, I might add."

• • •

Lady Anne's eyes brightened, and she smiled at Lucien. "Of course, my lord, I am delighted to host your meeting."

"I can call it off," he said lazily. "That is, if I have presumed too much by instructing them to meet me here."

"Nonsense. You knew I would agree. May I be present while you talk?"

Lucien chuckled and raised a brow. "I am surprised you felt you had to ask."

"One does try to be polite," she said demurely.

"When it pleases you, my lady."

As the sound of voices at the front door indicated their visitors had arrived, Lady Anne merely threw him a pert look. The new arrivals were announced, and Lady Anne welcomed Constable Harrison and his friend Nate Barnes.

"Please be seated," she said. "Tea shall arrive shortly."

"Thank you, milady."

"Nate, I do not believe we have met before," Lucien said. "Do you live in the village itself?"

"I do, sir." The young man with a thatch of strawberry hair sat on the edge of a chair, looking mightily uncomfortable. "You be right 'bout not meetin' b'fore, but I seen you around."

"The constable tells me you and he are long-time mates."

"That's true, m'lord." Nate grinned at Harrison. "We go way back. Got into a lot of mischief as young'uns."

Harrison laughed. "No telling tales."

"Saved by the tea tray," Lady Anne said, her eyes twinkling as the maid entered. She poured for everyone and passed the biscuit and sandwich plates.

Lucien waited until Harrison and Barnes had made their selections before claiming their attention again.

"I am concerned that someone local was involved in the recent death—and it may be tied to the smuggling of certain documents."

Nate's face blanched, and Lucien added, "Not the harmless luxury items. Someone among the smugglers is carrying secret war documents back and forth to France."

"You mean, spying? And murder?" Nate asked in disbelief. "Wot's he talkin' about, Harry? Gor', tell him he's wrong."

"Hold on, mate. Don't get all het up. He's not accusing you of nothing bad," Harrison said. "But he's sure about the spying going on, and the dead woman was left in the caves the smugglers use. It's hard to say they ain't connected."

"Hard, maybe, but they ain't." Nate's gaze flitted back and forth, his appeal settling on Harrison. "Are they?" When Harrison hesitated, Nate shook his head and swore under his breath.

Harrison sighed heavily. "I can't say for sure, Nate, but Lord Ware believes that's what happened—that she somehow got caught in the middle of it all."

Not exactly, Lucien thought, but it was as good an explanation as any, so he let it go.

Nate rubbed his chin warily. "Why are you tellin' me all this? What do you want?"

"We need your help to expose the traitor." Although Nate started shaking his head again, Lucien continued. "You've been on a run or two to France—think back…did you see anyone acting suspiciously, talking to strangers, maybe slipping a packet or letter to someone on the French side?"

"You're serious, ain't you?" Nate had a trapped look on his face, and he turned to Harrison. "You never said you wanted me to peach on my mates."

"Nate, that girl is dead," Harrison said.

"We didn't kill her!"

"Someone using the caves did. And someone is using our smuggling runs to aid the Frenchies."

"If you say so, but..." Nate trailed off as though he didn't know what to say.

"Just answer his questions," Harrison urged. "It won't come back on you or your friends, if they're not in on it. I promise."

"As do I," Lucien said.

"Gor', I hate this," Nate muttered. "And I ain't never seen nothing suspicious."

"Tell me about the smuggling set up," Lucien urged. "How long has it been going on? Who organized it?"

"I can answer that," Harrison said. "At least twenty years, every month or two. Old Ben Buxton started bringing stuff in his fishing boat. More and more fishermen got involved as the restrictions got tighter."

Nate nodded, seeming more at ease with Harrison doing part of the talking. "When Old Ben died, the Patel brothers took over... sort of. It really became a village thing."

"Do the same people go every time?"

"Pretty much, unless someone can't. We try to take eight."

"Who are the regulars?"

Nate frowned, balking again now that it came to names.

"Quit acting like a milksop," Harrison said, impatiently. "You can trust him."

Lucien wished he could write things down, particularly a list of names, but that would alarm Nate for sure. Lady Anne was remaining uncharacteristically quiet, and he hoped that meant she was paying close attention. With her ability to recall whatever she saw or heard, her presence was a definite asset. He exchanged a quick glance with her, and she flashed a smile as though she could read his mind.

Returning his attention to Nate, Lucien prodded him. "I need the names, Nate, and those of any frequent substitutes. One of them may be a willing spy or unwittingly taking messages back and forth for someone else without knowing the contents."

"If he won't tell you, I know two or three for certain," Harrison declared. Once he revealed those names, Nate sighed and gave up the others—not without throwing an angry look at Harrison.

Lucien noted that several prominent villagers were regular smugglers or frequent substitutes, including the blacksmith, the postman, and Justice Colby's land steward. No wonder Colby and Harrison were ignoring their activities.

"None of them are traitors," Nate grumbled. "I'm sure of that."

"I hope you are right," Lucien said. "If so, they have nothing to fear."

"If that's all you wanted," Nate said, fidgeting in his chair, "I got chores to do."

"We won't keep you any longer," Lucien said agreeably. The lad was clearly through talking. "Thank you, Nate. We would like to keep this chat quiet."

"Well, I ain't gonna tell," Nate said, jumping out of his chair. "I don't want no one to know I was here. Promise me that, Harry."

"You got my word," Harrison said. "But if you see anything on future runs that looks like spying, you need to come to me."

Nate thought about it. "Eh, sure. If it's something clearly suspicious, but I ain't reporting everything we do."

"That's fine," Lucien said. "I assure you, Nate, we're looking for a spy, not a smuggler."

Nate started for the door, then stopped and turned back. "Are you gonna question all my mates?"

"Not if we don't have to," Lucien said.

"That's good then." Nate nodded and backed toward the hallway visibly anxious to be quit of the house. He turned and nearly fled out the door.

"We may have cost you a friend," Lucien remarked to Harrison.

"Naw. I'll talk him around. He's a good mate."

Lucien wasn't sure it would be that easy. Nate had been shaken, and not the least bit happy he'd been singled out. But that was

Harrison's problem to solve. He turned to Lady Anne with a smile. "I assume you got all the names?"

"Naturally. Would you like me to write them down?"

"If you please."

Harrison waited while Lady Anne wrote two lists of the smugglers' names. She handed him one with a thoughtful look. "You have the best chance of watching activities around here. The villagers are used to you poking around. Since Lord Ware and I are both leaving for London in the next day or two, it should ease tension, and the guilty person may lower his guard."

"She makes a good point," Lucien said. "Are you willing to taking charge of the inquiry from now on?"

"Spying on my mates and neighbors?" the constable asked. "Sorry, I didn't mean for it to come out that way. I guess Nate's reaction has got me wound up." He nodded slowly. "If one of them, even of those I call friend, is a murderer and a traitor, I want him found out. And, yes, I know it's my job."

"Good man," Lucien said. "I will run these names by authorities in London. If any of them are known in the wrong circles, I shall send word and any other information I think may help you."

"Thanks. I'll send reports as I can. Nate might not have anything soon, as they just did a channel run."

"I'm not sure what is being planned in London," Lucien said, "but perhaps something will come up that forces the traitor to arrange a special run to get an urgent message to France."

Harrison nodded, his eyes gleaming. "I'll let you know of any unusual activity."

• • •

Lucien spent his remaining time in Seaford nosing around the village to determine where each of those on the smuggler list lived. Although the operation was likely linked to Señorita Hidalgo's death in some manner, it was not a sure thing, and he kept his eyes open to other possibilities.

Since most of the village cottages were one or two rooms, there was little space to conceal a captive for any length of time. More likely, she'd been kept in one of the larger houses on the outskirts or at the farms and manors just outside the village—possibly even a hunting shed or storage building. One thing for sure, if she'd been confined in one of the larger houses—such as Colby's—or even on the farms, the owners or tenants should have known.

Lucien was suspicious of Justice Colby due to his handling of Lady Anne's report—and the Colby property just outside the village was extensive enough to hide any type of activity—but Lucien credited the man with more sense than to keep a kidnapped woman on his own land. A shrewd man would not take that risk. From what Lucien had heard, Colby was many things, but he was no fool.

By the end of the day, Lucien had identified four properties that had the privacy and space to secure a hostage, and he gave those four names to Harrison as possibilities to watch.

Lucien made an early night of it. Now that Señorita Hidalgo was confirmed dead, he was keen to get back to London where he believed the leader of the spy operation—and ultimate blackguard—could be found. He would be leaving Seaford at daybreak.

Chapter Thirteen

London, 24 June 1813

The June morning dawned clear and bright with birds noisily calling to one another outside Lucien's room at the inn. He was up and on the London road early, leaving behind a message for Lady Anne that he would see her in town. As he loosened the reins to urge the horses to a faster pace, his lips twitched into a smile. She would be following him shortly, and it appeared her father, the Earl of Chadley, was going to establish London as his primary residence for the foreseeable future.

But Lucien did not dwell on Lady Anne for long. A sense of disquiet roiled in the pit of his stomach, ignited four days ago when he'd viewed the decomposing body of Rosa Hidalgo. It was barbarian that a seventeen-year-old child had been held hostage and murdered by agents of an evil dictator suitably called "the Corsican plague." In one way or another, Lucien had been fighting Napoleon for more than six years. He and Sherbourne had taken down a number of enemy agents in that time, but he had never wanted one more than the man responsible for Rosa's death.

Going on eleven in the morning, Lucien arrived at Sherbourne House and attempted to roust Sherry from bed. "The day is nearly half gone, my friend," he said, shaking the bed.

"Devil it, Lucien," Sherry moaned from under the covers he'd pulled over his head. "Only half gone? Then it is much too early. I was following Hensley until four."

"Six or seven hours of sleep is more than plenty. Did your efforts yield anything new?"

"Only if you're interested in knowing he has taken an actress as his current mistress."

"Do tell. Get up. We have much to do." Lucien snatched the pillow from under his friend's head.

Sherry lunged to take it back, missed and fell back, rolled over, and sat on the edge of the bed. "Oh, very well. You are a harsh taskmaster."

"I'm impatient to find the scoundrel who murdered Rosa Hidalgo."

His partner jerked his gaze up. "So, you're sure it is her? It seemed a foregone conclusion after Carmen de Leon recognized the sketch, but knowing all doubt is gone…her father will be devastated."

"Eventually yes, but I'm not sure Rothe will want him told yet. Until he gives the go ahead, we have to pretend we're working on a rescue."

His valet entered carrying a dark blue jacket which Sherry approved before turning back to Lucien. "It seems harsh treatment of the father."

"Tough either way," Lucien said. "Finding the Frenchie involved would put an end to his waiting."

"So, get out of here. I shall meet you in the breakfast room in ten minutes. Surely you need another cup of tea or coffee?"

"Don't primp for long," Lucien warned, "or I shall return." Wearing a grin on his face, he retreated to the morning room. The Sherbourne cook kept good coffee on hand, and he had nearly finished a cup when Sherry bounded in, no more than a few minutes beyond the promised time.

"There, was that fast enough?" he asked, grabbing a plate and filling it from the sideboard. "Coffee for me too," he instructed the footman. He turned to Lucien as he sat down. "Tell me about Seaford."

Lucien quickly brought him up to date. "She was held in the village or nearby. I'm convinced of that."

"And the smugglers are involved?"

"I believe they're part of the chain passing secrets between England and France. Someone in the spy operation knew Seaford well enough to hide Rosa there. They would also have known about the smugglers. It couldn't have been too hard to find a weak link among them."

"If Rosa's killer is down there, why aren't we?"

"The one who stabbed her may be there—although it's more likely he was a London thug and has returned—but young Constable Harrison is looking for him and the location where Rosa was held. Regardless, her killer is not the only person responsible for her death."

"You think the French agent is in London."

"Absolutely."

Sherry lifted his brows in agreement. "I suppose you're right. He'd want to be here to obtain Hensley's reports and send on what he deemed important." Sherry set down his coffee cup and leaned back. "Following Hensley should have taken us to the head of this gang by now, but we're getting nowhere."

"Why hasn't Whitehall speeded matters by sending a false message to Wellington? We have worked the deceit before. Successfully, I might add. Why is Rothe hesitating?"

Sherry shrugged. "I'd say he is fearful of making a false step. It has become personal, and he is blinded to all else by Hidalgo's plight."

Lucien arched a brow. The marquess was not a cold man, but he was pragmatic. Country and crown came before all else. What was different this time? Lucien grew uneasy when someone or something broke from the usual pattern. In spy work, those little discrepancies could come back to haunt you.

"Rothe has talked about the idea. He is concerned that if the French caught on, they might kill their hostage. With her death confirmed, maybe he'll change his mind."

Lucien thought about it. "Why don't I leave you to finish your breakfast in peace. I'll sound out Rothe and meet you at White's in…say, an hour?"

"Perfect," Sherry said, talking around a bite of biscuit.

Lucien stopped by his townhouse first to drop off his bags, freshen his clothes and switch horses, then he headed for Whitehall. The best way to determine what was going on with Rothe's end of the Hidalgo inquiry was to ask.

• • •

"Good morning, Mr. Sloane. Is his lordship in?"

Rothe's secretary gave a nod. "He is, Lord Ware. He has an appointment in half an hour. Will that be sufficient time for you to conclude your business?"

Lucien smiled. "I assume you will toss me out when my time is up?"

Sloane pushed his wire-rimmed glasses up on his nose. "Certainly not, sir, but I shall scowl deeply to remind you."

Lucien's smile widened. "And I promise to take the hint."

When Sloane announced him, Lucien found Rothe pouring over a map spread out on a side table. "Tell me what you think, Ware. Boney has rebuilt his army and appears headed in this direction. What would you say is his goal?"

Lucien looked over the map, marked with the positions of various armies and units. "Dresden."

"Yes, I thought so too. I hope Field Marshall von Schwarzenburg adheres to his orders not to engage directly with Napoleon. He may be vulnerable." Rothe straightened. "But that is not my problem nor yours. I will express my concern, beyond that…his field orders do not originate with me. So, what can I do for you, Ware? Any success in Seaford?"

"Not as much as I'd like." Lucien told him of the confirmation Rosa had been in Seaford for weeks before her death and of his strong suspicion of the smuggling activities.

"It would not be the first time that smuggling and spying have gone hand in hand," Rothe agreed. "Does your return to London mean you have given up finding the courier on that end?"

"Only temporarily. I left the task to Constable Harrison while Sherry and I concentrate on this end. Harrison is young and well-intentioned. Many in the community do not take him seriously, and that may work to his advantage. Our London spy—and the courier—may resume their activities, thinking they are safe, and Harrison has a friend among the smugglers watching for any unusual activity. In the normal course of things, however, it will be a month before the next smuggling run, and I felt my time would be better spent in London."

"I'm sorry to say we are at a standstill. Hensley has made no contact."

"Yes, Sherry told me. He says you have resisted planting false orders to draw them out."

"And you're both wondering why I am so slow to act."

"I cannot speak for Sherry, sir, but I am."

Rothe gave a wry laugh. "It is the next logical step, I know." He pinched the bridge of his nose, a sure sign of disquiet. "In the beginning, I hesitated for fear of endangering the girl, but now…I can't quite put my finger on it, but something about this situation is not right. Hidalgo said that Hensley contacted him every few days to keep him in line. That hasn't happened—and then they killed their only leverage. Did they know we'd discovered Hidalgo's activities?" Rothe turned and stared at Lucien. "How could they? We kept the information close."

"How close?"

"Very." Rothe listed less than a half dozen people, all highly trusted government officials experienced at keeping secrets. "Thank God Prinny showed little interest in the matter, and I have not kept him informed."

Lucien nodded. It was well-known their sovereign and his friends loved to gossip, but they weren't on Rothe's list. "Perhaps Hidalgo or someone in his household said something in an unguarded moment."

Rothe gave him a sharp look. "Not likely. As you know, we have an agent living in Hidalgo's home, and he swears the father has been fanatical about maintaining silence. I rather hope our man is wrong. Otherwise, the finger points at this office or the Spanish

Embassy again. Those who work in both agencies are trained not to talk out of hand, and if they have, it was likely deliberate."

"You're suggesting another leak." Lucien said, taken by surprise.

"Not here, I hope to God. If we have dirt on our hands again, it will hardly inspire confidence in us with the Prince Regent or the other war offices."

"With good cause," Lucien murmured, thinking of the spy they had discovered in their midst eighteen months ago. "You're worried that setting a trap will tip our hand if the leak is here, that he'd realize we knew there was a spy."

"Exactly."

"So how do we proceed?"

"I wish I knew."

Lucien was surprised at Rothe's response. His lordship was rarely without an alternate plan. "Have you talked with Sloane?"

Rothe gave a start. "Why? Surely, you do not suspect him. He has been with me forever."

"No, sir. He is above reproach, but he will have been extraordinarily vigilant of staff since the prior incident. You might want to discuss your concerns with him."

"Normally, I might have, but I've been unwilling to voice them aloud. You make a good point, and I shall speak with him yet today. Perhaps I have been too close to the situation to see it clearly."

"A frank discussion with the father might also be in order. I heard what your agent inside has said, but he hasn't been with Hidalgo every minute, and the man may have shared his fears with someone he shouldn't have. If Sloane feels this office is clear, I could ask Hidalgo to stop by my residence."

"Very well. I shall send word as soon as Sloane and I have talked." Rothe sighed. "If we have to query the security at the embassy again, it will not be an easy conversation."

"Diplomacy will be tested for sure," Lucien agreed. "Especially if you have to question his family—his wife, his son, his deputy."

"Egad. You know I'll have to unless we find the answer elsewhere. What a conundrum. I would like to avoid running afoul of Carlos de Leon. The man has a terrible temper." He shook his head and turned to go.

Lucien swore silently as it occurred to him he had his own touchy situation to handle. He had confided in Lady Anne, and now he must ask if she had spoken to anyone else. She had spent an hour alone with Lady Julia, and it might have seemed natural to tell her a bit of the story—but even mentioning Rosa's name would be dangerous. And who then might Lady Julia have told? At risk of offending Lady Anne, he must speak with her the moment she arrived in London.

"Say, Ware," Rothe said, turning back. "Has Sherbourne told you the good news? His father has been elevated to the title of earl, and Prinny made some special changes to suit them both." He laughed and explained the terms briefly. "Leave it to Prinny. I must go before I'm late. I'll get back to you on the other matter."

Why that sly dog, Lucien thought to himself. Sherry had not mentioned a word. What a great honor for his father, but of little practical use to a second son. Lucien sighed. It did not seem fair.

• • •

Upon leaving Whitehall, Lucien went straight to Lord Chadley's lodgings and wrote a brief note on the back of his calling card. He handed it to her butler.

"Please see Lady Anne receives this the moment she arrives. It is most urgent."

"Very good, my lord. I shall personally place it in her hands."

From there, he went home, sent off a note to Sherry regarding the change of plans, and settled in his study to await word from Rothe.

A half hour later, Sherry arrived. "What happened at Whitehall? Your note wasn't very helpful."

"Got you here, did it not?" Lucien told him of Rothe's concern over another leak. "If Sloane convinces him there isn't another spy in our office—as I believe he will—I'm waiting for the go-ahead to speak with Hidalgo."

"Since you won't be pressuring him as we would a suspect, shall I sit this one out? It might be less intimidating."

"Actually, I was thinking the opposite, that you might keep the conversation casual, rather laid back, and less like a one-on-one interrogation."

"I can do that." Sherry grinned, sitting down and stretching out his legs. "Perhaps adding a few jokes or amusing stories?"

"Do you know any?" Lucien asked with mock disbelief.

"You wound me. I am quite known for my wit."

"By whom?"

"Why, everyone. Do you doubt it?"

"Name one person. Go on. I challenge you."

"My mother." Sherry gave a long-suffering sigh. "Oh, all right. How long before we hear from Rothe?"

"Any time now. His meeting should be over."

"It is early for brandy, but I wouldn't mind a glass of port to while away the time."

"Then pour it yourself." Lucien waved a hand toward the sideboard. "You think an earl's son should wait on the lowly offspring of a baron?"

"A good host would," Sherry grumbled, getting to his feet. He set out two glasses. "Can the lowly offspring pour you a glass?"

"If you would, thank you," Lucien said, looking at him and raising a brow. "Well, are you not going to tell me?"

"Tell you what?"

"That you are no longer the lowly offspring of a baron but are the lowly offspring of an earl."

"Oh, that. Well, yes, it was quite the honor for Father. Happened quite quickly while you were gone. One of Prinny's whims, but Liverpool agreed."

"Do you know what was behind it?"

Sherry grinned. "I do. Officially, it's a reward for getting through a coveted piece of the Prince Regent's legislation—which Father did—but the real reason for such gratitude was Father headed off Prinny's long-time mistress Mrs. Fitzherbert the other evening until our fearless leader could shuffled another of his ladybirds out the rear entrance. I understand it was a close thing."

Lucien laughed. "I suppose that is worth an earldom, but I heard your father was going to refuse the honor until Prinny made some concessions."

"That's true." Sherry chuckled. "Father is a stubborn man. Since there was no new land attached to the title, and Father felt he was too old to change names, he asked that the official title be Earl of Sherbourne, and Prinny being Prinny, agreed. Consequently, the barony was changed to Calney, named after the village, and the baronetcy of Audley, where my half-brother has been living since he married is now the Viscounty of Audley. Graham may use the courtesy title of Viscount Sherbourne of Audley, although he may be too wrapped up in his historical research to care."

"In any event, I believe congratulations are in order." Lucien raised his glass. "A toast to your family's rise in the realm."

"We've become quite grand," Sherry said, taking a swallow of his own drink. "But a second son is still a second son."

"You'd think with all those titles, they could spare one for you," Lucien teased, knowing his partner had no such aspirations.

"Egad, Lucien, and all that responsibility that comes with one? Not for me."

And since Lucien knew he meant it, he dropped the subject. After all, the advancement up the ranks of the peerage had little real effect on younger sons.

He turned his head toward the sound of footsteps in the hall.

Hughes appeared, gave his usual dignified half-bow, and handed him a message from Whitehall. "Stay if you will, Hughes. If the contents of this note are as expected, I will need Robert to deliver a message immediately."

"Very good, sir." Hughes stood by the door.

"Yes, as I thought." Lucien handed the note to Sherry and then picked up a quill pen to compose a message to Hidalgo, asking him to call at his earliest convenience. He gave no reason. While

Lucien hated to raise the man's hopes, he knew Hidalgo would come without delay on the slightest chance there was news of Rosa.

"Tell Robert to wait for a response," Lucien instructed.

"Yes, my lord."

As soon as the tall, stately butler departed, Sherry waved Rothe's note at Lucien. "What does he mean, that Sloane knew about Rosa, but he's sure no else does? Who is sure?"

"Sloane. Rothe had not apprised his secretary of Rosa's situation or her death, but Sloane is no fool. I knew he would have figured it out by now. What we needed to know was whether anyone else in the office knew who could have leaked the information. Sloane says, no, and I trust his judgment."

"Two in-house spies in eighteen months would have ruined us."

"Rothe should be breathing a bit easier."

They had been discussing other possibilities no more than another fifteen minutes when footsteps were again heard on the stairs, and Robert appeared in the open study door. "Beg pardon, my lord, but Señor Hidalgo said he will call promptly. He asked if you had news of his daughter. Of course, I told him I did not know."

"Very appropriate, Robert. Thank you."

When the footman left, Lucien gave an audible sigh. "I knew this would raise the poor man's hopes. I dislike deceiving him, but due to Rothe's orders, I—thankfully, I might add—will not be the one to reveal the terrible truth."

• • •

Lucien and Sherry descended to the drawing room and were chatting casually by the open windows, a gentle breeze stirring the drapes, when Hughes announced Hidalgo's arrival ten minutes later. He ushered in a slightly built man with dark hair, light olive skin, and troubled brown eyes.

Lucien rose. "Do come in, sir, and be seated. I am Lucien, Viscount Ware. Are you acquainted with my friend, Andrew Sherbourne?"

"I am not, but I am pleased to meet you both."

"My pleasure entirely," Sherry said with a smile. "May I pour you a glass of port?"

"Not for me, thank you." Anxious eyes said he was impatient to get on with it. "Have you word of my daughter Rosa?"

Lucien shook his head. "I am sorry. I have nothing new to tell you."

Hidalgo frowned. "Then why am I here?"

"Let us be seated." Lucien urged him toward the seating near the window and seated himself. "It's about Hensley. Do you have any thoughts why he has not contacted you?"

"None, and it is worrying me. Should I reach out to him?"

"No. Not until we know the reason for his lack of contact. One of the possibilities we must consider is if he has learned of Whitehall's involvement."

Hidalgo's face paled, and he made the sign of the cross. "Mother Mary, I pray not. They will harm my Rosa."

Lucien refused to lie by denying it. "Let us not dwell on our fears but assess the situation. Have you shared your troubles with anyone? A friend perhaps?"

"No, of course, not," Hidalgo snapped. "I would not endanger Rosa. She is everything to me."

Lucien chest tightened, but he kept a calm expression. "I beg pardon, sir, but I had to ask." He was worried his guest was about to break down or leave, when Sherry chimed in with a welcome intervention.

"I cannot imagine how frightening the situation must be, sir. Señora de Leon told us Rosa is a lovely young woman with a sweet disposition."

Hidalgo swallowed hard. "She is that. A gentle soul, very like her mother was." He turned back to Lucien. "Pardon my outburst, my lord. I am not myself. What else can I tell you?"

"No apology needed, sir. What about your household? How much do they know?"

"I have told them nothing. That is…nothing of the truth. They believe she is visiting friends in the country."

"Could they have learned the truth by overhearing a conversation or reading a message? Is there one among them that you don't trust?"

He shook his head. "No, I don't talk or write about her abduction. Nor would I employ anyone in my home I didn't trust." His eyes widened in sudden alarm. "Are you suggesting there is a spy in my home?"

"Don't take our questions to heart," Sherry said, soothingly. "We toss around a lot of possibilities in hopes one of our theories will eventually help us sort out Hensley's odd behavior."

Hidalgo took a deep breath and appeared to settle. "Yes, all right, but it is difficult to consider I may have an enemy under my roof."

"If one of your staff knows and shared the truth, it was likely innocent," Sherry said. "A word said at the wrong time, the wrong place."

"Tell us about your household," Lucien said. "How large is it?"

"Small. A manservant, two maids, a footman, and a cook. The manservant and housemaid came with me from Spain. The second maid, an English girl, was Rosa's abigail. The cook is English too, but she has been with me more than a year, and she rarely comes above stairs, and well, you know Jose, the footman."

"And Jose's reports support your trust in you servants," Lucien said, not wanting the man to go home worried his home was filled with spies. "Have any friends or acquaintances been persistent in asking about Rosa, or shown unusual interest in what you do at the embassy?"

Hidalgo shook his head thoughtfully. "Nothing that stands out. A few friends have asked where she is but appeared satisfied with my answer that she was visiting in the country. I cannot think of a single soul whose behavior has been anything but ordinary."

"Have you discussed the situation outside your home? Anywhere—a walk in the park, in a coach, on the street?"

"No, never." The Spaniard shook his head adamantly. "My lord, surely you must comprehend—I am afraid to even speak her name. I've said nothing—except at the Embassy, Whitehall, and now here."

Lucien gave a sympathetic nod. "I regret the necessity for such plain-spoken questions, and I am truly sorry for your trouble. Thank you for talking with us." Lucien stood, bringing the interview to an end. He had not expected to hear anything indicating Hidalgo had been careless, and he hadn't. "If you hear from Hensley or anything worries you, let us know at once."

"Yes, my lord. I should be getting back." Hidalgo stood and hesitated. "How long do you think the kidnappers will keep her?"

"We have no way of knowing," Lucien said as he rang for Hughes.

"Do you think she's all right, my lord?"

Lucien's throat tightened, and he bit back the temptation to tell him the truth.

"No borrowing trouble, sir," Sherry cut in smoothly. "We are doing everything we can to discover what happened to Rosa and bring the kidnappers to justice."

Hidalgo nodded with obvious effort. "I shall try to keep that in mind."

Hughes answered Lucien's summons, and when Hidalgo's departing footsteps could be heard on the front stairs, Sherry slumped back in his chair. "He is going to be devastated when he learns the truth. Egad, Lucien. This is the most damnable case."

"Just so." Lucien stared at the floor for several moments, wondering if Hidalgo would ever recover from the loss. "Let's get out of here and discover what Pettigrew has to say after examining the remains."

"And yet another cheerful topic," Sherry said, rising. "Although I shall enjoy meeting the good doctor again, now that it isn't my neck in the noose."

Chapter Fourteen

London, 24 June 1813

Noah Pettigrew looked up from packing his medical bag, swiped a lock of dark brown hair off his forehead, and scrutinized the visitors to his Lawry Street surgery.

"Lord Ware…and Lord Sherbourne, if I am not mistaken. I am delighted to officially meet you, sir."

"The pleasure is mine now that I am no longer invisible," Sherry said with a grin. Pettigrew had refused to be introduced to him at their meeting eight months ago in order to avoid an obligation to report a fugitive to Bow Street.

Pettigrew's eyes twinkled in return. "As neither of you appear injured, I assume you are interested in the body from Seaford. I just finished my examination."

Lucien nodded. He and Pettigrew had met and conferred over several corpses, and Pettigrew had tended his injuries on more than one occasion. Lucien had learned to trust the doctor's opinion. "You assume correctly." He looked around the empty room. "It appears we have come at a good time, unless you are headed out."

"I have an appointment, but my apprentice has gone ahead. As he is skilled enough to take care of the immediate needs, I can spare a few minutes. Step into my office where we can be assured of privacy."

Lucien entered the office last and closed the door. The room looked much as it had on prior occasions, with walls lined with medical books. A large one he'd seen before lay open on a small table. As Pettigrew had explained, this was his bible when asked to handle death cases, a voluminous book written by Givanni

Morgagni in 1761, detailing the results of nearly 700 dissections and comparing those findings with the symptoms and observations at and prior to death. He'd seen Pettigrew refer to it before when a cause of death was eluding him.

He took a seat with the others and asked, "Well, doctor, have you new information for us?"

Pettigrew hesitated. "I believe I have. First of all, let me speak to one of the questions Rothe asked. He was concerned she may have died as a result of Whitehall's involvement, but by my calculations—based largely on Lady Anne Ashburn's description of what she saw and considering the cool temperature inside caves—the señorita was dead a day or two before discovery. She was already dead when Whitehall first spoke with her father."

"In a way, I guess that's good to know," Sherry said. "At least we weren't the cause."

"I fear the rest of my report has no good points."

"I'm not expecting any," Lucien said.

Pettigrew acknowledged his comment with a single nod. "She died of a severe injury to the lower chest, but it wasn't a knife. The wound is jagged, and I found a sliver of wood. I believe in was inflicted by a broken pole or chair leg."

"A crude weapon," Sherry said. "Could she have fallen on it accidentally?"

Pettigrew shook his head. "I don't think so. The placement, the angle all lead me to believe this was a matter of self-murder."

"What?" Lucien and Sherry exclaimed in unison.

"You must be mistaken," Lucien protested. "Did Rothe not explain she was abducted and held hostage by cutthroats?"

"Of course, he did, but hear me out. I also know she was beaten and interfered with repeatedly."

"*Bloody hell.*" Lucien was stunned. *Rape.* "Why the devil would they treat her so?"

Sherry shook his head as though he could not take it in. "If you're right, she must have been desperate…and lost all hope of rescue."

"I daresay she chose the only way out she could see," Pettigrew said.

"*The bloody vermin.*" Lucien struggled to suppress his anger at this hideous treatment of an innocent young woman.

"I thought I was inured to the worst of what men do," Pettigrew said. He opened a bottom desk drawer and took out a bottle of whiskey. "I could use a nip. Anyone else?" When Lucien and Sherry nodded, he produced three small glasses from the same drawer.

Not surprisingly, they downed the single fingers of whiskey in one swallow and Pettigrew filled them again.

"The brutes never meant to release her," Lucien said. "I wonder if they were told to kill her, that she was a throwaway, and they kept her alive for their own base pleasures."

"If so, she would have realized that, perhaps they even told her," Pettigrew said. "What she did took courage…she decided to take back control of her life in the only way she could."

"Hanging is too good for the likes of them," Sherry muttered.

• • •

Outside Pettigrew's surgery, Lucien watched Sherry swing onto the saddle of his riding horse. Neither of them had much to say, each caught up in his own dark thoughts. Lucien lifted a hand in farewell, and Sherry nodded. Struggling to contain his anger over Pettigrew's report, Lucien drove straight to Gentleman Jackson's boxing club on Old Bond Street. After a workout of nearly an hour, he was dripping wet but was calmer and no longer had the urge to murder the next man he saw.

While wiping down and getting dressed, he tried to set his temper aside and figure out how this disclosure affected the inquiry. It didn't really, except to harden his determination to track down every last person culpable for her heinous abuse and death. His and Sherry's task remained the same—hunt down the French spy who set up her abduction and every other low-life involved.

Once properly attired again, Lucien drove to Whitehall. Sloane was not at his desk, and Lucien strode into Rothe's office unannounced. "Have you read Pettigrew's report?"

Rothe looked up, slightly taken aback by Lucien's abrupt entrance, his face clearing with understanding at the question. "Dreadful, was it not?"

Lucien lowered his brows in a black scowl. "It was vicious, unthinkable. Every one of them has to pay."

Rothe rose. "I agree, but we must remain patient."

"Why? For what? They must know everything by now."

Rothe's gaze shot to his face. "What makes you say so?"

"Their failure to contact Hidalgo again."

"Yes, that is bothering all of us. However, it could be that Hensley or the man he reports to may be busy with something else."

"More treasonous activity, you mean?"

"Perhaps, but Hensley has a life outside of spying for France. His only daughter was betrothed to Lord Lambert's heir little more than a week ago."

"George Reeves?" Lucien cocked his head in surprise. "A cousin to one of the old and wealthy families, is he not? What a step down for him to align with the daughter of a mere scholar. I wonder what the family thinks of Hensley's secret activity."

Rothe frowned. "I doubt they are aware, but George is not from the wealthy side of the family. He is about your age. Do you not know him?"

"I have seen him, of course. Rather too self-assured…with a poor reputation at the betting tables. To my knowledge, we have never been introduced."

"Perhaps you or Sherbourne could make a closer acquaintance," Rothe mused. "He might be a source of information."

"I'll discuss it with Sherry."

"I've decided to spread the rumor of new urgent orders for Wellington. If we get no reaction from Hensley, I shall have to accept that they are on to us." He paused and gave Lucien a thoughtful look. "There is one source of information we have not considered."

Lucien stiffened. "Cade, you mean."

"Yes, but do not concern yourself. If I decide to seek his help, I shall make contact myself. You have been placed in an untenable position, becoming personally indebted to a crime lord on England's behalf."

That was not the half of it. Lucien shrugged as though it didn't matter, but of course it did. "I am hesitant to approach him too often. Whatever else he is, Cade is a businessman and will always expect something in return."

"Then he can deal with me this time."

Lucien suppressed a smile. He would like to be an unseen observer at those negotiations.

• • •

Two hours later, a note from Rothe arrived at Hays Mews stating Cade would only meet with Lucien. "I apologize for even mentioning it," Rothe wrote, "and I will understand if you choose to decline."

Well, Rothe sure hadn't thought very long before approaching Cade.

Lucien snorted as he crumpled the note and threw it on the desk in his study. *As though he would say no.* But his irritation was not with Rothe. Cade had brought him into this…again. And why? Naturally, Lucien would go, but he disliked being used in this manner.

It was in that peevish frame of mind that he arrived at Cade's Club a half hour later. Reginald, the club manager, met him at the door and waved him toward the staircase.

"He is in his office," Reginald said. "I assume you can find your way."

"Unfortunately, yes." Lucien crossed the room and climbed the wide staircase, turning down the main hallway on the first landing and stopping at the second door. He tapped, and Cade's voice bade him enter.

"Ware," Cade said rising from the chair behind his mahogany desk. "I hope I have not disrupted your day."

"As it happens, you have not," Lucien spoke crisply, "but I object to being a lackey carrying messages between you and Rothe. Could you not talk with him like one gentleman to another?"

The corner of Cade's mouth twisted in a smile, which further annoyed Lucien, and he made no effort to hide it.

"I think you could use a drink," Cade said, moving to the sideboard. "Brandy?"

"Let us just get on with this." Lucien made no move to be seated, watching Cade with a frown as the club owner known as the Gentleman Thief continued to pour two drinks. It was in Cade's capacity as a crime lord that the two men had met—several times now. He had an impressive web of spies throughout London that had been useful in Whitehall's fight against French spies within England on more than one occasion, and he had personally aided Lucien and Sherry only months ago. There was no question that Lucien owed him, but he didn't have to like it.

"Oh, sit down, Ware. I did not ask to speak with you on a whim. I have something specific to discuss, and I do not know Lord Rothe well enough to entrust a message of this importance to him."

Lucien's brows shot up. "I beg your pardon?"

"As well you should," Cade said with a half grin, clearly choosing to misinterpret Lucien's query as an apology. "Please be seated, Ware, and I shall come straight to the point." He held out a glass of brandy.

Lucien sighed, accepted the drink, and chose one of the upholstered chairs in front of Cade's desk. "So why am I here?"

"There is a price on your head." Cade spoke matter-of-factly, his eyes and voice conveying nothing. "Five hundred pounds. Enough to tempt every cutthroat in town."

Lucien's eyes narrowed, and he paused with the glass half-way to his lips. "Who?"

"That, I do not know. The funds are being held by a publican on the docks until someone shows proof they've earned them. The publican refused to name the money man."

"Perhaps I should visit this publican myself."

Lucien took a swallow of brandy, but he was not feeling nearly as nonchalant as he sounded. Cade was correct, that amount of money would have assassins coming at him from every dark corner. The timing suggested the French agent controlling Hidalgo was behind this…and yet, Lucien had made a lot of enemies in his past. It would not be the first time that trouble had followed him and Sherry from their spying days on the Continent.

"If you think he will tell you anything, it will not be so simple." When Lucien only shrugged Cade continued. "Rothe said you are looking for a French agent. Perhaps he has decided to strike first."

"It is possible," Lucien said, "but that would mean he knows more than we hope." He glanced at Cade. "How much did Rothe tell you?"

Cade picked up a note from his desk that Lucien could see was written in Mr. Sloane's hand. "He suggests we meet to discuss—and I quote 'a delicate situation regarding a young woman's abduction by a French agent and her subsequent death.' What detail can you provide?"

Lucien considered the question. The more Cade knew, the more likely he could be helpful. There really was no reason to hold back.

"I'll tell you the entire story, but for reasons soon to become apparent, most of the detail can go no further than this office." Lucien related the events of the past weeks—the abduction, the spying, the finding and losing of the girl's body, even the Seaford smugglers.

"Hensley," Cade said with a disdainful curl to his lips. "He is well-known in London's underworld. This is not the first time he has served as a go-between for illegal activities."

"Are you saying he is for hire to the highest bidder?"

"Not by me, if that is what you think. I have to have some level of trust in those I employ. But you are essentially correct, he answers to the largest bag of quid."

"What if Whitehall approached him with the required funds?"

"Doubtful. He would have to weigh the risk of double-crossing this spy, and if he had any sense at all, he'd want more than money—immunity from his own crimes."

Lucien frowned. "Rothe would balk at that. Not only is Hensley a traitor, he's responsible for this young woman's death."

Cade shook his head. "Government justice is too fastidious."

Lucien didn't ask him to explain, but he was certain neither Rothe nor Hensley would like the club owner's form of justice.

Cade took a cigar from the box on his desk, offered one to Lucien, who declined, and lit his own before going on. "Do you want me to find out who currently holds Hensley's reins?"

"Can you?"

Cade shrugged. "Is your inquiry at an impasse?"

"Not completely, but Rothe is—we're all growing piqued by the lack of progress, or I would not be here. I'm unraveling a portion of their operation, but the head of it remains elusive."

Cade nodded. "I fancy my resources are a bit better than those of Whitehall."

Lucien scowled at him. "What the devil are you about, Cade, to be so deliberately irritating?"

"Ah, did I touch a nerve? I don't mean to disparage your efforts, but it does please me when my help is required by the likes of Whitehall."

Cade was in a strange mood, and Lucien had no patience for it. "What shall I tell Lord Rothe?" He set down his brandy glass and stood. "Will you help him or not?"

"I shall do what I can."

"His lordship will be pleased."

"Oh, give way, Ware. We must discuss the bounty before you rush off. How do you plan to deal with it?"

Lucien cocked his head. "While I appreciate the warning, sir, I believe it is my concern now. But since you asked, the simple solution is to find the person behind it. My best guess is that he and the French spy are one and the same—capture him, and the bounty goes away. Now, if you will pardon me, I shall relay your message to Whitehall."

Cade leaned back in his chair and gave Lucien a long look. "As you wish. I should have news by later today or tomorrow."

"*Rothe* shall be waiting," Lucien said, making a point.

As he walked out and closed the door behind him, he heard Cade chuckle.

• • •

Lucien knew he was scowling when he returned to the curricle. It was enough to keep Finn quiet, and they drove toward Whitehall in silence. Cade had annoyed him more than usual today. Perhaps it was the man's high-handed demand to speak with Lucien, or even the warning he'd delivered, as if it was any of Cade's business. Whatever the reason, Lucien was on edge. When he pulled up in front of Whitehall, he decided not to go inside but sent Finn with Cade's respond.

He made no mention of the price on his head…not until Finn return to the curricle.

On the way home, Lucien told him about the reward. His servants deserved a warning that his activities might put them at risk from attempts on his life. The house might find itself under siege from nighttime intruders or those nosing around to learn Lucien's daily routine.

Upon arrival at Hays Mews, he discussed the matter with Hughes and Talbot.

"I shall take extra care with your pistols, my lord," Talbot said. "You may rely on them always being loaded and concealed in whatever carriage you choose for the day…unless you prefer to carry one."

"I believe I shall," Lucien said. "Just one, the other goes in the carriage." Lucien rarely went unarmed. During his days on the Continent, he had adopted the habit of carrying a knife in his right boot. That custom persisted into the present. "I am more concerned that each of you take precautions, in and away from the residence. We may have intruders or be accosted on the streets."

"I shall inform the household," Hughes said. "We shall be prepared."

Talbot nodded his agreement. "Most assuredly, my lord."

“Thank you. Now, I must inform Sherbourne. He too may be at risk.”

“If you are leaving again, should Robert not go with you?” Hughes ventured with a worried frown on his normally stoic face.

Lucien sighed. It would be the sensible thing, of course. “I am taking the curricle. There is no room.” He lifted a brow. “Before you suggest it, the closed carriage is too hot for a summer day and too cumbersome in London traffic. I did not tell you of the bounty so you could worry about me, but I had hoped you would be prepared if you needed to protect yourselves.” He turned away before they could protest further. It was impossible to chastise them when he knew they were in the right of it.

• • •

Lucien arrived at the Sherbourne residence as Sherry was coming out the entrance. Lucien leapt down. “Going out? May I offer you a lift somewhere?”

“Only the sale at Tattersall’s. My sister is looking for a new riding mount, and that husband of hers has no eye for horse flesh. I thought I would buy her a prime one for her birthday.”

“Surely you have plenty of time. Her birthday is in the autumn, is it not?”

“Yes, October, but one can never start looking too early.” Sherry gave Lucien a speculative look. “Have you something else in mind?”

“I saw Cade this morning.”

Sherry frowned. “Did Rothe send you to him *again*?”

“Not exactly.” Lucien explained Cade’s request to see him. “It turned out Cade wanted to relay a warning. Someone—as yet unidentified—has placed a price on my head.”

“Here in England? Egad, Lucien. How much?”

“Five hundred pounds.”

Sherry whistled. “The devil you say. Have you told Rothe?”

“I have not, nor can you. He would doubtless pull me off the Hidalgo inquiry, and I intend to see Señorita Hidalgo’s killer dead or in gaol.”

"How do you propose to stay alive in the meantime?" Sherry asked with a hint of asperity in his voice. "That amount of blunt will attract every low-life cutthroat in town."

"It is a complication," Lucien admitted.

"Complication! By Jove, Lucien, you can be much too careless of your own person. What would you say to me if the situation were reversed?"

"The same as I am saying now—watch your back. If I have drawn this kind of attention, it is likely you have too…or will soon." Lucien arched a brow, and Sherry reluctantly nodded. "The only way we put a stop to this is by exposing everyone in this spy chain—all the way to the top."

"How many do you reckon that is?"

"A half dozen or more." He ran down the list. "Hensley, his unknown boss, Hidalgo, one or two smugglers in Seaford, the actual kidnappers—and Rothe believes we have another leak somewhere. I'd lay down a heavy wager that he's right. They stopped using Hidalgo as soon as we knew he was spying for them. And now it appears they know I'm looking for them. Whoever they are, they couldn't know so much without having a secret informer."

"If he is not at Whitehall, and Hidalgo has been discreet, then where is the leak?"

"My wager is on the Spanish Embassy again. I shall talk with Lady Anne, but I doubt she has confided in anyone."

"What about Prinny and his friends?"

Lucien sighed. "Always a possibility, but Rothe has not kept him apprised of developments, so he considers it unlikely."

"I hope he's right. Otherwise, everyone in town must know our every move by now. So, what's next?"

"I shall urge Rothe to tell Rosa's father the truth. I must question Hidalgo and his household for details of the actual abduction and the days preceding it, and her father will not cooperate as long as he believes he'd be putting Rosa in danger."

"I don't envy Rothe the task."

"Nor I, but it is his to do. I just have to convince him it's time. When we learned of the abduction, it was already weeks old, and we fixed our attention on rescuing her, then Lady Anne found the body at Seaford, and I concentrated on that identification. Now, it's time to focus on how this happened—the when, where, and how she was taken. We may discover something overlooked or not considered before." When Sherry remained silent, Lucien shrugged. "It's an angle we haven't tried."

"I don't disagree. I was just wondering why we had not done it before, but you're correct, we were rushing to locate her and bring her home, not worrying about what happened four weeks earlier." He pulled out his pocket watch. "I just have time to make the horse sale. Why don't I meet you at your place in a couple hours?"

Lucien nodded. "Don't forget to examine the length of the pasterns." He grinned as he turned away. Two years ago, Sherry had been so taken with a showy gelding that he neglected to pay close attention to the hooves. It's short pasterns gave him a terrible, choppy gait, and he was eventually sold at a loss.

Sherry snorted in response.

Chapter Fifteen

London, 24 June 1813

Lucien arrived at Lord Chadley's residence to find the household in a bustle. Lady Anne hurried into the drawing room with a smile.

"My lord, you catch us unprepared for company," she said, holding out a hand. He took it and bowed, returning her smile.

"I apologize for coming unannounced, but what is all this?"

"I arrived late yesterday evening to find we are moving today. My father has bought a house in town and had hoped to complete the move before I arrived. As it is, we are all at sixes and sevens, and the housekeeper has hinted more than once that I am in her way." She laughed prettily. "I had your message, my lord, and I do apologize, but I have not had a moment to answer it. I had hoped to do so by this evening."

"I would not have rushed you, but I have a question that urgently wants answering… Get your bonnet, and we'll take a quick turn in the park. Your housekeeper can be about her business, and we shall have an opportunity to talk in private."

"You are being very mysterious," she said, giving him a quizzical look. "I suppose you are deliberately playing on my curiosity, but you're correct, Mrs. Pearson would do better without me." She smiled up at him. "Shall we go?"

She wasn't a fussy woman, and it only took her a matter of moments to put on hat and gloves, select a parasol, and join him.

"How was your journey from Seaford?" he asked as he handed her into his curricle. They continued to chat about this and that as they traversed the streets and entered Hyde Park. On such a beautiful summer day, it was a popular place with walkers, drivers, and riders enjoying the paths and fragrant gardens. Lucien navigated his way from the entrance to a less congested area, before turning the conversation to the Hidalgo inquiry.

"I wish you would not take offense, dear lady, but I must ask if you have spoken to anyone about Rosa Hidalgo, her death, or even mentioned her name."

She cocked her head. "Only you and Constable Harrison. Of course, there were many who knew I had found a body, but her name was unknown to them and remains so to my knowledge. Why do you ask?"

"Not even to Lady Julia?" he persisted. "It would have been natural for her to ask you."

Lady Anne shook her head, frowning at him. "She hinted at it, but when I changed the subject, she accepted it. What is this about, my lord?"

"The spies have cut off contact with Hidalgo, leading us to fear they know his part in the espionage has been discovered. We are trying to determine how they know. There may be another spy in our midst."

She turned to looked at his face, her eyes widening. "Surely you are not accusing me."

Lucien was so taken aback he laughed. "Absolutely not, my lady. Before we go hunting for spies, we want to eliminate all the innocent ways the information might have slipped out."

"I see."

"Come, now, Lady Anne," he coaxed. "We would be remiss if we did not ask everyone. Rothe even dispatched a man to Seaford to question Constable Harrison."

She pursed her lips. "You should know I would be discreet."

"I do know. Yet I had to ask."

"Oh, very well." She shifted her parasol to her right hand and laid her free fingers lightly on his hand holding the reins. "We shall talk of it no more."

He turned to smile at her in response to this conciliatory gesture and realized they were effectively hidden by her parasol. Sorely tempted to steal a swift kiss, he learned toward her.

The loud report of a rifle startled them apart as a bullet ripped through her parasol. Lady Anne let out a quickly-stifled scream, and Lucien shoved her to the floor of the curricle. The horses attempted to bolt, rearing and plunging, and Lucien fought to control them until Finn reached the horses' heads. Lucien then leapt from the carriage and swept his gaze in the direction of the shot. He saw a distant, quickly-vanishing figure.

"Stay with her, Finn. If I'm not back in a few minutes, take Lady Anne home." He plunged into the trees to reach the path on the other side and took off running.

As he ran, he searched for another glimpse of the shooter, but he knew he had little chance of catching him. While the parasol had probably saved his life and Lady Anne's, it had also kept him from getting a look at the shooter. He hadn't run far before he halted, realizing their assailant had gotten cleanly away.

He returned to find his curricle and Lady Anne surrounded by other riders and carriages.

"Did you see the shooter?" someone called.

Lucien shook his head. "Long gone. Did any of you see anything?"

While it was clear, everyone wanted to help, no one had seen the shooter—although they had all heard the shot. Lucien reached the curricle and swung aboard. "Are you all right, my lady?"

"A bit shaken, perhaps, and my parasol has seen better days." She held out the dainty white and lavender umbrella. It had a jagged tear.

He smiled at her for putting on a brave face in such a frightening moment. "I shall buy you a new one."

"You certainly shall."

"What's going on, Ware? Was it a freak accident?" someone called.

"I have no idea. I saw no one, just the bullet that ripped through Lady Anne's parasol. Some lunatic, I suppose. Or perhaps a drunk shooting at birds."

"Shooting at birds?" one man asked indignantly. "In Hyde Park?"

"The gall of it," remarked another.

"Thank you, gentlemen, for coming to our aid, but I must take Lady Anne home after such a shocking event."

"Yes, yes, of course."

The carriages and horses began to pull away. When Lucien could move his curricle, he turned around and headed out of the park.

"My lady, my apologies," he said through gritted teeth. "This is my fault. I should have anticipated it."

"What do you mean? Have there been other attempts on your life? For I assume they were not shooting at me."

"Yes. I'm sorry. I was warned and should have taken it seriously."

"Do please explain."

Her voice was so calm that he wasn't sure if she was angry or worried.

"Cade told me there is a bounty on my head of five hundred pounds. Confound it. I knew that amount would attract cutthroats eager to make such a tidy sum, but I miscalculated in assuming they would not attack in daylight or in such a public place." He pulled up in front of her current home, where many of the trunks where now loaded on wagons. He handed her down and urged her inside the house. "Is Lord Chadley at home?" he demanded of the butler.

"No, sir, he retreated to White's, I believe."

"Then I shall find him there and explain what happened."

"Lord Ware, please wait," Lady Anne urged. "We need to talk before you terrify my father."

He gave her an astonished look. "You cannot expect to hide this from him. This was my fault, Lady Anne, and I owe your father an explanation and an apology."

"For heaven's sake, Lucien," she said sharply. "The drawing room. Please."

He lifted a brow. "Very well, my lady. I shall join you in a moment." He waited until she turned and walked away, then he had her butler dispatch a message for him. When he entered the drawing room, she was seated near the window. "Now, my lady, I apprehend you have something you wish to say to me about recent events."

"Not about the shooting...well, not exactly, but about your wish to castigate yourself before Lord Chadley. He will not appreciate it nor understand it. You will embarrass him and alarm him unduly. By now, he is used to his daughter's involvement in unusual *incidents*."

Lucien's lips twitched despite the seriousness of the situation. "Being shot at is a common place thing for you, my lady? I had not realized that. Perhaps it is you who has endangered me."

"Don't tease me about this. I was only pointing out that you would distress him without cause. I am unharmed. It would be wise that he could see that for himself before he hears the details of the shooting."

"My dear, I did not intend to throw myself at your father's feet—unless you think I should." His lips twitched as he eyed her, then he went on more soberly. "I had hoped to inform his lordship you were unharmed before someone else told him you'd been the victim of a shooting. The news will be at White's by now."

"Oh, I had not thought of that." She looked uncertain. "Perhaps we should send word to the club."

"Already done."

She arched a brow.

"Your butler sent a message at my request. No doubt we should expect your father shortly."

"Unless he's talking politics," Lady Anne said with a slight smile. "In that event, he will accept your assurances of my safety and continue his discussion, giving you ample time to explain this bounty to me. Who would do such a thing, and why?"

Lucien sighed. "I assume it is connected to the Hidalgo inquiry."

"If so, would that not mean the spies know you are onto their game?"

"Exactly."

Lord Chadley strode into the room, precluding any further discussion. Although of only medium height with his graying fair hair tousled from his haste, the earl had a commanding presence, and the household came to an immediate halt. His worried blue eyes found his daughter, and Lady Anne hurried toward him. He kissed both her cheeks and looked her up and down. "Is there no place you are safe, my dear daughter? A murderer in Seaford, and now a shooter in Hyde Park?"

"I am perfectly unharmed, Father." She returned the cheek kisses before stepping back. "But you are ignoring our guest."

"Yes, you are correct to remind me. Lord Ware, thank you for your message. I shall not be surprised if you snub my daughter if she keeps this up."

"My lord." Lucien stepped forward. "I am afraid this incident rests on my head."

"How so?"

Lucien had thought about how to answer this question. "From time to time I have assisted Whitehall in certain matters I am not at liberty to discuss. I believe my current inquiry led to today's shooting. I was aware of some risk, and under the circumstances, I should not have taken your daughter driving."

"I see." Chadley studied him thoughtfully. "One hardly thinks of Hyde Park as a dangerous place—not during the day."

"Someone has placed a price of five hundred pounds on his head," Anne added indignantly.

Not helpful, Lucien thought.

"Oh, now I do see your point, Ware." Chadley frowned. "Rather thoughtless of you, my lad."

"It was, sir."

"Father, honestly."

"Anne, I cannot have you driven about town by escorts likely to be attacked at any moment."

"I understand and shall not repeat the mistake, sir," Lucien said.

"Now wait. Am I to have no say in this?" Anne demanded.

"No," Lucien said.

"Not a bit," her father agreed.

Lucien turned toward Lady Anne. "We now have the measure of how reckless these people can be. I cannot knowingly endanger others, particularly you, my lady. I am afraid our excursions are at an end until the situation is resolved. I shall once again beg your pardon and take my leave." He bowed to both of them. "Good day, Lord Chadley, Lady Anne."

• • •

As Lucien approached Whitehall for the third time that day, he was marshalling his arguments to convince Rothe to inform Hidalgo of his daughter's death. He drove up just in time to catch Lord Rothe leaving the building. Another meeting, Lucien assumed. Palace or Parliament?

He tossed the reins to Finn and jumped down. "Lord Rothe, may I have a quick word?"

The marquess stopped abruptly. "Ware, are you all right? And Lady Anne? I heard there was a shooting."

The devil was in it now. Lucien had not considered that Rothe would already have heard of the incident. He could no longer avoid telling him of the bounty…but perhaps he could use it to bolster his argument.

"We were unharmed, sir…this time. Cade says there is a price on my head, which places everyone around me at risk. I'm convinced our spy is behind it, adding even greater urgency to finding him. Thus, I have a request. In order to move the inquiry forward, we need the father's active cooperation. We won't get it as long as he believes Rosa's life is in danger."

"You want me to tell him she is dead."

"Yes, sir."

"How will that help? What more can Hidalgo tell you?"

"Since following Hensley has produced nothing, it is imperative Sherry and I take a hard look at the original abduction—where was she taken, how she happened to be there on that particular day. To determine that, we must start with her daily life, details we can only learn from Hidalgo and his household. It should add new angles, new suspects to our inquiry."

"He may refuse to help you," Rothe said. "He'll be angry we kept the truth from him so long. I would be."

"So would I, but I would also want her killers punished."

Rothe nodded slowly. "All right. I trust your judgment in this and shall talk with Hidalgo yet today. First, I must soothe a disgruntled Lord Chancellor on another matter."

"If you wouldn't mind, sir, I would like to know when your meeting with Hidalgo is set. I will try to talk with him before he leaves Whitehall. If I can offer him something, such as taking him to the cave where Rosa was found, he may be more inclined to assist us."

"It is worth a try. Providing I can reach him, you should hear from Sloane within an hour or two."

• • •

Lucien forced himself to work on correspondence while he waited. When he heard someone at the front door, he stood to meet whom he assumed would be Hughes with a message from Whitehall. Instead, he heard his father's voice say, "I shall find my own way, thank you, Hughes."

The Earl of Salcott appeared in the study doorway, impeccably attired as usual, his face a mixture of worry and anger. He looked his son up and down. "Well, you seem uninjured. Were you going to tell me about this shooting? Or the price on your head? Really, Lucien, this is too much." He tossed his hat on the desk and headed for the sideboard, picked up the decanter of brandy, and poured himself a drink.

"Good day, sir. Do help yourself."

Salcott turned to stare at him. "You appear rather cool about this. Were you the same when someone was shooting at Lady Anne? Confound it, Lucien, you should have come to me."

"You already appear to be well informed."

"Someone is always eager to relay the latest on-dit regarding my heir. Is Lady Anne unharmed as well?"

"She is." Lucien sighed. "It was careless of me to take her driving."

"You knew about the bounty?"

"I did," Lucien admitted. "Cade told me. I assume it's related to my latest inquiry, but I don't have a name for the person behind it." He gave a reluctant smile. "Do sit down, Father, and enjoy that very fine brandy." He waved a hand to a cushioned mahogany armchair and took his seat behind the desk. "I beg pardon that my affairs have caused you this concern."

Salcott gave a nod, sighed heavily, and took a seat. "Did Chadley ring a peal over your head?"

"Not exactly, but I am not to escort Lady Anne until this is resolved."

"Sensible. I suppose you would not consider giving up this inquiry to one of Whitehall's other agents."

"You know, I would not."

"Yes, of course, I know. Have you taken *any* steps to protect yourself?"

"I've informed my household and Sherbourne, and I have my pistol." Lucien patted his pocket. "Another is in my carriage."

"Hardly sufficient." Whatever else Salcott was about to say was belayed by a tap on the study door.

Upon Lucien's command, Hughes entered and handed him a folded note. "Just delivered, my lord."

It was a message from Sloane—Hidalgo was on his way to see Rothe.

Lucien turned to his father. "I beg pardon, sir. I am needed at Whitehall."

Salcott rose, placing his empty glass on the desk. "I shall make what inquiries I can regarding this bounty, but if it is coming from London's underworld, I doubt I will learn anything." He hesitated and cleared his throat. "Do take care of yourself, my son."

Lucien nodded, hearing the emotion in those words. "I shall do my best, sir."

"See that you do."

They left the house together, and Lucien set off in the curricle with Finn up behind. He was waiting in Rothe's outer office a half hour later when the marquess's door flew open and Hidalgo burst out, his head down. Lucien moved to intercept him, stepping between the man and the hallway door.

"Señor Hidalgo, I need to speak with you."

"Not now." The Spaniard's voice was choked, clearly holding back tears of grief or rage, more likely a bit of both.

"I am sorry, but it is rather urgent."

Hildalgo pulled up short, realizing Lucien had blocked his path. "Sir, I have just received terrible news. Please do not detain me."

"I know, sir," Lucien said gently. "I am truly sorry for the loss of your daughter. But I need your help in catching the people responsible. I will try not to take up much of your time."

"I cannot. Not at the moment." The man's chin trembled. "I knew this news was coming, but I had hoped… Yes, I want them punished," he said with a brief flash of anger quickly extinguished. "Come to my home in the morning, at ten, if you would. I will assist you in any manner I can."

"I appreciate it," Lucien said. He decided not to mention Seaford, not now. There was plenty of time for that journey later if Hidalgo wished to go. At the moment the *where* she died was probably unimportant to her grief-stricken father. "You have my sincere sympathy, sir."

"Thank you, my lord."

Lucien stepped aside and watched in silence as Hidalgo walked away, a heartsick man trying to hold himself together. He was in no shape to answer questions this evening. Lucien had known that, but he had gotten what he wanted. In the morning, he and Sherry would search the señorita's room and interview everyone in the residence. Somehow this avenue of inquiry felt right. They needed to go back to the day of the abduction and follow Rosa's movements—and the Hidalgo household was the obvious place to start.

Chapter Sixteen

London, 25 June 1813

At the agreed hour, Lucien and Sherry presented themselves at the Hidalgo lodgings, a modest suite of rooms just off Piccadilly, and found Señor Hidalgo awaiting them in the main parlor with his household assembled. His five servants—a Spanish manservant, a female English cook, a Spanish housemaid, Rose's English abigail, and Jose, the footman—stood around their master's chair as though to protect him. Their solemn faces and the women's puffy eyes indicated they'd been given the sad news.

Hidalgo had himself under control this morning, but Lucien could see the facade was thin. He would have to interview him with care.

As they had discussed on the way over, Lucien spoke with Hidalgo alone, and Sherry took the servants to a separate parlor.

Lucien and Hidalgo settled into chairs in the parlor the Spaniard used as a study. A desk and chair stood in one corner, and bookshelves covered the wall opposite the fireplace. The single window had been opened to catch the morning breeze and with it came the sound of singing birds and the scent of honeysuckle from the garden.

"I am sorry to intrude at a time like this," Lucien began.

Hidalgo shrugged. "There will not be a better time. Ask your questions, Lord Ware. I can hardly bear to think about Rosa's suffering, and I will do whatever I can to see the brutes punished."

"We want that too, sir," Lucien said gently. "I'd like to go back to the day Rosa disappeared. Our answers may lie there. When did you last see her?"

"That morning in the breakfast room. We chatted about nothing in particular as I recall. My mind was already on work. I had letters to write and a minor delegation to greet. Nothing important…if only I had known."

"How did Rosa act? Any different than usual? Did she mention her plans for the day?"

"She was as always, soft-spoken, cheerful. I don't believe she talked about her plans. She expected to be home by evening because she said she would see me at dinner." His chin started to tremble, and he took a deep breath.

Lucien paused, giving him a moment to collect himself, before asking, "What time did you leave?"

"About eight. I wanted an early start on the day."

"And when did you learn she was missing?"

Hidalgo sighed. "Not until I came home that night about seven. The servants know how important my work is, and they had not wanted to interrupt me. They assumed Rosa had just been delayed and that I likely knew where she was." He shook his head sadly. "I did not. Whatever assurances they had told themselves, it was clear they were alarmed. Our manservant met me at the door and reported she wasn't yet home, that she had left around two in a hired hackney and had not returned. I sent the footman to locate the hackney driver, but my first thought was of an accident. I sent the other servants and two street boys to check the hospitals and our family physician."

"What time was this?"

"Half seven or closer to eight, I suppose. Before any of them returned, I received the note."

Lucien sat up straight. "What note?"

"Telling me she'd been taken."

"Who brought it? Did you keep it?"

Hidalgo shook his head. "No. I wish I had, but all I could think was to follow their instructions. Our manservant found it. He answered a knock on the front door. No one was there, but the note lay on the step."

"What exactly did it say?"

"That they had my daughter, and her life depended on what I did." He stopped and looked at Ware. "But I did everything they said, why did they kill her?" He cut himself off. "I beg pardon, my lord. I know you don't have the answer. Where was I? Oh, yes, I was told to burn the note, wait for further orders, and to tell no one." He hung his head. "I nearly sent word to Envoy de Leon. I wish now I had, but I was terrified for Rosa."

"So, you burned it."

"Yes. I felt I had to."

"Can you describe it for me? The type of paper, the handwriting?"

"How could I forget? The sight of it is burned in my memory. Cheap paper you can get everywhere. Rather sloppy writing, the words and spelling suggested the lower classes, a man's bold stroke, I'd say. The appearance of that note frightened me even more—to think of her in the hands of low-life ruffians."

Her captors were indeed brutal cutthroats, but there were more intelligent minds behind this. "When did they contact you again… and how?" he asked.

"Another note, directing me to the Blue Goose pub, to go alone, and again, burn the note and tell no one. It said someone would meet me there. So, I went. Hensley sat down at my table and explained what I had to do to save Rosa."

"Had you known him previously?"

"Not at all." Hidalgo frowned as though baffled how this could have happened to him. "I don't recall ever seeing him before that night."

That was unexpected. Lucien narrowed his eyes in thought. If they weren't acquainted, how had Hidalgo been chosen? He had access to the Spanish Embassy, but so did others. Who had made the assessment that Señor Hidalgo was vulnerable?

"Think back to those weeks before the kidnapping. Had anyone been asking about the embassy, your work there? Had you or Rosa added someone new to your household or circle of friends? I'm looking for anyone who might have approached you and studied your—and Rosa's—activities."

"I can't think of anyone..." Hidalgo slowly shook his head, clearly going over the past, searching for something or someone who in retrospect appeared suspicious. "Rosa had only been in England two months," he finally said. "I came with the de Leons eight months earlier and left Rosa behind with my sister. But she wrote, repeatedly begging to join me, and I eventually agreed. I wish now I could take it all back." He swiped a hand across his face. "She made new friends right away, but mostly with the Envoy's family or their acquaintances. I hired the English abigail for Rosa, but that was the only new staff. I didn't notice anyone watching us. Nor do I recall anyone expressing an uncommon interest in Rosa or the embassy." Hidalgo's shoulders sagged. "Obviously, I should have been more vigilant. I seem to be no help at all."

"Every bit you recall helps us, sir." Lucien pulled a paper from his waistcoat pocket. "Would you look over this list of Rosa's friends and acquaintances? It's the one you gave Lord Rothe a few weeks ago. I want to be certain it's complete. I noticed there are no gentlemen callers. She was a pretty young woman. Surely there was someone."

Hidalgo lips parted in the ghost of a smile. "She had callers all right *and* flowers, but no one she favored or encouraged. I do not recall their names. She had a sweetheart at home in Spain. Nice young man. They might have wed in time..." He sighed. "As for female friends, the ones I recall are on the list, but her personal maid, Betty, or Señora de Leon might be better able to say. The señora had been kind enough to make a few introductions for her into polite society."

"I believe I need bother you no more today, sir. I have enough to start other inquiries." Lucien rose, and Hidalgo stood with him. "Again, sir, let me extend my sympathies."

"Thank you, my lord. I wish I could tell you more. Perhaps after my mind has cleared..."

"You know how to reach me. Oh, I nearly forgot to ask—did your footman locate the hackney driver?"

"He did. The jarvey had let her down at Grimley's bookstore, and he was supposed to pick her up in two hours. She wasn't there when he returned."

"And the bookshop proprietor?"

Hildago nodded. "Yes, he talked to him too. She made one quick book purchase and left. He didn't know where she went from there. She came in and left alone." Hidalgo sighed. "I do not know what she was thinking not to take her maid."

"Thank you, sir. I shall keep you informed as best I can."

Hidalgo nodded and turned away to stare out the window. Lucien stepped into the hall and quietly closed the door behind him. Jose, the Spanish-looking agent on Rothe's payroll, was waiting.

"A word, my lord."

"Is something wrong?" Lucien asked.

"I'm not certain. The last two nights, I thought I saw someone watching the house, but when I looked around, I found no one. I might have attributed it to shadows if I hadn't seen a man following Hidalgo when he went to meet with Rothe yesterday. He fled before I got close enough to catch him or even get a good look—a large, rather non-descript ruffian."

"A common thief?" Lucien mused, thoughtfully. "I suppose not. This is not a wealthy household. But why would the villains who took Rosa be hanging around? Do they hope to use Hidalgo again? How could they imagine—? Beg pardon, Jose, I'm thinking aloud. Keep watch but don't scare them off."

"I'll be cautious. I suppose you're right—it's the same gang, sir, but how could they gain his cooperation again?"

Lucien shook his head. "Is there anyone else he values so much? A lady friend, perhaps?"

"Not that I've heard about. At night, he stays close to home. Could they be looking for an opportunity to silence him? Perhaps he knows something that could expose them."

"If he does, I'm not aware of it. Have you mentioned the incidents to him?"

"I did...both nights. He brushed them off saying he had nothing left for them to take."

"Ah, well, he is a bitter man...with good reason."

Jose swiveled his head toward the back of the house. "Someone is coming. I'd rather they didn't overhear us talking. I should go, but I'll figure this out."

As Jose disappeared down the hall, Lucien tapped on the door where Sherry was interviewing the other servants. He found him speaking with a young girl in a maid's uniform.

"Lord Ware, this is Betty, the Señorita's abigail," Sherry said. "I asked her to stay behind so you could hear what she has to say."

"A pleasure to meet you, Betty. I expect you knew your mistress better than most and were privy to secrets no one else knew."

She looked uncertainly at Sherry. "Well, I suppose. There was the note."

"Which note is this?" Lucien asked, wondering if she was referring to the notes Hidalgo received.

"The one I gave to Señorita Rosa."

Lucien's interest spiked at the unexpected reply. "The day she disappeared?"

"Yes, milord, just past mid-day. A street boy brought it, and I took it to her."

"Who was it from? Did she tell you what it said?"

"No, milord. I don't know anything except it was pretty writing."

"How did your mistress react?"

"After reading it, she put it in her pocket," Betty said. "Then she asked for her hat, gloves, and parasol. She said she was going out for a while, and she left."

"She did not say where?"

"No, my lord."

"Why didn't you or the other maid accompany her?"

"I asked, milord. She said we were not needed. I thought she was meeting someone who would act as chaperone."

"Had she done that before?"

"Once or twice. One time I recall she met a group of ladies at the museum."

"Yes, I see how that would be. Going back to the note, did she seem surprised or concerned by what she read?"

"Oh, no. It made her smile."

Possibly an offer of a pleasurable outing by someone she knew and liked. An invitation to a soiree? A trip to the museum, an afternoon play, a shopping trip, or just a visit with friends? It could be any of those or a host of other entertainments.

"You said a street boy delivered it. Did you know him?"

"No, sir. Never seen him before."

"She gave me his description," Sherry said.

"Very good." The likelihood of finding a street boy was poor. Perhaps Finn could make those inquiries. He knew the street life much better, and his diminutive size was non-threatening, allowing him to blend into parts of the city where Lucien could not.

"Had she received similar notes before? Same paper maybe, same handwriting?"

"I…I don't really know," Betty said with a thoughtful frown, "but it was very pretty handwriting."

She'd said that before. It must have stood out. Cultured and probably feminine, Lucien said to himself. A lady suggesting an outing. Was this woman part of the plot to lure Rosa out that day, or had the kidnapper been watching the house to catch Rosa whenever she left? Identifying the writer should answer that question.

"Would you recognize the writing if you saw it again?"

"I might." Betty nervously twisted her hands in her apron. "The mistress has a drawer where she keeps her letters, but it doesn't seem right to go through her private things."

"Mr. Hidalgo gave his permission," Lucien assured her, "and it might help us find those who harmed her. If you could show us her room now, we shall take a look."

Señorita Rosa's bedchamber suited a young woman—pastel colors and delicately styled furniture. The top of her dresser held a few jars of creams, a bottle of perfume, a jewelry box, brushes, combs and a small glass container of hair pins. The wardrobe was filled with gowns and colorful bandboxes for hats.

"It looks as though she was fond of shopping."

"She loved hats and ribbons, in particular, and her papa was most generous," Betty said with a smile. She directed them to a rosewood desk near the window. "The letters are in there."

Lucien opened the top and found a packet of letters and notes tied with pink ribbon. He wanted to read every one of them, but that could come later. For now, he shuffled through the stack, showing each one to Betty.

"Do you see the writing that was on the note that day?"

"I'm not sure. It was weeks ago, milord, but it might have been this one or this other one." She pointed to two letters that to Lucien's eye were written by similar but different feminine hands. He set them aside. He was surprised by the number of letters in masculine writing until he recalled her young man in Spain. He handed those to Sherry and hoped his partner's Spanish was good enough to read through them. Señorita Rosa had likely told her young man about her new friends and her activities since coming to England. Perhaps his comments in response might yield something useful.

"Thank you, Betty. You have been very helpful, but we won't keep you from your duties any longer."

"You're not keeping me from much, my lord. Now that Miss Rosa is gone, there isn't much for me to do, and I must seek a new position."

Lucien nodded in sympathy. "I am sure you will find something soon."

Engrossed in a letter, Sherry barely looked up. "Thank you, miss."

As soon as the door closed behind her, Lucien turned to his partner. "What has you so enthralled?"

"Oh, nothing, really. Her young man in Spain was quite smitten, and he intersperses fond phrases and endearments throughout his letters. It's difficult to glance through them and pick out what is important."

"Nothing yet?"

"Not much. He mostly talks about what their friends and family are doing in Spain. A little about the war, but nothing significant. He does say it is nice she has made new friends, in particular another woman." Sherry looked up. "Of course, he doesn't mention her name. He felt such an established acquaintance would be beneficial to show Rosa the expectations of English society."

"Established," Lucien mused. "Sounds like an older woman, but given his age—which I assume is close to Rosa's—that could mean anyone beyond one and twenty."

"Then you and I are nearly ancient."

"No doubt. At seventeen, ten years is a world of difference," Lucien conceded. "Perhaps a young matron had taken Rosa under her wing. Strange that her father wouldn't know…unless it was Señora De Leon. She has denied it but may not realize how important the acquaintance was to Rosa."

Lady Anne would be the perfect person to look for such a connection, and seeking her help would be an excellent excuse for him to call upon her. The attendance of an earl's daughter was always sought for parties and soirees, and she could quietly ask around to see who might have established a friendship with Rosa. While he couldn't take Lady Anne around town with him, she should be in no danger in her own home or attending social events with her father or other female friends.

With such an agreeable visit in mind, Lucien parted from Sherry outside the Hidalgo residence and headed for the address on James Street near Grosvenor Square where Lord Chadley had moved his household on the previous day.

The very proper butler received him with only a slight hesitation and a flicker of the eyes revealing he was disconcerted by Lucien's appearance. He recovered his aplomb with a bow and said he would inquire if Lady Anne was receiving.

Chapter Seventeen

25 June 1813

"Lord Ware is asking to see you, my lady."

Anne looked up from her reading, a quick smile crossing her face. After the events of yesterday, she had feared he might stay away for a while. "Show him in, Staves. His lordship is always welcome here," she added, hearing the question in his voice. "Please order a tea tray for us."

"Very good, my lady." Staves bowed and departed.

Anne set down her book and smoothed her skirts; a tingle of excitement brought a faint rush of warmth to her face. She was pleased Lucien was not being deterred by her father's worries…or his own scruples. She had already been scheming how she could arrange to see him and remain involved in the Señorita Hidalgo inquiry.

"Lady Anne." He crossed the room with a confident stride and bowed before her. His grey eyes twinkled as though hiding some secret amusement. "I am delighted to find you recovered from yesterday's unfortunate incident."

She returned his smile. "As I mentioned before, it is not my first unfortunate incident, my lord."

"Do not remind me." He gestured toward the hallway. "Your butler was hesitant to announce me. Have I been banned from the house?"

"To be sure, you have not. Father was disturbed by the shooting, but he will have forgotten it by now."

"Somehow I doubt that," Lucien said. "He has every right to expect your gentlemen callers to keep you safe. Until this bounty is lifted, I shall not be escorting you anywhere. Indeed, I fear I will have to work hard to regain your father's trust." Lucien cleared his throat. "Nonetheless, I am here with a request I am doubtful he would approve."

Anne straightened eagerly. "Oh, tell me. For I am certain *I* shall very much approve."

Lucien frowned. "You must make me a promise first. No overstepping the bounds this time. If you do anything to place yourself in danger, your father will not forgive me—and I shall not ask for your assistance again."

"All right, I promise. What am I to do?"

"Lady Anne, have you been listening to me?"

"Yes, I have," she said with exaggerated patience. "You don't want me to put myself in danger, and I just promised I would not." In truth, she had never *deliberately* gotten herself into danger. She might have misread a situation or two…but never by intention. "Have you learned something new? How can I assist you?"

"Allow me first to explain our current area of concentration. To pull off her abduction, someone watched Rosa's activities in the weeks before she was kidnapped, likely someone close to her. As she was only in London two months, we hope to trace her movements—and identify everyone who befriended her in such a short time." He went on to tell her about the note Rosa's abigail had described. "After they studied her activities, I believe they used the information to lure her from the house—by way of that note. But to where? If we can discover that, it could break open the investigation."

Anne tilted her head. "It is strange no one saw her taken or reported it at the time. Where could she have been that there were no witnesses?"

"A very good question," Lucien said. "A remote location, perhaps. Or inside a house or shop. If only we had that note."

"Since that is not possible, the woman who wrote it must be found." Anne pursed her lips in thought. "How were you able to talk with the abigail and discover the note existed without arousing the father's suspicion?"

"I should have mentioned that before—he was told the truth last night."

"Oh, that poor man. I daresay he was devastated."

"As you would expect, but he and his servants are doing everything they can to assist us. Without her abigail, we wouldn't have the other notes for comparison."

"Notes?" Anne leaned forward. "Was there more than one?"

"She took the last one—the critical one—with her, but we went through the correspondence we found in her desk, hoping to find letters or notes from the same person. Most of the letters were from a young man back in Spain, but her abigail Betty picked out two notes with similar handwriting to that final message."

"May I see them?"

He smiled. "I anticipated your request and brought them with me." He handed her the letters from the pocket of his waistcoat. "As you can see, the handwriting is definitely feminine."

"Not by the same hand," she said after a swift glance. "There are similarities but these were written by different women."

"I agree, and although it seems likely, we cannot be certain either matches the message that prompted Señorita Rosa to leave her home that day."

Anne continued to study the notes. "The women are educated in proper correspondence, which in all likelihood puts them among the upper-class."

He nodded his agreement. "The one signature seems to be 'Nora' but the other is written with such flourish I cannot make it out."

"I believe it is an initial," Anne said. "May I keep these and study them?"

"Yes, to be sure. You will need them more than I do."

She looked up. "Oh, for what? Am I to identify the ladies who wrote them?"

"If you can. Her young man in Spain also mentioned an "established" woman who had befriended Rosa. That might give you a place to start."

"Might that not be Señora de Leon?"

"It could," Lucien said. "I am rather counting on you to find out."

Anne grew thoughtful. "If I am to fulfil such a task, how much of Rosa's story can I tell? I will need a good reason for showing so much interest in her."

"News of her death should be around town by tonight if it isn't already. You might say you were in Seaford at the time of discovery and became intrigued with her story. It would be natural to ask about her and her friends…and to mention how sad it must be for them."

"A good story, my lord, based on a piece of the truth."

"The best ones are."

She cocked her head at him. "You are much too good at this. How shall I ever know whether the things you tell me are true or not?"

"Would I dissemble with you?" His look was amused.

"If it suited your purpose."

"You sorely misjudge me, my lady."

"Oh, give over, sir." She laughed. "You'd deceive your grandmother in pursuit of one of your inquiries."

Lucien shrugged with mock remorse. "You have caught me out, dear lady. As you have such a low opinion of me, I suppose I must look elsewhere for assistance."

"Now, you *are* being absurd, sir. You know I am delighted to help. Since I am due at Madam Carwell's soiree this evening, I shall begin my inquiries there and report to you as soon as I have something of interest."

"You must be cautious. Bear in mind we are dealing with traitors and cutthroats."

"I shall not forget."

"What was the situation in Seaford when you left? Had Constable Harrison made any progress in identifying the smuggler passing secrets?"

She lifted a doubtful hand. "I am not sure. I saw him once in the village. He said he had someone in mind, but he was not ready to accuse anyone without proof. I thought he was rather upset by the prospect."

Lucien nodded. "I am not surprised he is finding this difficult. It is hard to doubt those you know, and he knows everyone in the village and the surrounding countryside. Perhaps I shall write and inquire if he needs assistance. I'd hate for the lad to get himself in trouble. I have my own suspicions, and if they prove true, the answers will cause him no end of grief."

Anne studied Lucien's serious face. He was unhappy with whatever he was thinking. "Is it someone I know?"

"I'm afraid so."

She wanted to ask for a name, but his tone made it clear he would not tell her until he was ready. So be it. For the moment, she was satisfied to be part of the inquiry again.

"Have you considered asking Lady Castlebridge for help?" she asked.

"Sophia or Lady Julia?"

"Lady Sophia. She has been your past source for society gossip, has she not?"

Lucien frowned. "Yes. Before her marriage."

"Are you concerned that contacting her might start tongues wagging?" she asked, stealing a peek at his averted face.

"I am concerned how Lord Castlebridge might view it."

Anne wasn't quite sure what he meant. Was he seeing Sophia in secret? "Has she given him reason to doubt her?"

"Certainly not." He shook his head with a hint of a smile. "I daresay Sherry's words of caution have made me uncomfortable over a situation that does not exist."

"So-o, if I see her at the soiree, may I enlist her aid?"

Lucien gave her a look as though debating her motive. "If you wish. Remind her to be discreet."

Anne chuckled. "I hardly think the lady needs my advice on discretion." She went on quickly as Lucien appeared ready to protest. "But I will mention it. Honestly, my lord, we ladies are fully competent of prevarication when necessary."

Lucien threw back his head and laughed as he rose. "Now that has put me in my place. Thank you, Lady Anne. I shall take my leave and await the results of your foray into the world of social intrigue."

Anne stared at the empty archway, listening to his departing steps in the hall. She didn't move until she heard Staves say, "Good day, my lord," and the outer door closed.

A grin slowly spread across her face, and she rose, hurrying up the stairs to plan what she should wear that evening and to consider how she might phrase her inquiries naturally so as not to rouse suspicion or the interest of gossipmongers. Anne found that she felt protective of Rosa and resented the thought of her name being bandied about. Perhaps Lady Sophia Castlebridge would have some ideas on the best, most subtle approach.

She nearly giggled when she recalled Ware's face when she suggested conferring with Lady Sophia. Clearly he was disconcerted by the prospect of the two ladies spending time together. She wondered what he thought his former mistress might tell her.

• • •

The soiree might have proved insipid if Anne had not had her inquiries and the presence of Lady Sophia to keep her entertained. She had sent a note to Sophia Castlebridge as soon as Lucien left, received her delighted reply, and the two women had met briefly upon arrival at the party to discuss strategy. The evening had barely started, however, when they realized they would have to move more quickly than they'd planned. The music for the evening was provided by the hostess's niece—a harpist whose skills were apparent only to her doting aunt—and guests were beginning to leave early.

Anne found it was easy to get people talking about Rosa. As Lord Ware had predicted, the news of her death had spread and was already the center of gossip. Everyone Anne spoke to was shocked and sympathetic, but none had known the señorita beyond a passing word or two.

Two hours into the evening, Lady Sophia approached Anne with the brief flash of a confiding smile. This would be their third tête-à-tête to talk things over. Anne returned the smile. She rather liked the lady and her quick wit, but Anne acknowledged to herself she might have felt otherwise if the Widow Stine had not recently married again to become Lady Castlebridge.

"Any luck?" Lady Sophia asked.

Anne shrugged. "No one really knows her. I suppose it's the wrong kind of crowd. Wouldn't her father have chosen a more political gathering?"

"I believe you are right." Lady Sophia pursed her lips. "I hear they are terribly boring though, and most are only attended by politicians and their wives."

"We would be sadly out of place."

"Very true." Lady Sophia said. "We shall have to choose just the right affair. If you trust me to look into it, I shall send word when I discover a likely event."

Anne's face brightened. "By all means. I am too recently come to London to know such things. I shall be happy to rely on you."

"Did Señorita Hidalgo's abigail not know her mistress's acquaintances?"

"Apparently not. I know Ware and Sherbourne questioned her."

Lady Sophia titled her head. "I wonder if one of us should try. No, forget that. Lucien would have asked for help if he felt she was holding back."

"I believe he would," Anne said.

"Then it's up to us to question the ladies. I *do* hope to find a suitable gathering soon." Lady Sophia smiled conspiratorially. "We make a good team, do we not?"

• • •

26 June 1813

Another chance to test their skills was not long in coming. Late the following afternoon, Anne received a message from Lady Sophia and shortly thereafter an invitation to a rout at the Galways' that evening.

The lady works fast, Anne thought, already wondering what one wore to a meeting of politicians. Something serious and conservative no doubt. Her half-mourning clothes in lavender should be just the thing. Perhaps she could convince her father to attend; his escort would create the perfect excuse for her own presence.

With that in mind, she successfully prevailed upon him over dinner, and the Chadley carriage dropped father and daughter at the Galways at a quarter past ten that evening, a fashionable hour. Anne had chosen a lavender gown with ivory trim and had a matching shawl of lavender lace draped over her arms, purely for fashion given the heat of the late June evening.

She swiftly spotted Lady Sophia but remained on her father's arm as he introduced her to his acquaintances. When he became involved in an intense political discussion, she tugged on his arm and whispered, "I see a friend and will find you later."

"Very good, my dear," Chadley said absently. "Enjoy yourself."

"Yes, Father, you too." She smiled to herself. He was barely listening to her and had already turned back to his discussion. She did not mind at all for it fit in with her own plans for the evening. And, to be sure, she was delighted to see him so engaged with society again.

Anne slipped across the room, idly glancing at some of the political pamphlets on one of the tables, and finally stopped beside Lady Sophia. "How long have you been here? Anything of interest so far?"

"Lord Castlebridge and I were only minutes before you, and I have not had much of a chance to chat yet. However, looking around, I'd say, we have a likely crowd. Do you know many of the guests??"

"Very few. Only those who are my father's particular friends."

"Then let me point out a half dozen you should know. The dark-haired lady in poloma green across from us is Carmen de Leon, the wife of the Spanish Envoy. That is her husband, the short, slender man who just joined your father's group."

"The señora is older than I expected," Anne remarked, studying the matronly woman in her late thirties with shiny black curls surrounding her round face. She was conversing quietly with two other women. "And the ladies with her?"

"Wives of diplomats. I do not know their names. Their husbands represent small countries, I believe." Sophia moved on to point out other groups, including two daughters of diplomats who were about Rosa's age. "I will try talking with both of them. They will have known her, of course, but I shall find out how well. Perhaps one of them will know who 'Nora' is."

"I should start by meeting Carmen de Leon," Anne said.

"She is not an easy one—rather aloof and rarely socializes outside her small circle of friends."

"Which includes the two ladies with her?"

"Yes, but I see her more often with Mrs. Seymour, the wife of the under-secretary."

"Is she here tonight?" Anne asked.

"As it happens, she just arrived. The lady in the lovely pale-yellow gown. It's a trifle young for her age but fetching nonetheless." Sophia nodded with her head to indicate a tall woman standing with an even taller man near the front door.

"Since Señora de Leon appears to be somewhat of a challenge, can you introduce me to Mrs. Seymour first?" Anne smiled cunningly. "The señora seems worth the extra effort of a round-about approach to allay her reticence and suspicion. Since she knew Rosa and introduced her to others in society, she should be able to tell me much about Rosa's friends and interests if I can get her talking."

"You might catch her attention by mentioning the incident in Seaford." Lady Sophia took Anne's arm. "Let us meet Mrs. Seymour now. After that, it is up to you."

Anne smiled with a last glance at Señora de Leon. "I shall do my best."

• • •

While Anne chatted with the tall, amiable Mrs. Seymour about the party, its guests, and places a newcomer should visit in

London, she kept looking for an opening to mention Rosa and finally created her own.

"I was in London recently but only for the briefest visit," she said. "We drove up from Seaford for the day."

Mrs. Seymour's eyes lit with interest. "Isn't that the coastal village where the Spanish girl was murdered?" she asked in a hushed tone. "Did you hear about it?"

"Oh, my, yes, the story was all over the village. She was found in a cave, you know, and then the body disappeared. It was not found again for several days. All very mysterious."

Mrs. Seymour gasped. "You don't say. My goodness. Come with me, Lady Anne, my dear friend Señora Carmen will want to hear this. She knew the girl."

"How dreadful for her," Anne murmured as Mrs. Seymour nearly dragged her across the room.

"Carmen, dearest, you must meet Lady Anne Ashburn. She has just arrived from the seacoast." Mrs. Seymour thrust Anne forward as though presenting a prize.

Señora de Leon smiled with polite interest. "Which coast? Were you in Brighton? I do enjoy it there."

"No, no. Seaford," Mrs. Seymour interrupted. She lowered her voice. "She knows all about finding the body of Señorita Hidalgo."

Anne watched the Spanish woman withdraw, looking both pained and wary. "I am sorry about your friend, Señora. Mrs. Seymour said you knew the young woman. Her death must be quite distressing."

"We are all grieving. Her father works for my husband."

Anne searched for a way to keep her talking. "She was so new to London that no one appears to know her well. What was she like?"

For a minute Anne thought Señora de Leon might ignore the question, but Mrs. Seymour inadvertently helped by turning to her friend and saying, "She was a sweet child, was she not?"

The señora sighed. "She was, yes. Well-spoken, polite, and devoted to her father. I have not seen him since the news, but it will be so very hard for him. A tragedy."

"Also for her young friends," Anne prodded. "The young have such a hard time accepting death. I assume she had made many friends at parties and dances."

"Perhaps so, but she was a shy, reserved, and gentle girl." Her voice seemed to tremble, and she paused to compose herself. "I really did not know her well. I introduced her to a few ladies, but I am not sure she pursued those acquaintances." Señora de Leon gave Anne a stiff smile. "It was a pleasure to meet you, my lady. We must talk again one day. I must locate my husband now. We are due at another gathering this evening."

Anne accepted the dismissal with a nod. Talking about Rosa had made the woman uncomfortable, but was that not expected? She thoughtfully watched the señora urge her husband toward the door. Either they were very late for their engagement or the lady was anxious to leave. She had hoped the Carmen de Leon would know more about Rosa—and indeed, maybe she did. Anne frowned. It was tempting to conclude she was *hiding* something, but she might just be hesitant to confide in someone she barely knew. After all, Lady Sophia had said the woman was reserved. She might take special wooing. Anne nodded to herself. She would have to find a good reason for a second meeting with Carmen de Leon.

Chapter Eighteen

26 June 1813 evening

Lucien insisted Sherry take the following night off from watching the Hensley house. His partner had been on duty every evening while Lucien was in Seaford and deserved a break from the boredom of surveillance. Not that Sherry wouldn't be working as he had agreed to make the contact Rothe had requested with George Reeves, Hensley's future son-in-law. Since the young man was a gamester, Sherry would be making the circuits of the gentlemen's clubs the next couple of nights.

As a result of this shift in tasks, by late afternoon, Lucien was crouched in a copse across the street from Oscar Hensley's home, hoping a certain black carriage or a suspicious caller would make an appearance.

Twilight fell, candles and lanterns came on in the neighborhood, and Lucien's legs were getting cramped. He stood, moving carefully so as not to draw attention, and found a tree trunk to lean against that kept him on his feet yet provided a good view. Another hour passed with no action across the street. Lucien was bored, and his head almost ached from running over and over the various lines of inquiry they'd been following, hoping to find something he hadn't thought of before.

He whirled at a sudden movement behind him, his hand gripping the pistol in his coat pocket…until he recognized his footman Robert. He stepped forward and waved him over.

"What are you doing here?" Lucien asked, keeping his voice low.

"A message from Lord Rothe, my lord. You are needed at the Thames River Police station on High Wapping. A constable will meet you. Finn's waiting on the street behind us with the curricle."

Lucien felt a prick of unease. 'That is the entire message, nothing more?"

"No, sir. Nothing."

A curse on Rothe's brevity, he murmured under his breath. "Thank you, Robert. While I'm away, I want you to watch Hensley's house and note anyone who comes and goes. If a black coach appears with a small symbol on the door—it looks like an eagle—follow the coach until you know who owns it. Make certain you are not seen. The owner of the coach may be extremely dangerous. I'll return when I can."

"Yes, my lord. I shall do my best."

Lucien wasn't disappointed by the interruption, but he was worried what he would find on the docks. Rothe would not summon him into such a lawless area of town unless it was urgent—and that usually meant a dead body.

He slipped out the back of the copse, took the reins from Finn, and set the horses at a brisk pace toward Wapping High Street. Turning onto the street a few minutes later, he spotted a constable with a lantern standing just outside the front entrance of the River Police station.

"What has happened?" Lucien demanded.

"There's a body, sir. That's all I know."

Bloody hell. He had hoped to be wrong this time. Leaving Finn with the horses, Lucien followed the constable through a dark back street onto a wooden walkway beside the river's edge. Water lapped against the boards, and the smell of fish was strong. The tap of his boots sounded loud on the warped slats. Finally, he spotted a group of five men ahead, including the unmistakable tall, slim figure of Lord Rothe. Drawing closer, his gaze sought out the body on the ground. Dr. Pettigrew crouched beside it, his boots wet from the large puddle of water that indicated the corpse had been pulled from the river.

Lucien's chest tightened at the look on Rothe's face, and he pushed past the others—another constable and two seamen, to get a look at the corpse. Pettigrew turned, and Lucien glimpsed a bruised and beaten body. A younger man. The face was swollen and bloody—unrecognizable—but the hair was dark. Not Sherry's auburn locks. Lucien let out a breath he hadn't realized he'd been holding.

He turned back to look at Rothe. "Who is it?"

"Jonathan Dickson, the man you knew as Jose."

A fellow agent. That explained Rothe's look of personal loss. "Good lord. I spoke with him just yesterday."

"Did he say anything that would explain this?" Rothe asked sharply.

"He thought Hidalgo was being followed and the house watched, but he hadn't clearly seen anyone, not to identify. It was more that feeling you get. And he planned to keep a closer watch."

Rothe stared into the darkness. "I'd say he must have run afoul of whomever it was."

"But what is he doing down here?"

Rothe shook his head. "Pettigrew, what say you? Did he die by drowning?"

The doctor stood to join them. "I cannot be sure until I look at the lungs, but from the injuries inflicted to his head by a club or similar weapon, he was dead or unconscious when thrown into the water. Hard to say where it happened." Pettigrew gestured toward the constables. "I'll ask the lads to search this area along the bank for the weapon as soon as it's daylight, but I wouldn't count on them finding anything."

"Just so. Keep me informed." Rothe turned back to Lucien. "We need to talk with Hidalgo, find out if he went out tonight. If he did, Dickson may have followed him, so we need to know where he went. The odds of finding the actual crime scene are low, but we shall try."

"The other possibility is Dickson spotted someone watching the house, followed them down here, and was ambushed."

"Thugs and cutthroats," Rothe muttered. "Why are they watching Hidalgo?"

"Jose…I mean, Dickson and I talked about that. Could they be thinking of using him again?"

"They'd be fools. His daughter's death is talked about all over town. No, Ware, it has to be something else. Hidalgo must know something this gang considers dangerous."

"If so, I feel confident he doesn't realize it."

Rothe swore again. "We've learned nothing, Ware, and now Dickson is dead and his killers have vanished into London's underbelly."

"There is one man who might find them," Lucien said before Rothe could say it. If he had to deal with Cade again, he'd rather it be his own idea.

"I don't want to go there…not yet. For all we know, the man might be one of Cade's or in the pay of a rival crime lord. Either way, bringing him in before we know more might cause more trouble than we can handle. Talk with Hidalgo. Let us see what we can ferret out on our own."

Lucien was surprised. Was Rothe concerned that the agency's interests and Cade's might part company, leaving Lucien in the middle? Lucien had certainly thought about it. So far Cade had not called in any markers—that in itself left Lucien uneasy, not knowing what *favors* he might be expected to fulfill.

"It's late, my lord. I'll speak with Hidalgo first thing in the morning." Lucien wanted no part of Rothe's next task, a notification that could not wait. "Is there a widow, sir?"

"There is," Rothe said tightly. "With an infant a few months old."

• • •

27 June 1813

Lucien woke in the morning with that heavy feeling that something was wrong. Confused for a moment, he scrubbed his face with one hand until he recalled the body pulled from the Thames. Sending orders for his carriage to be brought around, he dressed swiftly, gulped down a cup of coffee, and grabbed a freshly-baked biscuit on the way out the door. He hoped to reach Hidalgo's residence before the man left for work and before he heard of his footman's death from someone else. Lucien could at least spare the man the shock of learning the news on the street or from a distraught widow.

Hidalgo rose from his breakfast table, his brows lifting in surprise, as Lucien was announced. "My lord, what brings you here so early? Not more bad news, I hope."

"I'm afraid so, sir. It's your new footman, Jose…he was killed last night."

"Good heavens, what happened?"

"His body was found in the Thames just before midnight."

Hidalgo sank back into the chair behind him as though his legs would no longer hold him. "Will this nightmare never end?"

Lucien didn't wait to be invited; he pulled up a chair, asking the manservant to pour a cup of tea for him and to refill Hidalgo's cup.

"When did you last see him, sir?"

"Um, it must have been about eight last night. He was hurrying out the back door. I don't believe I had spoken to him all day, so I don't know his plans for the evening. Could this be a random attack?" he asked, a hint of hope in this voice.

"I doubt it. Jose believed someone was watching the house."

"Yes, he told me, but I thought he was wrong. I have nothing of value to spies or thieves."

"Did you go anywhere last night?"

"No, I was home all evening. Why?"

"We're trying to determine where Jose ran into trouble. If he wasn't following you, he must have noticed someone watching the house and confronted them or perhaps was ambushed."

Hidalgo shook his head in dismay. "Why in heaven's name is anyone interested in me? What do they want?"

"I wish I could tell you. You know something that would incriminate Hensley, or they think you do. Perhaps you found something—a handkerchief, a glove? What about the messages—did you make any copies?"

"None of that. Hensley was never inside my coach or the house, so he could not have left anything behind. As I told you before,

I destroyed the notes, as instructed, and was too afraid to make copies of anything."

"I'm sorry to ask this, sir, but is there anything they could say or do—threats against someone you haven't mentioned, blackmail over something in your past—that might force you to resume spying for them?"

"After they killed my daughter?" he exclaimed angrily. "I'd rather shoot myself."

The French spy and his gang should know that, Lucien thought. If they wanted to keep Hidalgo from talking, it was way too late for that, and Lucien believed him when he said he'd rather shoot himself than work with them again. What the devil was this about?

Chapter Nineteen

27 June 1813

The day after the politicians' rout party, Lady Anne put on her gray visiting gown with blue trim and set out with Jenny to call upon Señora de Leon. She had decided an effusive apology over distressing her by asking about Señorita Rosa might soften the Spanish lady, and she put on a rather subdued smile as she was announced and shown into the de Leons' sitting room.

The señora rose. "Lady Anne, I had not expected to see you so soon. How delightful. Do sit and join me in taking your English tea." She pulled the bell for a maid and ordered a tray. "It is a lovely day, is it not? I went for a walk in the garden an hour ago."

"It is indeed," Anne agreed, seating herself, but she was not to be diverted by talk of the weather. "I am sure you are wondering why I am here, but I truly felt I should beg your pardon for my lack of sensitivity last night. I fear I made you uncomfortable by asking about Señorita Hidalgo. You must think my manners are lacking for bringing up a subject that was hardly suitable for a party. You have my sincere apology."

"Oh, my. No need for that." Señora de Leon appeared flustered. "I fear I have been unduly affected by Rosa's death. It is I who should apologize for my abruptness. I have not dealt well with her loss." She dabbed at tears that threatened to brim over and roll down her cheeks.

And they were genuine tears.

"I did not realize the two of you were so close," Anne said gently.

"We were not, but just the thought of a sweet child…I am horrified such a dreadful thing should happen." She sniffed, dabbed her eyes again with her lace handkerchief, and composed herself.

"Would it help to talk about her?" Anne asked. "I heard she liked to read." She'd heard no such thing, but she hoped to get the señora talking.

"Yes, I heard that too, but she did not mention it to me. I am not a reader myself, and we never talked about books. Mostly we chatted about shopping…and about Spain. She missed home too—and her young man. She had hoped to marry him." Señora de Leon teared up again. "Perhaps we should speak of something else."

"Just one more thing, do you know a friend of hers named Nora?"

"I do not. Why do you ask?"

Anne immediately knew how odd her question sounded, that she had overstepped, threatening to reveal she knew more than she should. "Oh, no matter." Anne was floundering. "Someone mentioned Rosa's friend Nora and acted as if I would know who she was. I…was just curious, but honestly it is of no consequence."

"She had not been in England long, but I believe she had a few friends among the younger set. Nora may be among them."

"A likely suggestion," Anne said. She changed the subject then, asking about the de Leon home in Spain.

A smile lit the señora's face. "It is lovely there. All the flowers—so very fragrant. Our gardens held orchids, red carnations, and several varieties of the beautiful lilies. I sat among them every morning and evening."

"You clearly miss your home there."

"So very, very much. Every day. But England is lovely too," she said, as though recalling she was a diplomat's wife and should do her duty by praising her host country.

"England has its moments," Anne agreed. "Surely you must enjoy all the political discussions. I'm afraid I know little about them, but being a diplomate's wife, I'm sure you've been privy to such discussions and perhaps even consulted."

"Oh, no. I know little about the politics my husband loves. I am interested in music and theatre. And shoes and gowns, of course.

Are these not fetching?" She exposed a slender foot, with a slipper that matched her gown. Shopping in Spain is an all-day event."

"You make your country sound very appealing. I shall look forward to visiting one day…if this abominable war with France ever ends."

"Yes, it is most unfortunate." Señora de Leon raised a hand to her forehead. "I am sorry, Lady Anne, I have developed the headache. I must lie down for a spell."

"Oh, dear," Anne rose immediately. "I beg pardon for having tired you. I can show myself out." She stopped at the door and looked back. "A cold compress helps me."

"Yes, thank you. I shall try that."

As soon as Anne reached the carriage, she told Jenny all about her visit. "What do you make of all that?" she asked.

"I don't think she had the headache," Jenny said.

"No, she wanted me to leave. Everything I said appeared to upset her except when we talked about Spain. She brightened up then, but I still heard an underlying sadness in her voice," Anne said thoughtfully.

"Could it be the señorita's death, my lady?"

"Well, yes, but why so affected? She had genuine tears in her eyes, and by her own accounts she and Rosa were only acquaintances. The señora appeared to be taking it quite badly."

"Some ladies just cry easily," Jenny suggested.

"I wonder."

Jenny launched into a story about a second cousin who could cry on demand, but Anne was barely listening. She was pondering the señora's behavior.

Even after they'd arrived home, and Anne was settled in the family parlor with a tea tray beside her and her embroidery in her lap, she kept going over her visit to the embassy. Something was off about Señora de Leon. She was obviously unhappy and homesick for Spain, but it went beyond that. Perhaps her marriage was troubled, although Anne had not heard that gossip. The señora was hiding something… but perhaps it was personal—and none of Anne's business.

She picked up her tea, but it had grown cold, and she poured a fresh cup. As she sipped the hot drink, she pictured Carmen de Leon's face when Anne had apologized for bringing up Rosa Hidalgo's death. She was still convinced the tears were real. Was Jenny right, and the lady just had a tender heart? Or could she be regretting something she'd said or done?

Her butler Staves interrupted her woolgathering by announcing Lady Castlebridge. Anne smiled and rose to greet her guest.

"Lady Sophia, how nice to see you."

"I was out and about and decided to satisfy my curiosity over your conversation with Señora de Leon last night. Did you learn anything of use?"

Over a fresh tea tray, Anne repeated last night's conversation and her morning call only an hour ago. "Everything I said seemed to make her sad."

"How suspiciously overdone," Lady Sophia remarked. "I suppose you might have caught her at a bad time." She paused with her hand on her chin. "If I had known you were visiting her today, you could have asked about something I heard. She and Señorita Hidalgo were seen shopping together."

"Suggesting they were more than mere acquaintances."

"Yes, it does, does it not? Perhaps I should have a go at her and mention the shopping trip. It seems a harmless activity and very gracious of her to befriend a young girl."

"Exactly," Anne said. "Why go out of her way to deny it?"

"I suppose they might have run into one another while shopping separately and stopped to chat. It needn't be indicative of a friendship, but I very much wish to know."

"I do too," Anne said, "but I certainly cannot go with you on a second visit. She'd be suspicious for sure."

"Then I shall take Mrs. Buxton. She has been collecting for the hospital fund, and that would be the perfect excuse to visit the embassy uninvited."

"Sounds perfect," Anne said. "The señora knows something—I can sense it—and it makes her sad. I believe her grief is sincere."

"We could be prying into an affair of the heart—by her or her husband. Titillating, but not important."

"I thought of that, but what if it's not?"

Lady Sophia set down her empty cup of tea and stood. "Precisely why I am going. I shall report back as soon as I am able."

Anne sighed after Lady Sophia left. Were they plaguing a poor woman whose only crime was a tender heart? Or having a troubled marriage? She would not wish an innocent woman to fall under unsubstantiated suspicion. But was she innocent? Or did she know something that would make sense of what happened to Rosa?

• • •

Two hours later Lady Sophia breezed into the Chadley drawing room one step ahead of the butler. "Darling, I simply do not understand that woman." She sat down with a flounce.

"Uh, Lady Castlebridge," Staves announced belatedly.

"Perhaps we could do with a little sherry, Staves."

"Yes, my lady." He poured two small glasses from the sideboard, presented one to each lady from a small drink tray, and then left the room, closing the door behind him.

Anne watched Lady Sophia take a large swallow of the drink. "Good Heavens, Sophia, what is the matter?"

"That woman is as blue-deviled as anyone I have seen, but she wouldn't give me the slightest hint as to what was distressing her. I fear I lost patience and pressed harder than I should about the shopping trip with Rosa, and the silly woman burst into tears. Poor Mrs. Buxton. I think she was appalled by both of us. My reputation may be in tatters."

"Oh, dear. As bad as that?"

"Oh, not truly. Mrs. Buxton is more discreet than to spread rumors about such a trivial incident, but I did lose patience, and the señora did cry," Lady Sophia said ruefully. She took a more ladylike sip of her sherry this time. "I am so sorry. I fear I have alarmed the señora without gaining one bit of information."

"And yet you confirmed how very emotional she is about Rosa," Anne said thoughtfully, taking a sip from her own glass.

"I've been thinking about it the last two hours, wondering why she was feeling the loss so deeply. Perhaps it is guilt."

Lady Sophia cocked her head. "About what exactly?"

"That is what we have yet to learn. It might be any number of things, to be sure, but if she wrote that note, perhaps she did it for someone else, not realizing they would kidnap or harm Rosa. She might have arranged a shopping trip, for instance. Wouldn't that explain both her tears and how touchy she is about the mere mention of shopping?"

"You could be on to something," Lady Sophia said scooting forward in her chair, "*I*, most assuredly, would feel guilty under those circumstances. But who told her to write the note, and how do we prove she wrote it?"

"Well…we start with the note itself. We need something in Señora de Leon's handwriting, her signature, in particular. I have the two letters Lord Ware took from Rosa's bedchamber, and I would wager the señora's writing will match one of them. With that evidence, we could leave the rest to Lord Ware."

"How do we get her handwriting? Burglarize her house?"

"A bit risky," Anne mused, "but so far I have not formed a better idea."

"I was merely joking," Lady Sophia said with a grin. "Have you resorted to burglary before?"

"Yes, but I do not recommend it. I was caught before I started—by Lord Ware."

"Truly. What an interesting story that must be. Will you tell me?"

"Yes, of course, but not today. We must concentrate on a workable plan. We could try writing to her, but would she not be suspicious that we are suddenly giving her so much attention?"

"Which I made worse today," Lady Sophia said, biting her lip. "It may be our best option, however."

"If she ignores the letter, we shall be no worse off than we are," Anne said. "If we are to be successful, we must think of a good reason to write, something that will interest her enough to respond." She propped her chin on her fingers and thought about her visit with the señora, trying hard to come up with something. The room was silent for several minutes. "She is missing Spain and loves to talk about it—we could ask about her home or something related," she suggested.

Sophia, who appeared lost in her own thoughts, absently nodded. "I've been thinking," she said. "Since she would view anything from us with mistrust, we need someone else to write the letter."

"Someone who wouldn't demand a detailed explanation," Anne added. "What about—"

"Lady Julia," Lady Sophia and Anne finished in unison.

They looked at one another, their eyes sparkling. Fifteen minutes later they were knocking on the front door of Lady Julia Castlebridge, Lady Sophia's cousin-by-marriage.

The butler showed them into a private parlor where Lady Julie sat by an open window, a book in one hand, a fan in the other.

"How delightful to see you." She rose eagerly and came toward them with both hands outstretched. After clutching her cousin's hands briefly, she turned to Anne. "Are you in London now? I had not heard."

"My father has bought a house here. I shall be living in London for most of the year. I hope you will call on me soon."

"Count on it." Lady Julia looked back and forth between the two women. "You two are nearly bursting with excitement. Am I right in thinking this is not entirely a social call?"

Anne and Lady Sophia laughed.

"You would be correct," Lady Sophia said as the two women quickly rid themselves of hats and gloves in the day's heat.

Lady Julie smiled at Anne. "This wouldn't have anything to do with the sketch, would it? Was it helpful?"

"Oh, yes," Anne said. "And in a way today's errand is related."

"I sense intrigue for sure," Lady Julia said. "Do be seated, ladies, and before you tell me what this is about, shall I ring for lemonade? Or would you prefer tea?"

"Lemonade sounds wonderful," Anne said, taking one of the chairs arranged near the windows. The faint breeze would make the warm day more bearable, and they could enjoy the delicate fragrances from the flower garden.

"Delightful." Lady Sophia sank into another of the chairs. "Such an interesting day, but I confess that conspiracy takes a bit of energy. Lemonade will be most welcome."

"Conspiracy? Oh, my. You really must relieve my curiosity," Lady Julia said as she joined them.

Lady Sophia looked at Anne. "I shall let you tell her. I am not certain how much of this story can be related."

"Well, *thank you*," Anne admonished with a grin. "You're going to make me take all the blame if Lord Ware becomes annoyed over this."

"Naturally. You are the one who told me."

"Yes, but he said I could."

"Ladies," Lady Julia said laughing. "Is one of you going to explain or not?"

Anne sighed and thought ahead carefully. "About the sketch you drew...there is a complicated story surrounding it—and most of it I am not at liberty to reveal—but we believe a woman in London knows something important regarding the girl's death. There are letters involved, and we need a sample of this woman's handwriting to compare with them."

Lady Julia looked bewildered. "How does this involve me?"

"We want you to write to her, asking something that requires a written response. Neither of us can do it because...well, she may already be suspicious of us," Lady Sophia admitted.

"Do I know this woman?" Lady Julia asked. "Who is she?"

Lady Sophia looked at Anne and shrugged.

"Well, we have to tell her," Anne said. "Otherwise, how could she write to her?" She turned to Lady Julia. "You must not repeat anything we say today, not even to your husband. It is a delicate matter, and we do not wish to besmirch a lady's reputation without proof."

"I shall not say a word...provided that you will one day explain what this was all about."

"If we are right, it may soon be all over town," Anne said. "But, yes, I promise." She was *fairly* confident Lord Ware would approve.

"So, tell me who she is."

"Señora Carmen de Leon, the wife of the Spanish Envoy."

Lady Julia lifted a brow in surprise. "At least I have met her. I was concerned you would ask me to write to a stranger with no introduction."

"The acquaintance is fortunate." Lady Sophia nodded. "But I would have asked you in any event."

"I know." Lady Julie laughed at her cousin. "And I would have said yes, but with much trepidation. So…what is it I am to say?"

They talked it over for a while and agreed Spain was the best choice of topics. Lady Julia suggested she could pretend to be arranging a visit to Spain as soon as she and her husband found safe passage, and she would appreciate the señora's recommendations of places to visit.

"I am a bit worried she might think my request odd on our very slight acquaintance," Lady Julia said.

"Not if you stress this is a once-in-a-lifetime visit, and you do not want to miss anything," Anne said.

"I like that," Lady Sophia said.

"Your request might be unusual, but I doubt if she will think anything amiss. Most likely she will be delighted for any opportunity to talk about Spain."

"How soon can you write?" Lady Sophia demanded.

"As soon as you leave." Lady Julia gave her cousin a pointed look. "I cannot properly compose my request with you hanging over my shoulder. Finish your lemonade, and then be off. I shall have it written and on its way before you reach home."

Lady Sophia's carriage deposited Anne at home a few minutes later, and then Sophia rushed off to change for a dinner party.

Consistent with half-mourning, Anne spent the evening at home and thought of little else than the letter over the next few hours. She tried to read the newly published *Pride and Prejudice*, but found she couldn't concentrate. Nor did embroidery claim her attention for long. She kept worrying about Señora de Leon's reaction to Lady Julia's letter. Would she respond? Would they be able to match her handwriting with one of the letters they had? And what then?

A chime from the clock in the hall reminded her of the late hour, and Anne rose, forcing herself to set aside her speculation for the night. She headed up the stairs with only one last thought—how soon might the señora respond?

Chapter Twenty

27 June 1813

Wearing well-worn, stained, and rather odorous clothing purchased from a street vendor, Lucien haunted the docklands the next two days with Finn at his side. By pretending to be out of town ruffians interested in the bounty on Lucien's head, they hoped to trace it back to its origins. However, they quickly discovered the offer had only been made to certain individuals, and one grizzled tavern customer predicted takers would be few due to fears of reprisal.

Lucien frowned. Had his ties with Whitehall become common knowledge? "What do you mean? That Bow Street would take an interest?"

"No, worse than that. They be whispers Mr. Cade has taken a special interest and warned off anyone who might be inclined to give it a go."

Bloody hell. Did Cade ever mind his own business? Albeit, he might see it as protecting his investment. A dead man could not repay the debt Lucien had run up. For the hundredth time, he felt a nagging unease.

"'Course, it be a lot of coin." The man rubbed his bristled chin. "Some might still take a chance."

An excellent reason Lucien could not relax his guard.

After failing to trace the bounty, he and Finn made the rounds of other dockland pubs and entertainment establishments, hoping to hear talk of Rosa's abduction or Jose's murder. Once again, they had no success. If those who frequented the docks knew anything, it wasn't being bandied about. Even a coin judiciously offered here and there produced nothing.

• • •

28 June 1813

By the end of the second day, Lucien was ready to call it quits. As he and Finn were leaving the docklands, putting the river and the all-encompassing smell of fish behind them, they walked with caution through the narrow streets. Ever-mindful of his surroundings, Lucien kept a wary eye on the crowded warehouses and dark shadows. Twilight had fallen, bringing wisps of fog, and he was increasingly uneasy.

He stiffened when hailed from behind. Poised to bend down and snatch the knife from his right boot, he turned to see a scrawny lad of eleven or twelve running toward them.

"Are you the ones been askin' about a dead Spanish man?" the lad asked, breathing hard from his efforts.

"What if we are?" Lucien asked.

"Know who done 'im. A bad 'un, he be. Big brute, scar on his cheek." He pointed to the left side of his own face before looking furtively around and dropping his voice. "Know where he be too, an' kin show ye, if y' like…fer a coin."

Lucien didn't like the lad's shifty eyes. Would he be leading them into a trap? Regardless, it was the first real interest they'd provoked, and he wasn't going to walk away. "What's your name, lad?"

The boy hesitated. "Newt."

"Well, Newt. I have a coin." He showed him a quid on the palm of his hand.

The young rascal's eyes lit with greed, and he reached out, but Lucien closed his fist. "Not till you take us there."

"Kin go to the alley where he be last seen. No farther."

Lucien's conviction grew that something was amiss, but he gestured for the lad to show them the way. "Fair enough. Lead on."

Newt took them from one alley to another. Notwithstanding Lucien's years of experience at marking his path through such labyrinths, he nearly lost track of so many twists and turns. The lad finally stopped at the opening to a narrow alley between two warehouses so close to the Thames that Lucien could hear the water lapping.

"Coin," Newt demanded. "He went through thar."

Lucien studied the dark opening. Although it was twilight, little light penetrated through the fog. "Where does this go? Where might I find him?"

"Ship Street." Newt paused, as though uncertain what else to say. "He goes to t' Barnacle Pub most days." He stuck out his hand, palm up. "Coin," he repeated.

Lucien paid him, took a step forward to look inside the alley, and when he glanced back, the lad was gone.

"Hey," Finn yelled, but Newt was already out of sight. "You want me to go after 'im?"

"No, let him go. You'd never find him, and he got us as far as promised."

"We ain't goin' in there, are we?" Finn asked, pointing to the alley. "I smell nothin' but fish and trouble," he said, wrinkling his nose.

"I have my own doubts," Lucien agreed. "That's why you shall remain here. If it's a trap, you can go for help."

"But, gov, I ain't leavin' you alone."

"You will if I say so," Lucien said firmly. Given his size, Finn would be little help in a fight, and if he escaped, he could tell Sherry where to start looking for him—or for his body.

Lucien bent down to take the knife from his boot. Straightening, he edged his way into the alley his back close to the left wall.

No one jumped out at him.

The light was indeed dim, but after his eyes adjusted, he could make out shapes of bins and discarded trash. He moved forward, keeping an eye on the bins, as they were the only objects large enough to hide a man. He was so intent on studying them for signs of movement that he nearly tripped over the body at his feet.

Lucien crouched, looking around to be sure he was alone, then dropped his gaze to the body for a better look. The victim was male, but where he lay was so dark it was difficult to determine anything else. No question he was dead—the body was already starting to stiffen. Lucien grabbed the man's arms and pulled him into the middle of the alley where light from a distant street light filtered through the mist.

Bending close, he noted the scar Newt had mentioned. The man's chest and drab clothing were covered with blood, and Lucien found what looked like three stab wounds. Without a doubt, this was the man Newt accused of killing Jose, but the boy had lied about one thing—the stiffness Lucien had seen before on the battlefield meant the body had been dead two hours or more—well before the boy came to him. No wonder Newt had floundered when asked where the big man had gone. He'd gone nowhere.

The boy hadn't led him into a trap—a good thing, of course—but the man's death was another blow to his inquiry. Where did he go from here? This corpse wouldn't be answering the important questions—whether he'd been hired to murder Jose and what he knew about Rosa's abduction.

Squatting again, Lucien searched his pockets, even those soaked with blood. He found nothing. When finished, he stood and wiped his hands clean with a handkerchief that he returned to his pocket. He wouldn't be leaving anything behind in the alley.

His gaze dropped again to the faint outline of the dead man. Was this a warning? Or a simple statement that he need look no further, that Jose's killer had paid with his life? It was something Cade might do…except he would have instructed Newt to tell the truth that the man was dead.

Who then? The Frenchman? Or had Newt simply seen an opportunity and seized it? And if someone *had* sent Newt…what the devil was the message?

• • •

When Lucien returned to the alley with the authorities, deep night had fallen, but the constables had brought several lanterns, and Lucien got his first good look at the dead man. Blunt features, bulging shoulder muscles, as well as muscular arms and legs.

Killing hadn't been his only job. He did some kind of heavy work. His hands were deeply callused, but that was common to most of the workers on the docks.

When Lucien had first reported the death, the constables looked askance at his clothing and the blood on his sleeve. Even now, they kept glancing at him as though he might run. Since he'd also sent word to Rothe and Dr. Pettigrew, he was keen for them to arrive and take over before he ended up under arrest.

The constables came to attention the moment Lord Rothe walked into the alley with the doctor by his side.

After viewing the scene, Rothe took Lucien aside. "Who is this man, Ware? I assume he has something to do with the Hidalgo inquiry."

"The lad who brought me here said this fellow killed Dickson," he said, using Jose's given name. Lucien related his dealings with Newt. "He ran off as soon as we got to the alley, so I didn't have a chance to ask if he saw what happened here. I can try to find him again, but the odds aren't good." Almost anyone could hide in the dockland if they were motivated, and street boys were exceedingly adept.

"Why did he come to you?"

"I'm not sure, sir. Could be an enterprising lad, but it felt like a setup. By whom or why…?" He just shrugged.

Rothe nodded toward the corpse. "I suppose he was killed to keep him from talking."

"I daresay. Or sending a message of some kind."

"Well, gentlemen," Pettigrew said, coming to join them. "I cannot tell you much you don't already know. He was stabbed, several times." He looked at Lucien. "Was he this stiff when you first found him."

"It had started."

Pettigrew nodded. "Putting his death three to six hours ago. I might be a bit more precise after a thorough examination, but I doubt if my findings are going to help you much on this one. I assume you searched his pockets."

"I found nothing," Lucien said.

"Nor did I. So, there we are," Pettigrew said, closing his medical bag. "I shall let you know if I discover something of interest."

Lucien walked with Rothe and Pettigrew to the end of the alley, and then the doctor climbed aboard his waiting carriage. Two men of the death trade were already loading the body on their wagon to deliver it to Pettigrew's surgery. Unless family could be found, the body would be buried at the Crown's expense and without ceremony when the doctor was through with it.

"Where are you off to now?" Rothe asked as the doctor's carriage pulled away. "Can I give you a ride?"

"Thank you, but no. Finn and I are going to have a drink at the Barnacle Pub," Lucien said. "Newt mentioned this brute frequented the place. Perhaps we can learn something there."

"Proceed with care," Rothe cautioned. "This is not exactly civilized territory."

• • •

Indeed, the Thames area known as the docklands was a world unto itself. Life was cheap, emotions raw. When not openly displayed by men thrashing one another, violence bubbled just beneath the surface. Lucien rubbed dirt onto his face and hands and pulled his cap low. Where he was going, the blood on his sleeve would be a nice touch.

He opened the tavern's heavy wooden door to the sound of drunken sailors, laughing and singing bawdy songs, and to the inescapable odor of stale ale, greasy smoke, and the sweat of unwashed bodies.

The Barnacle had probably stood since the fifteenth century, and it's low-hanging, rough-hewn beams were darkened by soot and grease. The floor was stained nearly black and worn smooth by thousands of feet. If it had been swept, that was hours ago before the dockworkers, seamen, and locals who wouldn't or couldn't find work had splashed it with ale and dropped bits of food, tobacco, and other detritus. It crunched underfoot as Lucien and Finn crossed the poorly-lit room under watchful eyes. Strangers were noticed here, and Lucien kept his eyes averted until he sank onto a wooden bench.

"Careful not to stare," Lucien reminded Finn. "Anything can be an excuse for a fight down here."

"Aye, gov."

The barmaid strolled over, her hips rolling out of habit, but she acted tired and disinclined to chat. They ordered two pints and didn't attempt to draw her out. While Lucien drank his ale, his eyes roamed over the room from under the brim of his cap, and he listened to conversations loud enough to drift their way. Some were unremarkable, others ranged from laughing mates to lewd talk, angry disagreements, and the everyday complaints of those soured on life.

Surprisingly, he heard nothing of a man with a scar or a body in an alley—not until he was on his second pint. Two men burst into the pub and announced, "Big Toe is dead."

Half the pub went quiet, those that were sober enough to comprehend and to whom the words meant something.

"Nah, you be daft," the publican said, leaning on the counter. "Not, that one."

"I tell you he's dead. Stabbed in an alley."

"Who's dead?" one of the rowdier men turned and asked.

"You know, big fella with a scar."

Big Toe? What kind of name was that for a cutthroat? Lucien asked himself. Even for the docks—where many hid their identity behind some kind of nickname—Big Toe seemed an odd choice.

"What happened to 'im?" the publican asked.

"Don't know. We seen the beaks, and one of them said he'd been stabbed."

"Well, it ain't no surprise," said a man seated in the corner. "He had a way of makin' enemies."

"Hey, you over there," the younger of the new arrivals said, pointing toward Lucien. "You was there. I seen ya in the alley."

Lucien's mouth went dry, but Finn intervened before his master's speech gave them away. "We both was. Jest walkin' by 'n' a 'course the constables accused us a doin' the deed. Ain't that true, Freddie?" He looked at Lucien.

"Yah. Bloody beaks." He kept his head down and mumbled his words.

"Was he really stabbed?"

"That's what they tol' me," Finn replied, standing up and puffing out his chest just a little, pretending to enjoy being the center of attention. "Kilt four or five hours ago, heard someone say," he continued, taking a couple of steps forward and drawing attention away from Lucien. "That be why they let us go. Figured we wouldna hang 'round so long."

"Done him in broad daylight," an older man said, shaking his shaggy head of hair. "Must a been three or four to take down Big Toe like that."

Everyone seemed to agree on that point. Considering his size, a reasonable assumption, Lucien thought, unless his attacker had been a friend…that is, a presumed friend.

"I didn't care for him much," said the man in the corner. "But I reckon we should drink to him…out of respect."

"Eh, gotta show respect."

They raised their glasses. "To Big Toe." Lucien and Finn joined in, and then Finn returned to his seat.

Most of the room resumed their earlier conversations, but a few continued to speculate on what had happened. The table next to Lucien was running through a list of potential enemies. Probably all killers and cutthroats, Lucien thought. It appeared Big Toe had been a bully and all too ready to settle things with his fists. Nevertheless, Lucien didn't believe his killer would be found among the docklands' thugs.

He leaned forward and said quietly to Finn, "Start a conversation with them. Ask how he got the nickname of Big Toe. See if they'll tell you his real name, who he worked for, his friends, that kind of thing. But don't push it. Just keep it casual."

Finn nodded. He got up and went to the bar, bought another pint, and on his way back, he stopped at the nearby table. "Excuse me, mates, but I been wonderin' why ye call him Big Toe."

The four men at the table laughed, and the oldest, a stocky man with gray creeping into his full head of brown hair, said, "'Cause he had a toe he complained about all the time. He'd hobble in here and kick off his boot. His toe would swell up the size of a fist."

"And gor he could be nasty when it were actin' up," one of the other men said.

"Just who was he?" Finn asked.

One of the four men scratched his head. "He's been Big Toe so long, I forgot. If I ever knew."

The older man looked up. "Take up a seat, mate. I'm Gerry by the by. Does your friend want to join us?"

"Naw, he likes to be by hisself." Finn tapped his temple, indicating Lucien was a little slow in the head. "Me name's Finn." When one of the men scooted over to make room on the bench, he set his pint on their table.

Lucien didn't even look in their direction and kept his eyes down until they'd turned their attention back to Finn. During the next few minutes, he kept one wary eye on the rest of the room and listened carefully to what Finn's new mates had to say.

None of the men knew Big Toe's given name. "Don't even know how he injured that toe," Gerry said.

"He musta dropped one of them cannon balls on it while workin' at the factory," one man jested. They all laughed, but agreed it might be true.

So, he worked at an iron factory, Lucien thought. Hence all the muscles.

As for friends…

"Dint have none," said a red-head from the next table, who'd been listening. "He was a mean one, Big Toe was." Having had his say, he turned back to his own table, downing the rest of his pint in one long swallow and calling for another.

"I can't say he's wrong about that," Gerry said. "Big Toe was a leery cove. Kept to himself. Oh, sometimes I saw him with Hank and Beanie, but even they scuttled off when he was in one of his moods. Saw him beat a man senseless over a spilled mug of ale one night. Most of us kept our distance."

Lucien felt someone's eyes on him, and he carefully swept his gaze over the room, landing on a man seated with the fellow in the corner who'd done so much talking. Lucien averted his gaze but kept an unobtrusive watch as the man glanced in his direction several times, showing more than a casual interest. When the conversation at the next table began to lag, Lucien got to his feet.

"Well," Finn said jumping up. "Looks like me mate is ready to go. Thank ye fer sharin' a pint."

As they left the pub, Finn started to say something, but Lucien hushed him and turned in the direction of the foundry. He moved quickly, listening for the sound of footsteps behind them. He was waiting to see if the man in the corner was interested in the conversation about Big Toe…or in them. After a minute or two, he relaxed.

"Good job back there, Finn. In addition to visiting the foundry, we have two men to find and question. I daresay the foundry can give us Big Toe's real name. We'll ask around about his friends, but Bow Street might already know them. If we can find them, they might be persuaded to talk."

Lucien shot another look behind them, and Finn asked, "Are we being followed?"

"Not sure yet. We were being watched in the Barnacle."

"Front corner table?" Finn asked, nodding. "He be starin' at us as we left."

"That's the fellow." Lucien wasn't surprised Finn had noticed. His groom had helped on earlier inquiries and knew how swiftly situations could turn dangerous, that one needed to be aware of everything—and everyone—around them.

A trip to the foundry did indeed give them a name—Barton Kemp—but visits to two other area pubs failed to yield anything further about Kemp or his friends. No one admitted knowing Hank or Beanie, but Lucien was sure they were lying. He figured friends of Big Toe must be cut from the same cloth—large, belligerent cutthroats. No one was going to openly inform on them.

He heaved a sigh, glancing at the dark streets and darker alleys surrounding them. "It is late, Finn. Sherbourne and I can continue this tomorrow."

They turned their steps toward the west and away from the river, moving quickly through the unsettled streets. After finding a hackney at a small inn on the outer edge of the docklands, Lucien was just entering the cab when he saw the man from the pub again. The stranger stood across the street, just looking at them. Of average height, brown hair, an unassuming face, and wearing working-class dark trousers and shirt—a perfectly ordinary-looking man who could blend into any crowd.

Lucien shouted, "Wait," to the jarvey, but the stranger swiftly disappeared into the shadows. Unwilling to chase him blindly in the dark, Lucien turned back. "Forget it. Drive on," he called up to the coachman. He entered the cab, and Finn scrambled up to sit on top. Lucien scowled out the window. He had lost his chance to question the stranger tonight, but he would not forget that unassuming face.

• • •

Arriving at his townhouse twenty minutes later, he found it unexpectedly lit from top to bottom and the household in an uproar. The cook and maids were huddled in the front hallway. Talbot was wide-eyed and nervously fidgeting, Hughes appeared quite affronted, and Robert brandished a loaded pistol.

"What the devil is going on?" Lucien demanded.

"We had intruders," Hughes responded.

When others started to interrupt, Lucien shook his head. "No, only one of you need tell me. Hughes, please go on."

"Yes, my lord. Two men, ruffians, came in the kitchen door and ran up the servants' stairs. When the maids saw them and started screaming, the scoundrels threatened to throttle them, causing additional shrieking. At this time, I arrived on the scene with Talbot behind me, and Robert came out of the back with the pistol. The intruders retreated down the stairs and out the kitchen door."

Good lord. What nonsense is this?

He turned to the two maids. "What did they say to you?"

"To be quiet or they'd kill us," the younger girl blurted.

"Is that all?"

"They kept asking, Where is he? Where is he?" the older maid said. "I guess they were looking for you, my lord."

What clumsy dunderheads. Hardly the type anyone would choose as assassins. More likely petty criminals who had heard about the bounty and thought to make their fortune.

"I'm sorry you were all put through such a fright. As it seems to be over now, I believe you can safely return to whatever you were doing. Hughes, a moment of your time."

"Yes, my lord."

"From now on we shall keep all the doors locked even during the day. While that will be inconvenient for everyone, I hope it won't last long. Let us post Robert and his pistol near the kitchen door, so the women will feel protected. But, for heaven's sake, tell him not to shoot anyone unless he has to."

"Yes, my lord. I shall see to it now." Hughes departed into the back.

Lucien stood for a moment, debating whether to go out for the evening. He *was* expected at a soiree, but he wasn't in the mood. If anything, he'd rather locate Sherry and discuss the inquiry problems. On the other hand, his household was unsettled, and he was dirty and tired. What he really wanted was a bath, a decent meal, and a good brandy. A quiet evening at home might be just the thing for all of them.

He stopped in the front hall to check the messages on the table and found a note from Lady Anne. She had spoken with Señora de Leon and thought her behavior rather suspicious.

Her grief over Rosa's death is excessive, Lady Anne wrote, *considering she claims only a passing acquaintance. Every mention of Rosa made her eyes brim with tears, even when I asked if the two of them had shopped together. She denied it, but that time she actually cried. It could mean nothing...but it was odd enough I thought you should know.*

She ended her note by saying she, Lady Sophia, and Lady Julia were working on obtaining a sample of the señora's handwriting to compare with the letters from Rosa's bedchamber.

Lucien sighed. As usual, she was going beyond what he'd asked her to do, and now she'd involved both Lady Sophia and her cousin. He hoped the ladies in their enthusiasm did not get themselves into trouble or alert the spies and send them fleeing. He had thought finding a body would provide Lady Anne with excitement enough for a few weeks—even for a female with her avid curiosity. He should have known better.

He read her note a second time and frowned in thought. He didn't find the señora's sadness over Rosa unusual, but what would distress her about shopping? The ladies obviously suspected she wrote the note that lured Rosa from her home to—what? A shopping trip? Well, why not? Perhaps he should speak with the abigail about Rosa's shopping habits. He knew the young señorita liked hats, but where did she buy them? Always the same place? What other shops did she frequent? What about jewelry, shawls, slippers? What were Rosa's favorite items she could not resist buying?

He nodded thoughtfully. A worthy angle to consider. If she'd gone on a shopping trip that day, perhaps he could finally track her last movements.

"My lord," Hughes said, coming up behind him. "There is a second letter that you may wish to read tonight. It was hand-delivered by a lad who had ridden all the way from Seaford. It may have gotten shuffled to the bottom."

"Quite right, Hughes. Thank you for telling me." He sifted through the pile and found a letter scratched in an unknown hand. "Ah, this must be it."

"Yes, my lord. Talbot said to tell you he is waiting with a bath, and we are holding dinner until you are ready."

"Excellent. I shall take the letter upstairs with me."

While Lucien soaked in the bath, he read Harrison's letter.

Lord Ware,

I'm sorry to say, but I'm getting nowhere. At first I thought Colby was involved, but I've searched his property and found no proof a woman was kept there. I'm beginning to suspect everyone, even my friends. I am sorry to bother you, sir, but I just don't know what to do next. I need advice.

Constable Harrison

Well, it had been a lot to ask of a boy, and it was to his credit that he had asked for help. Perhaps Sherry could go down tomorrow. Yes, that was just the thing. While Sherry was covering that end, Lucien could explore the shopping angle, figure out if there was a way to locate Hank and Beanie, and attempt to keep the ladies from getting into trouble.

Chapter Twenty One

Seaford, England 29 June 1813

After an early morning discussion with Lucien, Sherry was on his way to Seaford by mid-morning, mounted on his favorite horse, General. It was good to be on the road, particularly after spending the last two days in gambling dens, pursuing Hensley's rather empty-headed future son-in-law. After many hours in the young cub's company, Sherry had concluded that George Reeves had no political interests and even less interest in his betrothed's father. He certainly had no knowledge of Hensley's activities. The whole thing had been a waste of time.

Sherry drew in a deep breath of country air—the fresh scent of grasses, growing crops, and wild flowers. It was amazing that he forgot how bad London air was in summer until he got away from it. When they solved the current inquiry, he hoped to make an extended stay at his family's country seat at Sherbourne Manor… and spend time with Miss Emily.

The thought of Emily Selkirk made him smile, and then he grew pensive. He knew it was past time for him to declare himself. He had put it off for two years, not because his feelings were uncertain, but because of his work for Rothe. A spy's life was not completely his own, and it could be dangerous. Emily had not made a single protest—bless her—and continued to wait for him to speak with no explanation for why he had not. He owed her that, at least, to tell her of his concerns. Perhaps she shared them…or was willing to endure the risks.

Thus, caught up in his thoughts, he whiled away the hours until he arrived in the village of Seaford by mid afternoon. After stabling his horse and bespeaking a room at the Clifftop Inn, he set out on foot to find Constable Harrison. As Lucien had suggested, he started at the inn's pub, but Harrison hadn't yet been in, and the publican directed him to the blacksmith's shop or the constable's home on East Giles Road.

He found a young man fitting Harrison's description sitting on a pile of hay bales talking with the blacksmith. "Are you Constable Harrison?" Sherry asked.

"I am. What can I do for you?"

"I'm Andrew Sherbourne. I work with Lord Ware."

"By Jove, I'm glad to see you." Harrison jumped down from the bales. "This is business, Ed. Thanks for the chat. See you later."

"Eh, whenever," the big man grunted. He went back to work without showing much interest in Harrison's guest.

"How long have you and Lord Ware worked together?" Harrison asked, as they walked back toward the main thorough-fare.

"Several years. It started in the war."

"Then you work for the military?"

"Ware didn't tell you?" Sherry asked, amused by the young man's probing.

"Well…no, but I didn't ask."

"You wouldn't need to if he felt you should know." Sherry sighed as though giving in. "All I can tell you is we have the necessary authority from the Crown for such inquiries. Anything else is best kept secret."

"Yes, of course," Harrison hastily agreed. "I didn't mean to pry."

"No matter. Ware said you wrote to him for help. Why don't we sit down somewhere and you can tell me what you've learned so far?"

"All right, sir. The pub shouldn't be too crowded at this time of day, and I reckon we can find a private corner."

The pub was no busier than when Sherry had stopped in earlier. Only a few regulars sat at the bar, talking among themselves. Sherry and Harrison picked a corner table and benches near a window where they might catch a little breeze and wouldn't be overheard by those already giving them curious glances.

As Sherry listened intently, Harrison went over the events of the last two weeks, beginning with Lady Anne's report of a dead body in the cave. When he mentioned the meeting he'd had with Nate, Lord Ware, and Lady Anne, Sherry interrupted.

"Has Nate discovered anything?"

"That's just it, sir. I don't know," Harrison said with a frown. "Nate and me, we've always been good mates, but since that day, well, I think he's avoiding me. It's got me wondering if maybe he lied about not knowing about the spying."

"Let us not jump to conclusions." Sherry trusted Lucien's instincts, and his partner had said Nate was a good lad, although he suspected the young man knew more than he'd said. "Isn't it more likely he is reluctant to inform on his friends?"

"I suppose…but why doesn't he just say so? When he sees me coming, he takes off."

Sherry shrugged. Nate might feel guilty, embarrassed he'd talked about the smuggling at all. "Why don't you try again? If he fails to respond, we can talk with him together and find out if he has changed his mind about helping you. Now, tell me more about Justice of the Peace Colby. What made you suspect him?"

"The way he treated Lady Ashburn for one thing. He was so quick to discount her story and to suggest she'd made it up. It was odd he was so disrespectful."

Sherry nodded. "Anything else?"

"When we searched for the missing body, he made himself scarce. And he's usually in on everything…giving the orders."

"Maybe he was out of town."

"He wasn't. I asked his stable lad."

"Did you ask Colby why he hadn't participated?"

"Eh? Definitely not." Harrison looked rather alarmed. "I would not dare."

"Like that, is it? Not exactly an approachable fellow?"

"He dislikes being questioned—about anything." Harrison looked uneasy that Sherry might ask him to do so.

Good to know when the time comes, Sherry thought.

Fortunately, he was not an inexperienced young constable, and he'd be the one conducting the inevitable interview with Colby.

"What have you done to follow up on your suspicions of him?"

"I searched every inch of his property—looked through all the out buildings and the root cellar, picking my times when the family was gone or asleep. I managed to do it all without getting caught," he said with a note of pride. "I even bribed a day maid from the village to look through the main house. I was nearly sure he wouldn't have kept her there—his wife wouldn't have liked it, mind you, not a bit—but I wanted to be thorough."

Sherry stifled a smile. It sounded as though Mrs. Colby was a force to be reckoned with. That might explain why her husband was such a bully outside the home.

"You've done well," Sherry said. "And disposed of a major task. A good inquiry isn't all about gathering evidence, but also about eliminating possibilities. Have you had time to consider other places in the countryside where she might have been held? Discarded shacks, hunting huts, and the like?"

"All of them were searched when we were looking for the body, and I went through most of them again—still nothing."

Sherry's money was on a wine cellar or attic somewhere. But where should they start looking? And how? Sneaking around occupied houses at night was bound to get them caught, and they didn't have time to watch every residence in and near the village and wait until its occupants were away from home.

"Are there other manors like Colby's around Seaford? The kind that might have underground cellars or upper floors that are unused?"

"Several, I'd say."

"Any abandoned or lived in only a few months of the year? I'm thinking of places where there might not be a lot of people around to notice unusual activity."

"Um, let's see. Two manors are only used when the London season is over. I think both have a caretaker though. There's an abandoned place in really poor shape. I think it was searched, but it wasn't by me."

"Shall we start with those three? They seem the most likely and should be relatively easy to search without arousing suspicion. And since local residents might be involved, let us keep this to ourselves."

• • •

Three quarters of an hour later, Sherry had collected his saddle horse, met up with Harrison, and was following the constable down a narrow path with overgrown brush on both sides. They were no more than a quarter mile from Seaford, and the abandoned house loomed directly ahead.

Quite clearly, it had been unoccupied for some time. The lawn was overgrown, vines hung heavily on the crumpling brick exterior of the house, the once painted portions had peeled and were worn gray by weather, and several window panes were shattered. Grass and weeds leading to the front entrance were untrampled, indicating no one had come that way recently.

They dismounted, secured their horses to a tree branch, and waded through the weeds. The door was locked, but Harrison climbed through a window, and opened it from the inside.

"The boards don't look any too solid," Harrison cautioned. "And I question if the stairs are safe."

"Let's try the cellar first." Sherry found the door and peered downward. If he left the door open, there would be just enough light to see if it had been used in the last few weeks. "I'll take the cellar if you want to look around the rest of the house," he said. "Don't bother with the upper floors if the stairs look unsafe."

The young constable nodded, and Sherry eased down the rickety steps, fighting off cobwebs—a sign of the cellar's disuse. He squinted in the dim light, but saw nothing out of place. Every surface was covered with dust. This looked as though it was once the servants' quarters. He found a door at the east end that opened into the old wine cellar. A broken bottle lay on the dirt floor, but otherwise it had been emptied—long ago.

"Sir, there's nothing up here," the constable called down. "Find anything?"

"Only dust and cobwebs." Sherry brushed another web off his face and climbed the stairs. "We should give a look outside before giving up, but this isn't at all promising."

The stable roof had caved in; only a storage shed, perhaps for garden supplies, looked steady enough to be usable. "I'll look for a root cellar if you want to see to the shed," Harrison offered. "I'm sure I remember a mound just to the north."

"Just so." Sherry struck off for the shed, fighting his way through tall weeds and bramble. As soon as he saw the lock on the door, he called for the constable.

"Yes, sir." Harrison came plunging through the brush.

"Someone has been here. There's a shiny new lock on the shed."

"There's also a clear path coming up from the woods," Harrison said, as he arrived out of breath. "Shall we break the door?"

Sherry eyed it. The wood was weathered. "A couple of kicks might do it. On three. One, two, three." Their boots struck it in unison and the wood splintered. Instead of evidence of a woman being kept there—blankets or remnants of food—they stared at crates of wine bottles, and boxes of luxury items, silk scarves, gloves and the like.

"Smugglers' goods," Sherry said. "We've found their hoard."

"Good lord." Harrison was clearly caught by surprise. "What do we do now?"

Sherry chuckled. "Depends on what you want to do. You can ignore it, confiscate the contraband without saying a word, or make a real issue of it."

"Well, um…" Harrison ducked his head. "The village kind of depends on this stuff. Can we just put the door back and leave?"

"Sure. This is nothing to me," Sherry said agreeably.

After fixing the door as best they could, it took another hour after that to do a thorough walk-through of the other two properties. Each had a caretaker, but at Sherry's suggestion Harrison explained this was official business, and they were given full access without questions being asked. Nonetheless, they came up empty-handed.

On the way back to the village, they discussed what to do next. Sherry was wondering if it was time to apply a little pressure on Nate.

"You know, Colby stopped to ask about you before we left town today—while you were getting your horse," Harrison suddenly said.

Sherry swung his head to stare at him. "Why didn't you mention it earlier?"

"Well…uh, thought about it, but I reckoned he was just being Colby. Has to know everything. He quizzed me about who you were and what you're doing here. I told him you were a friend of Lord Ware, that I wasn't sure why you were in Seaford, and that was all I knew. He didn't believe me and said so." Harrison shrugged. "But in truth, I don't know much more."

"Hence, you didn't lie to him," Sherry said with a grin.

"That's what I thought." Harrison returned the grin. "But seeing him reminded me he has friends whose homes might be worth inspecting."

"Because…?"

"Colby's acting funny. I said he was just being Colby, but it might be more than that. He demands to know what's going on, yet he hasn't offered to help. It don't seem right somehow. Now these two fellows I have in mind, they do whatever he asks."

"How far would they go?"

"Would they kill on his orders, you mean? Well, I guess they would."

"Good to know. However, I meant torture, depravity," Sherry said, thinking about Pettigrew's report of the abuse Rosa endured.

Harrison's eyes widened. "She was, uh, mistreated?"

"That's what the London doctor says. Keep that information to yourself, no one else."

"Devil take 'em," Harrison muttered. "I won't say nothing, but demme that is frightful." He frowned in thought and shook his head. "These two men aren't up to that, but they might walk away and turn a blind eye to what others were doing."

"Which could be what happened," Sherry said. "It's possible London cutthroats had charge of her." His jaw tightened recalling what they'd done to her, then he shoved those thoughts aside. If he let anger take over, it would only get in the way.

"How can I meet these two men without being conspicuous?"

"The pub. Most fellows stop there come evening, even Colby. And where he is, you can usually find Jed Harper and Marty Walsh."

"Capital. Shall we meet at the pub at eight?"

"Sounds about right, sir."

At the edge of town, Harrison split off to his own home, and Sherry turned toward the main road that led to the Clifftop Inn. As he exited the woods at the edge of the village, he noticed three men coming out the side door of a house that set back from the road and next to the woods. They seemed startled to see him, in fact the youngest of the group stepped back as though to duck into the house until the older, heavy-set man grabbed his arm. They turned toward the rear of the property and hurried off into the woods.

Sherry frowned, wondering what that was about. He shrugged—odd behavior but meaningless, no doubt. He'd grown too suspicious.

He returned to the inn and left his horse with the stable boy. His stomach growled, reminding him he hadn't eaten since early morning, and he stopped in the inn's public room for a quick meal. He just had time to hurry upstairs to freshen up. By the time he entered the pub a few minutes after eight, Harrison was already seated at a table and waved him over.

"Good evening," Sherry said as he sat on the bench across from him. "Are Colby and his friends here?"

"Behind me and to my right. Table of four. The older one with a paunch is Colby. Next to him is Jed Harper. Marty Walsh is directly across from Colby, and next to Walsh is Eli Green."

Sherry's eyes narrowed. "I saw three of them earlier as I returned to town. They were coming out of the last house on the lane, the one that sets so far back, and I got the impression they weren't pleased to see me." Sherry described the incident in greater detail. "Their behavior was off."

"Off, indeed," Harrison agreed. He grew thoughtful. "The Freeman house has sat empty for months. I cannot think why they'd be there."

Sherry lifted a brow. "You don't say."

Before he could ask Harrison more about it, Colby rose from his table and came toward them. "Evening, Harry. I understand your friend here—Sherbourne, is it not?—is acquainted with Lord Ware. I wondered if there was news of the body you found. Has it been identified?"

"I am Andrew Sherbourne, sir," Sherry affirmed with a nod. "To my knowledge the dead woman's name remains unknown."

Colby pursed his lips. "I had assumed news of her brought you to Seaford."

He might as well have said "to *my* town," his tone leaving the strong implication he had a right to know everything that happened there.

"I had certain matters to discuss with Constable Harrison," Sherry said keeping his voice affable.

"Perhaps you could share those with me."

"I'd rather not." Sherry suppressed a stronger reaction to the man's impertinence and allowed the simple words to hang in the air.

"Eh, truly? I am the magistrate, you know. Harrison, I assume in good time you will report anything I should know." He looked at Sherry. "You are leaving in the morning?"

"Perhaps," Sherry said lazily. "I have not quite decided."

"Not much to do around Seaford, unless you've come to enjoy the sea air," Colby said, eyeing him.

Sherry shrugged. "Never can tell. Nice to meet you, magistrate," he said, initiating an end to the conversation.

"I shall send over a pint for the road. I doubt we shall be seeing one another again."

Sherry smiled up at him. "As I said before, you never can tell."

Colby gave him a hard stare, then signaled to the publican to refill their pints and returned to his own table. Those at nearby tables, who'd been listening, resumed their own low-voiced conversations.

"You don't give an inch, do you?" Harrison said quietly. "He won't forget that."

Sherry took a swig of his own pint, ignoring the one Colby had sent over. "Your magistrate is a pompous bully, but I've met worse, and since I do not live here, I shall not worry if he carries a grudge. He won't hold it against you, will he?"

"Probably not. He'll just think I couldn't stop you—and he'd be right. Besides, he'll be too busy probing for everything we said and did while you were here."

"With any luck, it won't matter by then. Got a lantern handy? I know it's late for country folk, but we have a house to explore, and then I want to talk with Nate, even if we have to get him out of bed. I believe we are on the verge of learning something significant."

• • •

By the time Sherry and Harrison entered the empty house at the edge of town, it was going on ten, and they were obscured by the darkening shadows. The house smelled of dust and disuse, not a hopeful sign. Sherry paused until his eyes adjusted to the dim moonlight filtering through the dusty windows. He would not light the lantern until they couldn't avoid it.

"Have you been inside here before?" Sherry asked.

"No. The old couple kept to themselves. They died a few months ago, within days of each other. It looks as though the local lads haven't taken to exploring it yet."

Sherry nodded. "Shall we get started? Look for a room with few or no windows, possibly the attic, and naturally, we'll explore the cellar."

They began on the upper floor, Harrison stuck his head in the attic, and finding nothing out of the ordinary, they moved down to the main floor. Upon reaching the kitchen, they found the cellar door and opened it. Pitch black.

"We're going to need the lantern," Harrison said. "Why don't I light it and go first?"

"Lead on." Sherry followed the constable downstairs, and they stopped abruptly when the lantern's glow revealed dried blood on the floor.

"Good lord, sir," Harrison gasped. "I think we found it."

As the constable continue to swing the lantern around, Sherry spotted blood smears on a broken wooden chair. One jagged chair leg lay on the floor, heavily stained…and exactly the shape Pettigrew had described as the fatal weapon.

"No dust or cobwebs," Sherry remarked, putting the gruesome chair leg from his mind and continuing to explore. He found a second lantern on a shelf, lit it, and worked his way around the cellar. Off in one corner, he spotted two empty wine bottles, but they were covered with spider webs and might have been there months or years. As he moved back toward the stairs, a rat scuttled across his path and drew his attention to an object behind an empty canvas bag. Edging it clear with the toe of his boot, he picked it up and shook off the dirt. A gothic chapbook. Despite the cellar dust, it looked new. Could this be the book Rosa bought the day she was taken? It hardly seemed the thing her captors would have read—if they could read at all, which wasn't likely.

He stuck it in his pocket and resumed his search, poking into corners, looking for her reticule, her bonnet, or other personal items that might prove her presence. Those things weren't with the body, so they should be here or her captors got rid of them when they cleared out. He stirred up two more rats and a couple of large spiders, but none of her belongings.

After several minutes, he returned to the bottom of the stairs and showed the chapbook to Harrison. "They made some attempt to clean up and hide that anyone was here, but the blood and broken chair are rather obvious. Did you find anything else?"

"Not sure what I have, sir. An address maybe, but not one in Seaford." He handed a torn corner of paper to Sherry. "Mean anything to you?"

"*98 Canton.* Never heard of it, but I suppose it could be in London. I think the cutthroats that held the señorita are from town. Maybe this will lead us to one of them. In any event, I'll take it with me, and see if Ware or someone else can run it down." He was thinking this would be a good job for Whitehall.

Sherry took one last look around, thinking of the weeks of abuse Rosa had suffered in that inhospitable place. "Let's get the hell out of here."

Back in the kitchen, they exited through the back door and located a path beaten through the tall weeds ending in a small clearing in the woods. Hoof prints and horse dung indicated at least two horses had often been there. "This is how her captors remained unnoticed," Sherry said. "They used the woods to get close to the house, went in the back door, and straight down to the cellar, avoiding the windows of the front rooms."

"We need to talk to Colby, don't we?" Harrison asked.

"Eventually, but I want to know everything I can before we do. Let us talk with Nate first. I suspect your friend hasn't told us the half of it."

Harrison's face fell. "I wish you were wrong, sir, but he hasn't been acting at all like himself."

• • •

As it were, the Barnes family had not gone to bed. Not to say Sherry and Harrison were well received, but after only brief resistance, they were seated in the study talking with Nate and his father, who—as any good father would do—had insisted on being present.

"Just what is it you think my boy has done?" Mr. Barnes demanded.

"He has been smuggling—by his own admission," Sherry said gently. "But I am only concerned he is hiding what he knows of secret messages being carried to and from France. Beyond that, I can't say what he might know about the men who held the dead woman captive at Freeman house."

"Zounds, Nate." His father looked at him in dismay. "If any of that is true, you need to tell us."

Nate's face was pale, nearly white, and frozen, as though his worst nightmare had come to pass, and then he visibly slumped and shot a look at Harrison. "Demme, Harry, I wanted to tell you, but all that talk about dead women and spyin'...I got woefully scared. But I know nothin' about the Freeman house." He turned to look at his father. "Honestly, sir, you gotta believe me 'bout that. But...but I..." He looked away, staring at the wall. "I took them letters to France."

"Nate!" His father stared at him in disbelief.

"I aint no spy. At least I dint mean to be." Nate jerked his gaze from father to Harrison and finally appealed to Sherry. "I didn't know nothin' bad what was in 'em. Honest. She *said* they was love letters."

"Who is she?" Sherry asked.

"Sally, Mrs. Colby's maid."

"Son, what have you gotten yourself—" Barnes stopped and turned to Sherry, "I think you better explain what this is all about."

"Fair enough." Sherry related what facts he felt Barnes needed to know regarding the Seaford end of the situation without mentioning anyone's name.

Barnes eyed his son. "I guess you better tell us the rest."

"Sally came to me," Nate said straightening, "and ask for a favor—just to take a few love letters to France and bring back his replies. I didn't see no harm in it. I gave them to Pierre, one of the Frenchmen we usually see."

Poor odds of finding Pierre, Sherry thought. Even if that was his real name, it was common and likely untraceable without a surname. He'd leave the task to Rothe's agents in France.

"Sally said they was just love letters," Nate repeated.

"I heard you, Nate. We shall need to confirm your story." Sherry rose and looked at Harrison. "*Now*, we talk with the Colbys."

"What about Nate? How much trouble has he got?" Barnes asked anxiously.

"If Sally verifies he has told the truth, I have no interest in his activities," Sherry said. "I do, however, hope he learns from this incident."

"I shall see that he does." Barnes followed Sherry and Harrison to the door. "Thank you, he is my only son," he added awkwardly. "I wish you good luck in sorting out the sordid matter."

• • •

Their late-night arrival at the Colbys' caused quite a stir. The house was mostly dark when they knocked on the door about midnight, and within minutes, half the lights in the manor were on. Justice Colby expressed his outrage that his household was being disturbed, and he let his displeasure be known in such a large voice that Mrs. Colby came hurrying down the stairs, followed by several servants.

Eventually, Colby realized Sherry wasn't leaving until they talked with Sally, and he ordered his butler to bring her.

When the girl was ushered into the drawing room a few minutes later, she was white as a sheet and starting to cry.

"We'd prefer to talk with her in private," Sherry said.

"I don't care. I am staying," Colby announced. "You cannot deny me knowing what is happening in my own house."

"I'm staying too," Mrs. Colby said. "Sally is my maid, and if she has done something wrong, I want to hear for myself."

"Bollocks, Eudora," her husband said, impatiently. "Go back to your room—and take all these servants with you. I can take care of this."

"Really, Martin. Your language," Eudora Colby scolded while looking down her nose. For a moment, Sherry thought she was going to refuse, but she suddenly acquiesced, contrary to everything he had heard about her. Maybe she allowed her husband to win an argument now and then…or she just wanted to go back to bed.

When she closed the door behind her, Colby demanded, "Explain why you're here."

"I believe it will become clear as we go along," Sherry said. "If that is not acceptable, Magistrate, we shall be forced to conduct this interview elsewhere. I will say this, we believe Sally has gotten herself involved in acts of treason."

"Good lord." Colby stared at Sherry a moment, then gave a sharp wave of his hand. "Get on with it then."

Sherry turned to the maid with a friendly smile. "Sally, my name is Sherbourne. I'm going to be asking you a few questions, but before I do, you should know that we talked to Nate Barnes tonight. He said he carried some letters to France that came from you. Is that true?"

Sherry saw Colby's mouth drop open out of the corner of his eye, but he kept his attention on Sally. She stared at him in frozen silence.

"This is important, Sally. We must have the truth. Where did you get the letters?"

She continued to gaze at him in silence until Colby snapped, "Sally! Good lord, child, talk to him."

She jumped the moment he said her name. "Yes, sir. I…um, I…" She looked at Colby and then back at Sherry. "Yes, I gave 'em to him." Her voice was so small he barely heard her.

"Did you write them?" When she shook her head no, he asked, "Where did you get them?"

"I don't want to get her in trouble. They was just love notes."

"Nobody is in trouble yet. But they were not love letters," Sherry said.

"What were they?" she asked big eyed.

"Secrets. Important papers."

Her eyes got bigger. "My cousin Mary sent them. She asked that I find someone to take them to her sweetheart in France. Pierre, that is."

"Have you met Pierre?"

"No, sir. I barely know Mary."

Sherry frowned. "I thought she was your cousin."

"She is, but she lives in London, sir. I ain't seen her since I was little, five or six, maybe."

"Mary just suddenly wrote to you?"

Sally bobbed her head, her self-assurance returning now that someone seemed to believe her. "You coulda bowled me over, sir, but it was so romantic, sweethearts kept apart by the war, so I agreed to help. Did I do something wrong?"

Colby gave a disgusted snort.

"I'm afraid you were tricked," Sherry said.

Her brows knit in worry. "By Mary?"

"I'm not sure, but we shall soon find out." Sherry obtained Mary's last name and address and one of the letters written to Sally in which "a love letter" had been enclosed. When he had everything he needed, he dismissed the girl and turned to Colby, "And now, sir, I have questions for you."

"Me? I knew nothing about these letters or that any spying was occurring. I would have turned them in myself."

"Would you? It is all connected to the death of the young woman recently found in Singing Cave, and I observed you, Jed Harper, and Marty Walsh coming out of the house where she died."

Colby surged to his feet. "Now see here, are you accusing me of murder and espionage?"

"You tell me," Sherry said, giving him a cold look. "What is your connection to all this? Why were you in the Freeman house?"

Colby paced to the window, stood with his hands linked behind his back, and stared outside into the dark. One, then two minutes passed and Sherry continued to wait. Finally, his silence was rewarded.

"Believe it or not, Sherbourne, I care that justice is done. And I regret I did not give more credence to Lady Anne Ashburn's report. I have attempted to make up for my lack of diligence by discovering for myself what happened to the young woman. My friends and I have conducted our own investigation. When you saw us, we had just discovered the blood in the cellar. I would have reported it to Harrison in the morning." He turned away from the window and looked at Sherbourne. "That is the honest truth, sir."

"How did you know where to look?"

"We've inspected a dozen places or more. Freeman's house was just the next one on our list." Colby shrugged. "This is a small village, Sherbourne. Perhaps you didn't know, but Harry should have realized that you've been all the talk. Everyone knows you've been searching for an isolated spot where the woman was held captive and killed. We wanted to get there before you…and I guess we did."

It was Sherry's turn to shrug. "Well, you're mostly correct, so I won't quibble over the details."

"I still don't know who she is, why she died, or how she ties in with the smuggled documents. Are you going to tell me? I *am* the magistrate."

"Jurisdiction in this matter lies in London," Sherry said. "Only the ongoing smuggling of goods and the transport of the messages occurred here. As you are already aware of the smuggling, I assume you won't be pursuing those charges, and I believe both Sally and Nate were the innocent dupes of a clever French spy. Foolish actions on their part but hardly criminal. None of that entitles you to privileged information." Sherry sighed. "Nevertheless, sir, if you sit down and calm yourself, I shall give you the key points."

"They murdered that woman here. What about that?"

"In truth, they did not."

"Devil they didn't," Colby bellowed, leaning forward almost in Sherry's face. "We saw the blood."

Sherry sighed and stared at him, refusing to engage in a shouting duel. If Colby didn't get down from his high horse soon, Sherry was leaving.

Colby grimaced, but he returned to his seat.

"The young woman was abducted in London several weeks ago," Sherry explained. "She was used as leverage to force her father to steal secret war documents."

Colby interrupted. "The documents passed on by Nate?"

"Yes. With what we learned tonight, I hope this Mary in London can lead us to the French spy behind this scheme."

"But why did they kill the woman?"

"She wasn't murdered, sir, not in the sense that someone else wielded the weapon. The doctor's examination indicates she committed self-murder. It appears her captors never intended to send her home. After all, she could identify them. She must have lost heart that she would be rescued and could no longer endure the constant beatings and misuse of her person."

Colby scowled. "Misuse? She was interfered with?"

"Repeatedly."

"Good lord. The poor thing." The magistrate's face sagged. "The curs should be hanged ten times over."

Chapter Twenty Two

London, 29 June 1813

While Sherry was in Seaford and Lady Anne was conducting her own inquiry regarding the mysterious note to Rosa, Lucien made sure his household was adequately fortified against further intruders and then set out for the Hidalgo residence to speak with Betty. The new footman, a lad of eighteen or so, glanced at his calling card, and looked up eagerly.

"Betty is not here, my lord. She is interviewing for a new position, but she only took a half day. She should return within a couple of hours."

"If you would, tell her I shall call again. It is important I speak with her."

"Yes, my lord, I shall do so."

Lucien could tell the lad wanted to ask why. He would have been told of the household's recent tragedies and was curious if this was connected. Nevertheless, he stuck to his training and simply bowed as Lucien walked away.

Lucien had just reached his curricle when he looked up to see his footman running down the street. "A message, my lord." Robert came to a halt beside the carriage, sweat beading his face. He caught his breath and lowered his voice. "Lord Rothe requests you meet him at Bow Street station with all haste."

"What now?" Lucien muttered to himself.

"I do not know, sir."

Lucien smiled at his footman. "I appreciate your promptness, lad. You look mighty hot," he said eyeing his moist brow. He tossed him a coin. "Perhaps a pint of ale on the way home might cool you down."

Robert grinned and deftly caught and pocketed the coin. "That it would, my lord. Thank you."

Lucien urged his team into a trot. Bow Street? What was Rothe up to now?

He worked his way through London's heavily congested streets and turned onto Bow Street. Drawing the team to a halt in front of the station, he eyed the front entrance with misgiving.

The Bow Street Runners, the first organized policing force in London, had been established in 1749 by the Fielding brothers with only seven runners. It had grown to 68 by 1800 and added 7 magistrates. The runners had replaced the "thief takers,' a loose knit group of bounty hunters, who often showed little concern for getting the right man as long as they arrested *someone* and collected the reward. The runners still carried the stigma of those earlier men and were both feared and distrusted by many. Lucien and Sherry's experiences had been mixed, and their most recent memories were far from good.

"I hoped I'd never come through these doors again," he muttered to himself as he entered the station.

A young constable immediately came forward. "Lord Ware? Lord Rothe and the Magistrate are waiting right through here." He directed him into an office where Lucien found the two men deep in conversation.

"Ah, here you are," Rothe said rising. He handed Lucien a note before seating himself again. "Two men bound in ropes were delivered to the station this morning, along with a message addressed to you."

Lucien took the note silently and took the chair indicated by the Magistrate. He broke the seal, his eyes quickly scanning the short message. He heaved a sigh and read aloud,

"*Hank Fowler and Lawrence 'Beanie' Smith confessed to kidnapping and abusing Señorita Hidalgo, along with Big Toe Kemp. I regret we did not locate Big Toe in time for him to face your legal justice. I assume the law will punish these two men as they deserve.*

C. Cade"

"The audacity of the man," the Magistrate said. "Why would he do this? Is he attempting to curry favor with this court?"

Rothe hastened to respond before Lucien said anything. "He has assisted Whitehall before. The man lives by a unique moral code of his own, which fortunately for us includes loyalty to the Crown and a loathing for those who mistreat women and children."

"You have found him truthful?"

"Yes, sir. In our limited dealings, his information has been consistently trustworthy."

The magistrate pinched his lips together. "I had heard this said before but wrote it off to gossip. It is an oddity to see such contradictions in anyone. I had not thought to find a man in the underworld with scruples that were more than self-serving." He steepled his fingers and leaned back in his chair. "This adds a new layer to my judgement of the Gentleman Thief."

Good luck at figuring him out, Lucien thought. Cade was an enigma. Rumored to be the by-blow of landed gentry, young Charlie grew up on London's streets as a pickpocket. At age nine, he was transported for petty theft, and he returned at age eighteen on a privateer. The smuggler then became a wealthy receiver of stolen goods, eventually starting his own gang of thieves. Ten years later he opened a gambling establishment and assumed the outward appearance and manners of a gentleman. During the following eight years, he had worked his way into Society, and many of the haut ton now frequented Cade's Club. He had kept his ties to the underground, and Lucien was convinced he continued to run several gangs. His unusual background and success in society had earned him the nickname of Gentleman Thief.

"Tell me what is behind this," the Magistrate said pointing to Cade's note. "We cannot continue to hold these men unless I know what they have done."

"Allow me, sir." Rothe began by giving a brief summary of the abduction and Hidalgo's spying. Lucien was glad to have him do it, as the marquess could pick and choose those parts that Whitehall was willing to share. Rothe also covered Pettigrew's findings, which the Magistrate heard with a good measure of disgust. When they came down to the events in the docklands, Lucien took over, explaining how he found Big Toe's body and tracked down the names of Hank and Beanie.

"How Cade got their names, I do not know. It wasn't from us. He has his own spies all over town," Lucien finished. He looked at the Magistrate. "May I talk with the two men?"

"I shall be conducting an interview to hear their side of these charges. You and Lord Rothe, if he wishes, may attend and ask any additional questions you have at the end."

Lucien nodded, knowing this was the best he would get, but Rothe rose. "Much as I would like to stay, I am due elsewhere and shall await Lord Ware's report. Thank you for your time, sir."

The Magistrate gave a respectful nod to Rothe and turned to Lucien. "Shall we get on with it?"

They walked down a hallway to an empty room, and the Magistrate sent a constable to bring the prisoner, Hank Fowler. While they waited, the Magistrate brought up Cade's name again. "I dare say Whitehall is walking a fine line in dealing with a known crime lord, even if he does fancy himself a gentleman. Such a man is likely to demand favors in return."

"Perhaps, but Lord Rothe will hold a hard line. Most of Cade's activities on Whitehall's behalf were done out of loyalty to the Crown. Nabbing these men, however, was not at Whitehall's behest. He can hardly expect recompense for that."

"And yet, such a man is unpredictable." The magistrate paused before adding, "I suspect personal favors would be seen in a different light. Do you not agree?" He looked closely at Lucien, as though he knew the past deal that had been made to rescue Sherry.

Lucien shrugged, keeping his face unreadable, and was relieved when the door opened with the sound of clanking shackles. A constable entered with a tag-rag prisoner.

"This is Hank Fowler, sir." The constable turned away and sat on a chair by the door.

Good grief. Did a life of crime mean you never bathed? Fowler was disheveled, his black hair tangled, oily, and badly in need of a wash. His clothes looked as though he'd been rolling in dirt, and he smelled of week-old fish and stale sweat. His eyes were dark and defiant. Cade may have gotten a confession from him, but Fowler's attitude said he was ready to put up a fight.

Which he did, remaining belligerent and uncooperative until the Magistrate finally showed him Cade's note. "Take a look at this."

"Wot's it say?"

Rothe read it to him.

Fowler shrugged. "So?"

"He says you confessed to the kidnapping and murder of Señorita Hidalgo. Are you saying Cade is a liar?"

Fowler looked stunned—and rather fearful. "Liar? No. No, demme. I wouldna say that 'bout him. You think I be dicked in the nob?" He sighed and threw the Magistrate a baleful look. "Big Toe set it up and give us our orders. We kept the girl three weeks or so. But she done kilt herself."

Lucien drew in a long breath. Any doubt he'd had that Cade might have forced a false confession was put to rest. No one else would have known that Rosa stabbed herself.

"You didn't just keep her, did you?" he asked.

"We mighta roughed her up a bit."

"And raped her," the Magistrate said bluntly.

Fowler recoiled from the harshness accusation. "Not me. I swear. It was Beanie. He got bored."

Lucien wanted to beat him. He didn't believe for a moment that Fowler hadn't participated, and at the very least, he had stood by and watched. What a terrifying ordeal they put the girl through.

"If you were supposed to be holding her hostage, keeping her safe, how did she end up dead?"

Fowler shook his head. "That weren't how it was. Big Toe said to keep her somewhere outta town fer a week or two to see if she were needed, then we'd be getting' rid of her. So that's what we did, me and Beanie. Then one day Big Toe sends word she ain't needed no more but to make sure her body weren't found. Well, Beanie liked her a lot by then, if you get my drift, so we was gonna keep her a bit longer, then she up and kilt herself."

"How did she do it?"

"Gutted herself with a broken chair leg."

The Magistrate paused and shook his head as though in disbelief.

Keen to ask his own questions, Lucien took advantage of the break. "Who gave Big Toe his orders?"

Fowler shook his head. "He kept all that to hisself. Someone in London, I reckon, 'cause he come back quick from meetin' with him."

"Where did you kidnap the girl?"

He shrugged. "Big Toe done nabbed her and then picked us up in this big black coach. Brought us down to Seaford where he used to live." Fowler went on to describe how they'd taken Rosa to an empty house that Big Toe had found, and then he left them guarding Rosa with provisions for a few weeks. "And he never come back. Beanie and me had to find our own way to London."

"Why put her body in the cave and then move her again?" Lucien asked, wanting to hear his suspicions confirmed.

"Thought nobody would find her there. But before we done cleared the house, we heard this coach…it come tearin' down the road an' the coachman said somethin' about Singin' Cave. Well, we knew what it was and run all the way. Carried and drug the body down the cliffs, along the beach, and up a path to the woods. Put it in a thicket of brush where she shouldna been found."

The Magistrate took over the questioning again, moving on to other charges. "Quite a dreadful story, Fowler. And why kill Jonathan Dickson, who you may know as Jose? And if anyone else was involved in this sordid affair, I want their names."

"You got the only names I know—me, Beanie, and Big Toe. Big Toe got the jobs. We just did what he tol' us."

"You have no idea who was paying you?" the Magistrate asked. "I find that hard to believe."

"Can't help that. It be the truth."

"I cannot say I believe you, but let's talk about Jose."

"Big Toe had this job watchin' Hidalgo's house. Some box inside he was after. Don't know what was in it but it be worth a lot, we figured, and Beanie and me wasn't best pleased he were cuttin' us out. So, when he come to us at the pub the other night, say he's been seen and we have to help him get rid of the fellow, we ain't so keen to help. But Big Toe being who he is…or was, we did as we was told. And then, we dumped the body in the river."

"I have heard enough," the Magistrate said, leaning back in his chair. He nodded to the constable. Take him back and bring Smith."

"Beanie" Smith wasn't quite as disheveled as his mate. If he had washed his fair hair and cleaned up a bit, he might have looked half-way respectable. But Smith was in no mood to talk. Even when Cade's name was mentioned and he'd heard Fowler had confessed all, his answers were brief, mostly yes or no. All in all, his story squared quite well with Fowler's except on the abuse of Rosa.

"Fowler said that was you," the Magistrate said. "That you got bored."

"Well, he tol' you wrong. 'Tweren't me, but him. Hank was all over her from the moment we got to Seaford."

Smith crossed his arms and refused to say another word about the abuse—or anything else.

"Your silence doesn't matter," the Magistrate said, staring Smith in the face. "Fowler told us what happened, and you are legally responsible for anything that took place." He turned to Lucien. "I have more than enough to hold them over for trial. Anything else you want to ask?"

"Who killed Big Toe?" Lucien asked.

Smith rolled his eyes. "Know n'thin' bout that. Don't wanna know."

"Why have you confessed to the rest of it? Were you threatened?"

"By who?"

"Anyone."

"Not me."

"Are you certain?" the Magistrate interjected.

"Damned sure." Smith's mulish look said he was done.

While Lucien suspected Cade's men had pressed hard for the confessions, he didn't doubt the veracity. Nonetheless, he wondered what threats had been used, not that he'd ever learn. Even hardened cutthroats were not going to *gabble* on the crime lord.

"Well, that's that," the magistrate said as the constable led Smith back to the gaol cells.

"What happens to them?" Lucien asked.

The Magistrate's answer was matter-of-fact. "They'll be charged with the kidnapping of Señorita Hidalgo and the murder of Jonathan Dickson. As their guilt is not in doubt, they will face the hangman in due course."

Considering the weeks of misery the young señorita had suffered, it somehow did not seem punishment enough.

Lucien let the door of Bow Street station slam behind him. He looked around for his carriage, and a moment later Finn was standing in front of him holding out a message in Lady Anne's handwriting.

"Her footman told Robert it be urgent, m'lord."

Chapter Twenty Three

Earlier in the day, 29 June 1813

After waiting two days for a response to Lady Julia's letter to Señora de Leon, Anne had just finished a late breakfast when her butler announced that Lady Sophia Castlebridge and Lady Julia Castlebridge wished to see her.

She rose hurriedly, gathering the folds of her blue morning gown around her. "I shall see them in the private parlor, Staves, and please send in coffee, tea, and biscuits. No one else is to disturb us."

"Yes, my lady."

Anne and her guests arrived at the parlor together. "Have we a response?" she asked eagerly.

"We do," Lady Julia said with a conspiratorial smile. "I have it right here." She started to open her reticule when Anne stopped her.

"I have ordered tea," she said as they seated themselves. "Perhaps we should delay any discussion until after it arrives."

"I am not sure I can wait that long," Lady Sophia protested. "Can we at least see it?"

"Of course." Lady Julia opened her reticule but laid it in her lap when the door opened. A maid entered with the tea tray, set it on the table, and curtseyed when Anne said they would pour for themselves.

After the maid was gone, Lady Julia pulled out the letter while Anne poured their choices of tea or coffee.

"Where are the comparison letters?" Lady Sophia demanded.

Anne took a quick sip of her coffee, set it down, and went to her desk, taking out the two letters found in Rosa Hidalgo's bedchamber. She waved them in the air with an impish look, and all thoughts of coffee and tea vanished as the three women shoved the tea tray aside and spread the letters on the table, comparing them with the one Lady Julia took from her reticule.

"It matches this one with the fancy signature," Lady Sophia declared with gleeful indignation. "Señora de Leon was helping the kidnappers."

"Oh, no." Lady Julia said sadly. "How could she?"

"We don't know she did, not for certain," Anne said, having learned from earlier inquiries that one must be cautious of making swift assumptions. "All we truly know is the señora wrote the note Rosa received that day."

"I suppose there is some room for doubt she was part of the plan," Lady Sophia conceded, "but *I* am confident she was. Why else would the señora pretend she hardly knew the girl—when it is clear that is a lie—unless she had something to hide?"

"It is very suspicious," Anne agreed.

"Now that we have these letters, what should we do with them?" Lady Julia asked.

Lady Sophia spoke quickly. "We cannot let her get away with such villainy. I say we confront her, make her tell us the truth."

Anne was sorely tempted, but she knew they *should* turn the matter over to Lord Ware.

"What if she denies it?" Lady Julia asked. "Knowing we suspect her, won't she flee the country before we can gather other proof?"

Even Lady Sophia seemed taken aback. "Oh, I had not considered that…but we cannot do nothing."

"We should give the letter to Lord Ware," Lady Julia said.

"Yes, we should," Anne agreed, "but I do so wish to see her face when she knows she has been found out."

They fell silent, sipping at their coffee and tea. Anne was debating with herself, weighing the possibilities, and she supposed her friends were too.

"Would he allow us to accompany him?" Lady Julia asked.

"Doubtful," said Lady Sophia.

"No," Anne said. She knew what Lord Ware would say, and

perhaps it was that certainty that caused her to make the decision she did. "I agree with Lady Sophia, we should confront her ourselves. After all, how far can she run before Lord Ware would catch her?"

"Not far, I would think," Lady Sophia said. "Shall we go now?"

Lady Julia frowned in doubt. "Oh, so soon. Should we not think about it a bit more?"

"And talk ourselves out of it?" Lady Sophia snorted. "I think not."

Anne laughed, a little tensely. "If we are going to do this, we need a plan."

"What kind of plan?" Lady Sophia cocked her head. "We simply tell her what we know and demand an explanation."

"Then what?" her cousin asked. "Supposing she admits it—we can't arrest her."

"Lord Ware could," Lady Sophia said uncertainly. "Or the constables. Maybe it's different for Envoy's wives." She sat back, obviously pondering the question.

"We don't want her to escape punishment," Lady Julia said.

"Decidedly not, but I have an idea," Anne said. "I shall write a note to Lord Ware to be delivered as soon as we leave for the Embassy. That way we can confront her, and Ware shall arrive in time to take charge of the prisoner."

"Excellent plan." Lady Sophia clapped her hands together, and even Lady Julia nodded in approval.

• • •

At the Spanish Embassy, Deputy Envoy Pablo Ruiz, a short, dark Spaniard with a thin mustache, met them in the hallway. "Good morning, ladies. If you have come to speak with the Envoy, I am sorry to tell you has appointments all day. I can put you on his schedule for next week."

"Oh, no. That is not necessary. We wish to visit Señora de Leon," Anne said with what she hoped was a winning smile.

He returned her smile with a small bow. "Ah, yes, the señora is in residence. Allow me to show you in." He turned to the butler. "You may return to your post, and I shall announce the ladies."

"Yes, Deputy Ruiz."

"May I ask the purpose of your call?" Ruiz asked, his dark eyes flashing with curiosity as he gestured them toward a hallway.

"Just a social call," Lady Sophia offered gaily. "You know how we ladies love to chat."

"I am sure she will be pleased." He stopped at an arched doorway, stepped into the room, and spoke to someone they could not see. "You have visitors, Señora." Anne did not hear the response, but Ruiz announced their names, stepped back into the hallway, and motioned for the ladies to precede him.

Señora de Leon rose with a gracious smile. Anne wondered if she just imagined a wary look in their hostess's eyes. After all, the Spanish woman could not know they were going to accuse her of unspeakable crimes.

"May I ring for tea?" Ruiz asked as he crossed the room to the bell pull.

"Thank you. Will you stay and join us?" the señora asked him.

"Briefly. I have work to do, so I shall not remain for long." When everyone else was seated, he took a chair close to Señora de Leon.

Why was he staying for tea? Almost as though he was guarding her, Anne thought. Did he view them as a threat? Why had he asked their reason for coming? It was all a bit strange…unless Anne was seeing everything at the Embassy through a veil of suspicion. She glanced at Lady Sophia to see if she shared Anne's concerns, but that lady's face was giving nothing away.

Anne was loath to confront the señora with Ruiz present, and she sought other topics of discussion that could pass the time. "Have you seen the new collection of Kashmiri shawls from India at Benson & Sons?"

"I have not," the señora said. "Do you approve of them?"

"They are divine," Lady Sophia exclaimed. "I could not resist buying two, although they are costly."

That led into a discussion of the latest fashion trends, including the hemlines that were now off the floor. After ten minutes, Deputy Ruiz was visibly bored, and he finally excused himself.

The moment the door closed behind him, Lady Anne pulled out the two matching letters—the one sent to Lady Julia and the one with the elaborate initialed signature found in Rosa's room—and placed them on the tea table. "You were corresponding with Señorita Hidalgo, were you not?"

The señora looked at the letters and said hesitantly, "Now and then. Why do you have these? Why do you ask?"

Anne paused when she heard a faint noise in the hallway that made her wonder if someone—such as Ruiz—was listening. When the sound did not repeat, she forged ahead. "Rosa Hidalgo's maid said a note in your handwriting was received on the day her mistress went missing. The señorita left the house immediately after reading the note." Anne gave the señora a direct look. "Can you tell us what it said?"

"You have not said why you ask me such questions," Señora de Leon said, clearly offended. "But I shall tell you, I wrote no such note. The maid is mistaken. An honest mistake, I suppose, but a mistake nonetheless."

The door opened abruptly. Envoy de Leon and his deputy entered the room. "I heard we had guests, my dear, and as I had a few moments between meetings, I did not want to miss greeting them." He gave his wife a long look. "How are you, my dear? I know you had the headache earlier."

She reached out a hand, and he took it in his. "I fear it has returned," she said. "We were having a delightful visit, but I believe I must have a lie down."

"Certainly, my dear. What a pity your chat must wait for another day."

During this exchange, Anne slid the letters into her reticule. It was clear they were being dismissed. They had made a mull of it, but she was not going to lose the evidence.

The door opened again and the butler announced, "Lord Ware to see you, sir."

Sudden silence filled the room.

The viscount strolled in, looking as elegant as ever. He bowed gracefully to the Envoy and his wife but threw a look at Anne that said clearly he knew something was amiss. She shook her head subtly, unsure what he would make of that, but he seemed to get the point.

"I appear to have arrived at an inconvenient moment," he said.

"Somewhat, I fear," Envoy de Leon said. "I have an appointment waiting, and my wife has the headache."

Lord Ware gave Carmen de Leon a sympathetic look. "I wish you a swift recovery, Señora." He turned to the other ladies. "I came seeking Lady Anne. Since it appears you all rode together, may I escort you to your carriage?"

"A very agreeable offer," Anne said, giving him her arm.

Within a minute or two, the ladies were outside the embassy, and Lord Ware was handing them into their carriage.

"Well…" he said with a pregnant pause, holding the carriage door open. His gaze fell upon Anne. "I assume whatever you had in mind did not go well."

"I fear not. You see—"

He held up a hand to stop her. "I shall not stand in the middle of the street while you attempt to explain what I am convinced is a complicated tale. Where are you going from here?"

"Home. If you would meet us there, we shall tell you everything."

"Delighted," he said, closing the carriage door and stepping back as the conveyance pulled away.

Chapter Twenty Four

London, a bit later, 29 June 1813

After escorting the ladies to their carriage, Lucien returned to his curricle, leapt aboard, and set his team at a slow trot toward the Chadley residence. He had felt the tension in the room, heard it in the Envoy's voice. What the devil had the ladies done? Had they bungled his inquiry beyond repair? The prospect of hearing the answer filled him with equal amounts of curiosity and apprehension.

Upon arriving at the earl's home, he was shown into the drawing room. The three women were taking tea, but they sat ramrod straight and would not meet his eyes. He drew in a quick breath as his unease grew.

He gave the customary bow. "Good day, Lady Anne, Lady Sophia, Lady Julia. I am most curious to hear what transpired at the Embassy."

"Do sit, my lord. May I pour you tea or coffee?" Lady Anne asked.

"Coffee, if you would." He took the cup she offered and settled back in his chair, his eyes on her face. "What has happened, my lady?"

"We believe Señora de Leon sent the note to Señorita Rosa the day she was kidnapped." Lady Anne explained how Lady Julia had written, gotten a reply, and they had compared it with the letters the maid had selected. She passed the two letters two him. "I think you will agree that they match."

He looked at them carefully. The writing did appear to be the same, but he could not be certain without closer scrutiny, comparing each word…and then he smiled at his hesitation and looked up at Anne. How could he have forgotten her formidable memory? She could make a comparison in a matter of minutes or less. "I assume you have studied the two letters?" At her nod, he continued, "And you are confident they were written by the same hand?"

"A few strokes are different, but I believe one's handwriting varies a little. All things considered, yes, the same person wrote them."

"Then, the matter is settled. I deduce you confronted Señora de Leon with your suspicion, and she denied it."

"How did you know?" Lady Sophia demanded.

He failed to suppress a wry smile. "From the looks on your faces. So, tell me the worst, exactly what took place at the embassy?"

Lady Anne gave him the details, the others nodding and adding their comments. "She was angry and frightened. We might have gotten something out of her, but her husband came in."

"And tried to hustle her away," Lady Sophia said.

Lady Julia nodded. "It is true."

"I believe the deputy had been listening at the door, became concerned with our questions, and brought the Envoy to intercede," Anne added.

While all this suggested some guilt on the señora's part, Lucien's immediate concern was how he could fix the diplomatic uproar if the Envoy chose to make a formal complaint. Was there a way to avoid a crisis with Spain and yet get the truth from the señora? He drew his brows into a frown. This might be one problem Lord Rothe and the politicians would have to resolve.

"Have we ruined everything?" Lady Anne ventured.

"I trust not," he said mildly. "You have obtained valuable information we did not have before, but I think it best that Lord Rothe and Whitehall take it from here."

• • •

Leaving the ladies still chatting over tea, Lucien drove straight to Whitehall only to learn Rothe had been called to Bath by the Prince Regent and was not expected to return until tomorrow.

"Is it an urgent matter?" Mr. Sloane asked.

"I hope not. Have you received a complaint from Envoy de Leon?"

"I have not. Should I expect one?"

Lucien sighed. "Perhaps. If you do, would you send word to me? I'm not sure what kind of situation we have created. It involves the Envoy's wife. It could blow over, but then again..."

"I shall be certain to notify you of any communication from the de Leons."

"Thank you, Sloane. If needs must, I shall take the matter to Bath myself."

"Understood, my lord."

As Lucien descended the stairs at Whitehall, he pondered over what to do next. Clearly the de Leons were off limits for now. Ah, but Betty, the Hidalgos' maid should be home by now, and it occurred to him he could use Lady Anne's exceptional memory in questioning the maid and examining Rosa's room again. Since he dare not take her in his carriage due to the bounty, he sent a note asking if she would meet him at the Hidalgo residence in an hour.

In the meantime, he made a swift trip home, switched his curricle for a riding horse, and arrived at the Hidalgo property by the back gate. Having left his horse in the care of a neighbor's lad, he entered the residence through the servants' quarters, hoping this quiet approach would not bring potential assassins to the household or anywhere near Lady Anne.

After explaining the strange manner of his arrival to Mr. Hidalgo, he asked to speak with Betty and to view Rosa's room again. "I have also asked Lady Anne Ashburn to join me. If anyone asks, her presence is easily defined as a condolence call."

"Whatever you need," Hidalgo said wearily. "My residence and household are at your disposal. I shall be in my study."

A defeated man, Lucien thought. On an impulse, he turned back. "Sir, I thought you should know, the men who abused your daughter...one of them is dead, the other two in gaol. We're continuing to look for the rest of the spy ring. I regret we could not bring your daughter safely back to you, but we intend to get some measure of justice for her."

Hidalgo heaved a sigh. "Thank you, my lord. It will be good to know these same evil persons shall not shatter another family with this kind of grief."

Lucien watched Hidalgo walk away. Only time might lighten the man's despair. The sight of his suffering hardened Lucien's determination to unmask the spy who set this tragedy in motion.

He turned as the sound of voices from the front of the house announced Lady Anne's arrival. Lucien hurried forward and met her being escorted by the footman.

"Right on time, my lady." He took her arm as the footman led them toward Rosa's bedchamber.

She arched a brow. "I was surprised to receive your note, my lord. I was not certain you would be speaking to me after this morning."

"These things happen," he said evenly, as they entered the bedchamber. He had no desire to start an argument. What was done was done. "We must move on. This shopping matter you mentioned is yet to be explored."

She gave a light laugh. "You thought shopping required a lady's attention?"

"I had in mind your sharp eye for detail. If you would, take a close look at Señorita Rosa's room, her wardrobe, in particular."

A tap on the door announced the footman's return with Betty the maid. Lucien introduced Lady Anne and then turned to Betty. "I heard you had an interview this morning. Good news?"

She beamed at him. "I got the position and begin on Friday. Mr. Hidalgo has been so kind in letting me stay until I found a new post. I am sorry it is such a sad time for him."

"So are we. Shall we sit while we talk?" Lucien motioned toward a grouping of chairs.

When they were settled, Betty looked at him expectantly. "Was there something else you wanted to know?"

"We are hoping to discover where Señorita Rosa went the day she disappeared. It might help to know her regular habits—where she shopped, what she purchased. Were there certain things she bought frequently, certain shops she patronized?"

"Well, she had a fondness for sweets and would often stop at Gunter's Tea Shop in Berkley Square. She loved the ices. And naturally, she shopped the new fashions—gloves, shawls, and ribbons for her hats and gowns. She took a most particular delight in hats. Let me show you." Betty popped to her feet and opened the wardrobe.

Lucien and Lady Anne joined her there.

"Oh, yes, I see what you mean. She had quite a collection," Lady Anne said, smiling at the stack of pink and white bandboxes.

"Yes, ma'am, I cannot think what the master will do with so many," the girl said.

"I have seen bandboxes like those," Lucien said. "The first time I met Señora de Leon, she was returning from a shopping trip with two pink and white bandboxes."

"Those are distinctive to the Burgess Millinery," Lady Anne said. "The señorita and señora shared a hatmaker." She looked thoughtful. "Not unusual, I suppose. The señora may have recommended the establishment." Anne picked up the box on top and peeked inside. "My, my. The señorita must have been quite diligent in pursuing the newest styles. This is the very latest fashion."

"She went there often," Betty said. "It is so pretty, isn't it?"

The girl sounded so wistful that Lucien would have given it to her if it had been his to give.

"A shame she never got to wear it."

"Why is that?" Lady Anne asked.

"It was delivered the day she disappeared, just a few hours before we realized she was missing."

"Had it been ordered previously or purchased that day?" Lucien asked quickly.

"That day, I'm sure, my lord, but it was strange she had it delivered. The señorita always brought her purchases home with her, and before I put them away, she would wear them to admire in the cheval glass." She pointed to a full length looking-glass.

"Well done, Betty." Lucian gave her a broad smile of approval. "You have given us our first hint of where your mistress went that afternoon." He turned to Lady Anne. "Unless you see something else that might help us, I shall see you to the front door, and you can give me the direction of this milliner."

Lady Anne dipped her head to one side with a faint smile. "I can see you are eager to be off, my lord, but should we not look around a bit more while we have the opportunity? I also have a question or two for Betty."

"Of course, my lady." He grinned wryly. "I was getting ahead of myself. Let us continue."

Lady Anne looked through the rest of the wardrobe, inspected the shoes, and examined Rosa's jewelry. She shook her head at Lucien, indicating she'd found nothing else significant. Finally, she asked Betty about special ladies her mistress had been friends with, gathering nothing except names they already had, and ended with one last question. "How often did the señorita visit Señora de Leon?"

"Not often. Two or three morning visits, I suppose. But they also attended a ball together and visited the shops at least once when the señorita first came to London."

"No other invitations to the tea shops or the museum?" Lady Anne clarified.

"Not that I knew."

Friendly but not friends, Lucien concluded. Still, it was more than the señora had told him.

"Thank you, Betty," Lady Anne said. "You have been most helpful. Good luck in your new position."

"Thank you, ma'am."

Betty curtseyed and turned to leave, but Lucien stopped her.

"You have been particularly patience with our questions. I would like you to take this and buy yourself some pretty ribbons." He pressed two coins into her hand.

"Thank *you*, my lord. I surely will." She dropped another curtsey and quit the room with a grin on her face.

Lady Anne looked at Lucien. "Well done, sir. I found her last answer most interesting. If they did not normally go on outings together, it makes the señora's note that day all the more suspicious."

"Yes, I agree, my lady, and now, it is time for you to return home, while I make my way to the hatmaker."

"Kill-joy."

"You know we cannot go together."

"Yes, but it is tiresome," she said. "Can you not find this person who offered such an outrageous bounty?"

"We *are* trying. I am certain the person behind it and the spy are one and the same."

"Of course, you are. I do beg your pardon. But you will keep me informed of what you learn?"

Lucien laughed. "As though I would dare not."

• • •

He stopped by his townhouse to trade back his saddle horse for the curricle, and then he and Finn were on their way to the Burgess Millinery on Conduit Street. Even though it was late in the day, the establishment might still be open. At the very least, the milliner could be working on new hats for the shelves or on those bonnets that had been custom-ordered. He drew the team to a halt in front of the shop, glanced at the stylish hats filling the front windows, and nodded with satisfaction at the "open" sign near the door.

The moment he entered, a fashionably but modestly dressed woman came forward, a welcoming smile on her face. She was slim and her movements quick, as though she was rarely at ease. A faint fragrance of rosewater drifted around her.

"Madam Burgess?" he inquired.

"I am Sarah Burgess."

Lucien introduced himself. "I wondered if I might have a word with you."

"Certainly, my lord. Is your lady in need of a new bonnet? We have the latest fashions from Paris."

"Not today. It is information I seek."

"Oh? I shall do what I can. How may I be of assistance?"

"I'm interested in a sale that took place more than a month ago, in the middle of May."

"Oh, goodness," she interrupted before he could go on. "Was something wrong with it? We shall assuredly make it right."

"Nothing of the sort, madam. I believe a young woman, Señorita Rosa Hidalgo, purchased a hat in your establishment, which was later delivered to her home. Six weeks is a long time to remember, I know, but perhaps you have records that would provide details of the purchase or might jog your memory. It was a white hat with pink ribbons and some small feathers."

"You are correct, my lord, in thinking I do not recall it. Let me see what I can find." She went behind the counter and opened a drawer, thumbing her way through rows of cards.

Lucien took the opportunity to look around at the shelves along the walls that held a colorful variety of hats and bonnets displayed on stands. Tables held silk scarves, crocheted shawls, fine gloves of linen, leather, or silk, rolls of ribbons, and even a few pieces of paste jewelry to decorate hats or gowns. All of it was displayed to catch the fancy of the ladies of the haut ton. He assumed her work tables were kept out of sight in a back room.

"Ah, here we are. Yes, it was the 14th of May, but unfortunately that is all I can tell you about the sale. It was made by a girl who worked for us at the time. We had to let her go."

"Why is that?" Realizing he had spoken too abruptly, he softened his tone. "If I may ask, madam. It could be important.'

"My brother-in-law, the owner of this shop, caught her thieving."

"When did this occur?"

"About the same time." She paused, looking thoughtful. "If I recall correctly, this hat may have been one of her last sales. Yes, how very odd. I believe she left on the 14th."

That piqued Lucien's interest. Odd coincidence, indeed.

"I would be obliged if you could give me her name and direction."

"Certainly, my lord. I have it right here." Madam Burgess wrote it down, handed him the paper, and tilted her head, clearly puzzled by his interest. "You are certain there was nothing wrong with the hat or the service the señorita received in our shop?"

"I am certain. Thank you for your assistance, madam."

As Lucien exited the millinery, he shook his head, rather disappointed by how little he had learned. Of a certain, he now knew the señorita had been there on the 14th and purchased a hat, but so many questions were left unanswered—where had she gone from there, and why hadn't she taken her hat with her? It seemed as though every question answered was swiftly replaced by a new one: had the shop girl truly been dismissed for thievery or for something else perchance related to Señorita Rosa?

• • •

The Swansons' soiree that evening grew tiresome for Lucien after the first hour. Lady Anne was not in attendance, nor was Sophia, and too many match-making mamas watched his progress around the room. He decided to call it a night by half eleven, sent for his carriage, and stepped outside to wait for his coachman Gregory to bring it around.

The heat of the day had eased with the rain earlier in the evening, and a gentle breeze ruffled his hair. He brushed it back with one hand and strolled down the steps.

He paused, his shoulders tensing at a furtive movement in the bushes across the road, then his coach pulled up, and he got in. Taking his pistol from the carriage compartment, he stared out the window, studying the shadows until they were out of sight.

The bounty was making him jumpy.

He sighed, put the pistol away, and settled back in the seat, turning his thoughts to tomorrow's visit with the shop girl. Would it give him the answers they'd been seeking?

Swaying unexpectedly with the coach's sharp turn onto an adjoining roadway, Lucien was then thrown forward as the carriage rocked to an abrupt halt. A pistol shot rang out. He looked out the window and seized his pistol again as he saw a black coach had pulled out of an alley to block their path. A second shot from overhead had to have come from Gregory. Lucien was already half-way out the door with his double-barreled flintlock pistol in hand. He dropped down to the street, saw three men exit the other carriage, and he rolled under his coach, mindful of the wheels as Gregory fought to contain the terrified horses.

The handful of people on the street ran for cover, and as Lucien popped out from underneath the coach on the far side, he saw a fourth man, a large brute, holding a pistol in one hand and brandishing a club in the other. Lucien fired one shot, the man yelped, clutching at his pistol arm. The other attackers came running, and Lucien shoved the big man aside, dashing for the cover of a dark alley.

He was nearly there when something hit his shoulder, spinning him around, and he staggered, fighting to regain his footing. Hearing boots pounding toward him, he lifted his pistol to fire, but out of nowhere, someone tackled him, knocking his feet out from under. He handed hard, and for a moment, he lay still, struggling to catch his breath, his body held fast by the weight of this new assailant.

More shots. Shouting. Frightened horses snorted and squealed. Lucien twisted and turned to roll over—and suddenly he was free. He pushed himself up and saw the assassins' black coach was racing away from the scene at a reckless gallop.

"Are you all right?" a gruff voice asked.

Lucien turned his head to see the nondescript man from the docklands. "Could be worse," he said, pushing to his feet.

"Then I'll be on my way." The stranger disappeared into the dark alley before Lucien could ask who he was. But he suspected he knew, or rather he knew who the fellow worked for—Charles Cade. He really had to work toward getting his debt paid to the crime lord. If for no other reason than he'd like to have his life back and know he wasn't always being watched.

Lucien hurried toward the coach to locate Gregory. The street was filling with the curious and a few who had come to offer help. He noticed that two coaches had been struck during the assassins' wild escape, one of them knocked over. The occupants of both carriages were assessing the damage, and a constable was running in their general direction.

Gregory stumbled around Lucien's coach with blood running down one side of his face. Lucien put his good arm around his shoulders to steady him. "Are you badly injured?"

"Not as bad as those scoundrels. I think one of them is dead."

"No more than they deserve. Were you shot?"

"No, sir. One of them fellows caught me from behind with a cudgel." Lucien looked at Gregory's head wound. The bleeding had almost stopped. Regardless, Lucien wanted it seen by a doctor—and if someone was dead, they would be there a while.

He snagged a street lad and sent him off to find Dr. Pettigrew and to alert Lucien's staff. After finding another lad to calm the horses, he insisted that Gregory sit down inside the coach, and Lucien leaned against the outside to wait.

His shoulder was beginning to ache. He couldn't determine much about the injury. Whatever had hit him—he suspected it wasn't a bullet—had left a wound of some kind. His hand came away wet, but we wasn't certain whether it was blood or mud.

Finally, Pettigrew arrived. "Well, Ware, we meet again. At least it isn't a dead body this time."

"Unfortunately, I believe there is one," Lucien said ruefully, "but I sent for you to look at my coachman, Gregory. Afterward…I've banged up my shoulder," he added.

While Lucien was answering questions from the constables—two more had arrived by now—the doctor climbed inside the carriage to examine Gregory.

"What was this all about?" one of the constables asked.

Lucien, doing his best to look like a gentleman in his muddied clothes, arched a brow. "I assume it was a robbery. What else could it be?"

"What else, indeed, Lord Ware. Was anything taken?"

"They didn't get a chance."

"Did you recognize any of the attackers?"

"Hardly. I am not acquainted with many cutthroats," he said, annoyed by the question. "Nor did I get a good look at all of them—I'm not certain how many there were—but the two I saw were common ruffians. I shot a large brute in the arm or shoulder before they got away."

Pettigrew opened the door of the coach and stepped down. "Your coachman's injuries are not severe, mostly multiple bruises. He may have the headache for a day or two, and he was thumped pretty good in the ribs—a possible fractured rib or two. The head injury should heal with little attention other than keeping it clean." He turned toward Gregory as the coachman exited the coach behind him. "A little healing salve on that head wound wouldn't hurt, and keep those ribs wrapped for a day or two."

"Aye, sir," Gregory replied. "I'll see to it. Thank ye."

"Now, my lord, if you are through chatting with the constables, I'd like to take a look at your shoulder."

Taking the hint, the constables moved away. They stopped to speak only briefly with Gregory, even though he had killed one of the assassins. Lucien assumed they had heard the same story over and over from witnesses and didn't need to hear every detail again.

"My lord, what have you done to yourself?"

Lucien turned at the sound of that familiar voice to find Talbot and Finn had arrived—having run most of the way, judging by their appearance—despite his message to wait at home. "The doc was just about to tell me," he said. "Finn, since you're here, will you see to the horses?"

"Aye, gov."

While Talbot held a lantern and quietly scolded his master, Pettigrew slipped off Lucien's jacket and examined the injury.

"A broken bottle, I'd say. The slice it left appears clean. I don't see small slivers in there." He looked at Talbot. "You might want to check again when you get him home."

Talbot nodded. "Certainly, doctor. I shall be thorough."

Over the next twenty minutes, the overturned carriage was righted, the dead body was carted away, and the crowd began to disperse. After more instructions from Pettigrew and another chat with the constables, Lucien was allowed to go home. He had not told the constables about the bounty on his head or the timely assistance from a stranger. While the bounty was likely the cause of this attack, it wasn't something the constables could stop, and the stranger was irrelevant to their investigation. Not to Lucien, although it was hard to be annoyed—the man had shielded him at a vulnerable moment—and saved him from further injury.

It was time—or would be when this inquiry was over—for Lucien and Cade to have a serious talk. Surely no future favor was worth this kind of ongoing protection.

Chapter Twenty Five

Seaford to London, 30 June 2013

Sherry woke at dawn, ate a hearty breakfast downstairs in the Clifftop Inn's public room, and was on his way to London by eight. He was eager to get back and share all that he had learned—the location where Rosa had died and the unwitting pair who had smuggled secret documents to France believing they were love letters. As far as he could tell, all the true villains were in London. He was keen to track them down—and he was bringing two promising clues: the name of Mary Foster, the cousin who'd sent the letters to Sally, and a mysterious address, 98 Canton.

He rode into town about one and went straight to Lucien's townhouse in hopes of catching him before he was out for the day. He found him in the front hall just putting on his hat.

"Well met, Lucien. I have much to tell you."

"Sherry, my friend. Delighted to have you back. You must have been up early this morning."

"Egad, yes. The trip was hot and dusty, and I am sorely in need of a bath. Do you have a pressing appointment?"

"It can wait while you bathe yourself—as long as you don't dawdle."

"Give me an hour?"

"I can curb my curiosity that long."

Sherry dashed out the door. When he arrived at Sherbourne Hall, his valet Archie greeted him eagerly, then looked him over and bemoaned the state of his cravat, his coat, his boots and his hair. A bath was drawn, clean attire laid out, and he was just rinsing his hair when Archie dropped the news.

"I assume you heard about the attack on Lord Ware last night."

Sherry sat up straight in the tub, splashing water on the floor. "What attack? Drat the man. He mentioned nothing about an attack." In all fairness, Sherry knew he had hardly given his partner time to say much. He'd been in and out in a minute or two. Nonetheless…

"What happened?"

"As I heard it, a coach of four or five assassins blocked Farley Road, cutting off the viscount's coach. Shots were fired, a fight ensued with cudgels. It was quite an uproar, particularly when two other carriages were hit and overturned by the scoundrels' coach as they got away. Too bad they escaped, but one of them got his deserts and was shot dead. By Gregory, I heard."

"Was anyone else hurt?" Sherry interrupted impatiently.

"His lordship and Gregory both suffered injuries—nothing critical, I understand."

Sherry splashed more water getting out, and he grabbed a towel, grumbling as he vigorously dried his hair. "Send for a hunk of bread, cheese, and a glass of port. I can't take this in on an empty belly."

By the time Sherry was dressed, his hair mostly dry and styled, the food had arrived. After a glass of port, he was feeling calmer. Had he not seen Lucien with his own eyes? His partner was up and about, so his injuries were not disabling.

Astride his second favorite riding horse, Sherry arrived at Hays Mews in due course and within the allotted time. Lucien was seated at his desk in the study with a glass of port. He pushed his correspondence away when he saw Sherry and leaned back in his chair.

Lucien nodded toward the decanter on the sideboard, but Sherry waved it off. "Not for me. I just ate and washed it down with a bit of port. By the by, you might have mentioned last night's ambush."

"It was rather exciting for a while."

"So I heard from Archie. I don't see any bandages."

"A cut on the back of my shoulder. It's nothing except an excuse for Talbot to fuss and scold. Gregory was hit rather hard in the head, but Pettigrew assures me he will recover. I've sent him home for a few days. But enough of that, I have a shop girl to interview, and first I wish to hear about Seaford."

"What shop girl?"

"In good time. Tell me about Seaford."

"Oh, very well." Sherry kept it brief, hitting the main points that led to the discovery of the house where Rosa died, finding the unknown address, and how he discovered Sally's and Nate's part in the spy chain.

"I say, Sherry, that is impressive work. You are confident this maid and Nate were telling the truth?"

"I am. Their belief in the love letters was obvious. I was reluctant to acquit Magistrate Colby of guilt, because I don't like him, but he was not part of it."

"He knows about the smuggling."

"Oh, yes. The whole town knows and half the households are harboring smugglers. In any event, I believe those responsible for what happened to the Hidalgos are here in London, including the kidnappers."

"I agree. In truth, two of the bloody awful fellows who brutalized the girl are sitting in Newgate and the other is dead."

Sherry started. "*Bloody hell*, Lucien. That *is* good news! Tell me—how did it come about?"

Lucien explained that Big Toe Kemp had been found dead and that the other two had been tracked down and handed over to Bow Street by Cade's men.

"They confessed to everything, including killing Dickson—that's Jose, the agent Rothe had in the Hidalgo residence," Lucien said. "What they didn't know was anything about the French spy. Big Toe Kemp had made the only contacts."

"Thus, he had to be silenced."

Lucien nodded. "By the French spy, yes. That's my take on it. But we shall find him yet. I should tell you we are not the only ones investigating—Lady Anne, Lady Sophia, and Lady Julia have all taken part."

"Good grief. You fill me with trepidation. Dare I ask if it turned out good or bad?"

"A little of both. They have alerted a suspect that she is under scrutiny, but perhaps it was time to shake that particular tree." He described the tense scene he had walked into at the Spanish Embassy and what had taken place before he arrived.

"Has de Leon complained to Rothe?"

"Not yet, and I have wondered why. Regardless, the ladies' persistence led me to examine Rosa's shopping habits in greater depth—which then took me to Burgess Millinery."

"I don't follow. How did we get from comparing handwriting to a milliner?"

"Female logic, I believe. They reasoned if Señora de Leon had written to Rosa, it must have been about shopping as that appeared to be the only thing they had in common. And I confess that may be the truth of the matter. I noticed the band boxes at Rosa's were the same color as those I had seen with Señora de Leon. Lady Anne said those boxes came from Burgess Millinery. It all seemed rather tenuous until Rosa's abigail told us the latest hat was delivered shortly after Rosa disappeared."

"Suggesting the señorita had been there that day," Sherry interjected.

"Exactly, and the hatmaker has confirmed it. Now comes the truly interesting part. The shop girl who waited on Rosa was dismissed that very day, allegedly for thievery. I'd wager the girl knows something of what happened to Rosa."

"Ah, that is where we are headed—to interview the shop girl."

"Yes, I am keen to hear what Mary Foster has to—"

"Mary Foster!" Sherry interrupted digging in his pocket. He pulled out a piece of paper. "Yes, I thought so. See here? We are looking for the same girl."

"How so?"

"She is the London cousin who sent the fake love letters to Sally."

"That settles it. I say, Sherry, we are getting close." Lucien strode toward the study door and called to Hughes as he and Sherry descended the stairs. "My hat, my good man. We must be on our way."

"Very good, my lord." Hughes handed him the hat and a sealed note. "This just arrived for you."

Lucien nearly set it aside for later, but he recognized Lady Anne's handwriting, and curiosity won out. He broke the seal.

Dear Lord Ware,

Please call at your earliest convenience. I have had the most intriguing visit from Señora de Leon.

Yours sincerely,

Lady Anne Ashburn

Chapter Twenty Six

London, 30 June 2013

"What do you suppose this is about?" Sherry asked for the third time as Lucien brought the curricle to a halt in front of Lord Chadley's residence.

"You know as much as I do." Lucien swung down and strode toward the door. His knock was answered promptly, and they were brought to the drawing room where Lady Anne greeted them with a mischievous look. "I had hoped my note would bring you, but I had not anticipated it would be quite this soon."

"We were just leaving Hays Mews when it arrived," Lucien explained.

"Then I am glad I caught you. May I offer you tea or coffee?" she asked, gesturing them to be seated.

"Not for me. We cannot stay long."

"Nor me," Sherry said, looking around. "A pleasant house Chadley found."

"A room or two require new decorating, but Father chose very well," she said.

"We cannot stay long," Lucien repeated, impatient to be on his way. "I am eager to talk with a witness or possible suspect."

"Is this something you learned from Madam Burgess?" she asked with interest.

"Partly. She confirmed the señorita had purchased a hat on the 14th of May, but the girl who sold it no longer works there. We hope to talk with her today, and we may need to speak with Madam Burgess again after that. But you asked us to stop here," he reminded her, directing the conversation back to her message. "A visit from Señora de Leon, I believe."

"Yes. An odd visit." Lady Anne nodded. "She arrived quite unexpectedly this morning, very distressed, saying our visit yesterday had weighed on her mind all night. She feared we thought she had played a part in Rosa's kidnapping. So, I asked if she had."

"Did you?" Lucien's lips twitched. "And what did she say?"

"She seemed surprised I had asked but denied it, of course. I then pointed out the matching bandboxes from Burgess's, suggesting they had shopped together, and she said she had introduced Rosa to Madam Burgess a few months ago."

"Does that mean the bandboxes are meaningless?" Sherry asked.

"Not at all," Lady Anne said. "It may be significant they used the same millinery. Betty said the señora and Rosa had occasionally shopped there together. I think Rosa would have found it perfectly ordinary to receive a note from her suggesting they look at hats that day."

"But that is just a guess," Sherry said. "Did she admit the handwriting matched?"

"Oh yes. She agreed she had written one of the letters Lord Ware gave me, but she denied writing to Rosa that day. She suggested the maid had been mistaken, and I have to admit Betty was not certain." She looked at Lucien. "She chose letters from two different women if you recall."

Lucien frowned. "I do, but the Señora could easily be lying."

"I'm confused, Lady Anne," Sherry said. "You appear to be arguing both sides. Is Señora de Leon involved in this or not?"

"She is…or I think so." Lady Anne gave him an earnest look. "But I watched closely, and her tears were very real."

Lucien and Sherry exchanged a look. During their days spying on the Continent, they'd known women who could cry over nothing just for the effect it had on men.

"Tears don't necessarily mean she's innocent," Sherry said. "She could be crying for effect or because you found her out."

Nonetheless, Lucien shared her doubts, not due to the tears, but because he could not fathom her motive. Did that make Rosa's trip to the milliner a mere coincidence? He didn't think so, but the señora's conduct forced him to consider if the hat shop had just been a stop Rosa made on the way to meet the unknown writer of the note. If so, who could it possibly be—and where had she gone?

He had not an inkling.

• • •

"Well, if that ain't the sow's ear," Sherry grumbled as they exited the Chadley residence a few minutes later. "I thought we were onto something with the señorita going to the millinery."

"I think we are," Lucien said thoughtfully. "The note might still be from Señora de Leon—we just haven't discovered *why* she would be involved—and the shop girl Mary Foster remains a strong link."

"That's right, by Jove. In all the discussion of Señora de Leon, the girl had slipped my mind," Sherry said, brightening. "Miss Foster has a lot of questions to answer. Get this showy chestnut team on the move."

Talking with Mary Foster wasn't quite as easy as expected. The maid who answered the door at her home said Mary had taken a position in a shop making mourning caps. And when they approached her employer, a thin man with a pinched face, he was adamant they could not speak with her until the work day was over. "My girls are here to work. It they don't work, I don't make money, and they don't get paid."

"As you wish, sir," Lucien said, knowing to push further would cost the girl her employment. "We shall speak with her after closing, which is when?"

"Seven. She'll be free to leave at seven."

Seven to seven—a long, but not unusual, work day, Lucien mused. Nevertheless, it was a definite step down from Mary's prior position at Burgess. She must have been let go with no reference, but why? Her dismissal for alleged theft on the day Rosa disappeared was entirely too convenient. What had the girl done? Or what the devil had she seen?

• • •

When the back door of the workshop opened shortly after seven that evening and six girls came out, Lucien stepped forward from where he and Sherry had been waiting in the alley. "Mary Foster?"

A slender girl of sixteen or so looked him up and down, her brown eyes wary. "Who's asking?"

"I am Viscount Ware. If you are Mary Foster, I wish to speak with you regarding your former employer at the millinery."

"Why?"

"Is there somewhere we could talk privately?"

She shook her head. "Not here, sir. I'm going home. I don't know what you want, but if you need to talk to me, come there."

"I could offer you a ride," Lucien said, although he was sure she wouldn't take it.

She shook her head again, more adamantly this time. "My father would be angry if I accepted—you being strangers and all. Thank you, sir, but I shall walk."

Fifteen minutes later, Lucien and Sherry watched as she trudged up the street, obviously weary after her long day. They nodded to her as she entered her home and then they descended from Lucien's curricle. A man of only medium height but broad shoulders, opened the door before Lucien could knock.

"I'm Charlie Foster, Mary's father," he said, scowling at them. "What do you want with my daughter?"

"To ask her about the Burgess millinery. I am Viscount Ware, and this is…"

"Andrew Sherbourne," Sherry said, stepping forward.

"May we come in while I explain?"

After a brief hesitation, Mr. Foster stepped aside. "Of course, my lord. Please come through."

It was a small house, but clean and tidy. Mary sat on the sofa in the main parlor. She looked ill-at-ease. Mr. Foster gestured for them to be seated in the room's only chairs, while he joined his daughter.

Lucien heard the sound of childish laughter from another room and assumed the mother had retreated there with the younger children, leaving her husband to deal with their uninvited guests.

Foster cleared his throat. "Now, sir, would you tell me what this is about? If you have come about the theft, Mary did not do it."

"We are not here to accuse her of theft," Lucien said. "We are interested in what happened her last day of work for Madam Burgess." He turned his attention to Mary. "I understand you were dismissed on the 14th of May. Is that correct?"

"Um, about then. I'm not certain of the day." Mary looked at her father for help.

"Yes, that was it," Foster confirmed.

Lucien turned back to Mary. "Do you recall selling a hat to Señorita Rosa Hidalgo that day?"

"Oh, yes." The girl smiled. "She's a really nice lady, and she looked ever so pretty in that pink hat with the white feathers... what with her dark curls."

"I imagine she did," Lucien agreed. "Did anything unusual occur while she was there?"

Mary looked puzzled. "Not that I recall, but she was still there when I left on an errand, so maybe..." She stopped and frowned. "Oh, yes, maybe it did—she left her new hat behind."

"Was that unusual?"

Mary nodded emphatically. "She always took them with her. Since the sale was complete, I asked the delivery boy to take it to her home."

That explained the delivery, but what had happened while Mary was out of the shop?

"Was your errand an emergency? Why would you leave while you had a customer?"

"It was nothing really. Madam Burgess came out of the back room and asked me to fetch some blue ribbon from a shop down the street. She said she'd take care of the señorita if she wished to make further purchases. I was only gone a quarter of an hour."

"But the señorita left before you returned."

"Yes, sir. That's right."

"What went wrong that caused your dismissal?"

She hung her head. "It happened just after I got back. Madam Burgess said I had taken money from the drawer, but I didn't. She wouldn't believe me, and I was sent away."

"Without the pay she was owed or a reference," Mr. Foster put in bitterly. "I tried to talk to the owner a couple of days later, but he claimed no one else could have done it. He kept her pay, saying she took more than she was owed. It wasn't true, I know my girl, but there you be."

"It does seem unfair," Lucien said. "How much were you owed?"

Mary told him the amount, a mere pittance, which Lucien took from his pocket, added a bit more, and gave to her.

"We won't accept charity, sir," her father intervened before Mary could put the money in her pocket.

"It covers the salary she is owed, and a bit extra for the false accusation. I shall be speaking with her employer, and I'm sure he will want to repay me when he understands the situation."

Foster looked troubled, but nodded when Mary questioned him with her eyes. She quickly stuffed the money in her pocket.

Lucien had acted on impulse, knowing the family needed the funds, but he had seen the brief frown on Sherry's face. Perhaps he *had* acted prematurely when his partner hadn't yet questioned her about the spy letters, but Lucien simply could not picture the chit as a French spy.

"There is another matter we need to discuss," he said. "It is a bit more serious."

"You said you weren't here about the theft," Foster interrupted, his expression guarded.

"We aren't—"

"Then what?" Foster broke in again before Lucien could explain.

Was this the concern of a worried parent, or did Foster suspect what was coming? Could *he* be the spy behind the letters?

Lucien gave a nod to Sherry, and he took over. "Mary, do you have a cousin by the name of Sally Woods?"

"She does," the father answered rather sharply. "Why?"

"To be certain it's the same Sally, does she work as a maid for Mrs. Colby in Seaford?"

"Has something happened to my niece?" Foster asked, sounding worried now.

"No, nothing like that." Sherry looked at Mary. "She says you have sent her several recent letters."

"Me? No, nary a one. Why would she say that?" Mary's eyes were wide and questioning.

"I have one of the letters right here." Sherry offered her the letter Sally had given him.

Foster took it, looked at the writing, gave his head a doubtful shake, then handed it to his daughter. "Did you write this?"

"It looks sort of like me," she said in a small voice, still reading the contents. "But I truly didn't do it. Honest, papa, I didn't. I hardly know her, and this stuff about me having a sweetheart in France…it aint true. I don't know a Frenchie boy." She stopped, tears brimming in her eyes, and gulped twice. "I don't."

"I know that, love. She didn't write it," Foster said, glaring at Sherry then at Lucien. "My daughter doesn't lie. Least not when it's important." He took the letter from Mary and held it out. "What is this all about?"

"Sally has received several letters like it with sealed messages inside—allegedly love letters—which she passed on to someone else in France. Those so-called love letters contained secret documents obtained by a French spy."

"My God, sir, you cannot believe my daughter is working for a spy," Foster bellowed, coming to his feet. When Mary began to cry, he just as quickly sat down and lowered his voice. "It's all right, Mary. I'm sorry I got so riled." He turned a black look on Sherry. "What you are saying is ridiculous."

"I'm inclined to agree, sir," Sherry said. "To be certain, I need to see a sample of Mary's handwriting."

"Go get that diary of yours," Foster said to her.

"But, Papa. It's private."

"Now, love, there must be one page you could let them see." He turned to Lucien and Sherry, a bit friendlier now that Sherry appeared to believe his daughter. "Young girls and their secret diaries. I suspect she's been writing about the lad next door and doesn't want me to know."

Before Lucien could suggest that any writing of hers would do, Mary returned and opened the diary to a specific page. "I wrote this about Madam Burgess dismissing me. I reckon you can read that."

Sherry took the diary carefully, making sure the pages didn't flip. Lucien held up the letter from Seaford, and they compared the two. "There is a superficial likeness," Sherry said. "But many of the letters are very different and others are too perfect as though they had been copied over." He looked up. "Who would be capable of faking your handwriting? Someone who knows it well or has samples to copy from."

Mary shrugged. "No one except my family. And Aunt Irene. A friend or two, maybe."

Lucien rubbed his chin in thought. "What about at the millinery. You filled out purchase sheets and kept a log of sales, did you not?"

"Yes. It was required."

Sherry turned to Lucien. "Sally said she sent the letters from France to Mary at the millinery. Supposedly so the father wouldn't know about them."

"Easily intercepted." Lucien looked at Mary. "I assume you never saw those letters."

"Not a one, sir. All the mail is delivered to the back office."

"They thought of everything." Lucien raised a brow at Sherry. "Back to the Millinery. Madam Burgess has a lot of explaining to do."

"You think she is a spy?" Mary asked with a gasp. "I would not think so badly of her. Maybe it was him. He's not very kind, and it was he who insisted I be dismissed."

"Are you speaking of her son-in-law, the business owner?" Lucien asked. "Was he there that day?"

"I never saw him, but his coach was in back, the one with the bird thing on it, when I left to get the ribbon."

"Bird?" Lucien asked staring at her keenly. "With large wings?"

She nodded. "Madam Burgess says it's only part bird, and it came from some misty place."

Lucien frowned. "Are you sure that is what she—oh, mythology, perhaps?"

Mary seemed confused and bit her lip. "Uh, maybe. I don't know what that is."

Lucien smiled. "Never mind, Mary. Tell me about the owner. What is his name?"

"Mr. Griffin," she said. "He talks mean to everyone, even Madam Burgess."

"Thomas Griffin," her father clarified.

"Of course, it would be," Lucien said to himself, as it all began to fall together. "Was his coach there when you returned with the ribbons?"

She thought about it, one finger on her cheek. "I don't think so, sir."

Lucien nodded with satisfaction. "Thank you, Mary, Mr. Foster. You have been most helpful. Sherry, it is time to go."

Foster followed them to the door. "Does this mean everything is all right for us? Mary is not in trouble?"

"No trouble at all, sir," Lucien confirmed, turning back for a moment. "In fact, I believe she has just helped her country unmask a French spy."

• • •

"What a fool I've been," Lucien said, as he leapt into his carriage. "It wasn't merely a large winged bird on the coach, it was a gryphon, a mythological creature that is half eagle, half lion."

"A play on this Thomas Griffin's name. Egad, how obvious—once you know the rest of it, certainly not before we started looking at the millinery, and even then—" Sherry grabbed the seat as Lucien put the horses at a fast trot, weaving their way through the busy streets. "I suspected Madam Burgess was the spy until Mary told us the owner's name."

The millinery was dark, closed for the night. They went from there to Whitehall, where they found an address for Thomas Griffin in Sloane's records, but when they arrived at his modest lodgings on Sutton Street, Griffin was not at home.

"I'm sorry, sir. He did not say what time he would return or where he was going," the manservant said. "May I tell him who called?"

"Oh, no need. It's business that can wait. I had not realized it was quite so late. We shall speak with him another day." Lucien gave the man his most disarming smile and returned to the carriage. By making light of their visit, he hoped it would not forewarn Griffin and cause him to flee.

Lucien flicked the reins and urged the horses into a walk.

"Might he have fled already?" Sherry asked.

"His servant didn't act as though anything was amiss. I would expect him to be rather uneasy if his master was missing or had grabbed his clothes and taken off."

Sherry's face tightened in a scowl. "Let us hope he has not—for I would feel obliged to chase the bloody fellow all the way to the gates of hell."

"It will not come to that. Griffin may be ruthless, but he is not as clever as he thinks. He could not resist displaying the gryphon on his coach, and it has proven to be his downfall."

"In all fairness, Lucien, how likely was it that the symbol would be noticed or remembered?"

"Why take the risk? Arrogance, I'd say."

"I concede the point. So, are we watching the house until he comes home?" Sherry asked, as Lucien turned the corner and pulled over into a small park.

"Got a better idea?"

"I do." Sherry grinned at him. "I could go home to bed while you stand watch."

"Not bloody likely."

While they kept watch, they talked for a while but eventually sat in silence or quietly strolled the park. After futile hours of waiting, Lucien leaned against the curricle and stretched his arms. "What a boring evening."

Finn, who'd been dozing on the back of the carriage, sat up and rubbed his eyes. "Why not go home, milord? I can stay an' watch an' tell y' if he returns."

Sherry stifled a yawn. "He makes sense, Lucien. If Griffin comes home any later than this, he's bound to sleep late, giving Finn ample time to get us."

Lucien eyed his groom. "Are you sure about this? Naturally, you can have tomorrow off."

"'Course, gov. I'll keep a good watch."

With that settled, Finn slipped off the back of the curricle into the dark shadows, and Lucien drove Sherry home, arriving at his own townhouse after two. He suspected he was in for a restless night—listening for the sound of Finn's arrival—but some sleep was better than none.

Chapter Twenty Seven

London, 1 July 2013

Lady Anne woke early the following morning and rang for Jenny. Within minutes her maid appeared with a tray containing hot chocolate and toast.

"Oh, bless you, Jenny. How you spoil me," Anne said, taking in the mouth-watering smell when the maid set the tray on the bed. "Any news?"

"You mean from Lord Ware? No, my lady, not yet. I'm sure you'll hear something today."

"It's just that they seemed rather discouraged when they left here. I've thought and thought about it, and the millinery has to be at the center of this. It's just too strange that the shop girl was dismissed the same day."

"Lord Ware will know that," Jenny said as she started to lay out her mistress's attire for the day.

"Yes, I'm sure he does," Anne said softly, sipping her chocolate. "I believe they intended to talk with Madam Burgess again when they left here. They should have talked with both her and the shop girl yesterday. So why haven't I heard something?"

"Whatever they learned may have sent the gentlemen somewhere else."

"You are probably right." Anne nibbled on the toast. "I cannot help but wonder about it though. Perhaps I should stop by the millinery and look at the latest styles."

"As though you need a new hat," Jenny said.

"Don't be saucy," Anne admonish with a grin. "A lady cannot afford to let fashion pass her by."

"Yes, my lady." Jenny picked up the gown she had selected, put it back, and chose one more appropriate for an outing to the shops. "How soon would you like to leave?"

"Oh, no hurry," Anne said, setting the tray aside and slipping her legs off the bed. "I have time for a proper breakfast, but I do want to make the trip before the heat of the day. Say, an hour?"

Jenny chuckled. They both knew to leave in an hour meant that "Oh, no hurry" should be disregarded. They would have to rush through the morning routine, but Jenny didn't comment on her mistress's eagerness. Anne suspected her maid was just as keen as she was to hear what had taken place at the hatmaker's the previous day.

• • •

As her carriage drew closer to Madam Burgess's hat shop, Anne found herself growing uneasy. So much so that she moved the pistol she'd been carrying since the Hyde Park shooting from her reticule to the pocket of her gown. Not that she thought she would need it, but it made her feel better. Anne sighed and glanced at Jenny. Her maid didn't appear nervous, so maybe it was Anne's conscience nudging her. She knew Lord Ware would not approve of this trip. But why not? All she wanted was a chat with Madam Burgess.

Conduit Street was congested, and the coach stopped on the opposite side of the road to let her down. She and Jenny were half-way across the thoroughfare before Anne noticed Lord Ware and Sherbourne standing in the open doorway of the millinery. She halted uncertainly. A sharp sense of apprehension swept over her.

What was happening?

The gentlemen appeared equally shocked to see her. Lord Ware turned back as though to stop her, then Sherbourne shouted at someone inside the millinery, "Stay where you are."

A shot was fired.

Ware ran toward Anne, wildly gesturing for her to go back. Before he reached her, a horse and rider burst from the alley, charging straight at her.

"Watch out," Sherbourne yelled.

"Lady Anne!" That was Ware.

Anne grabbed her pistol and pulled the trigger in hopes the horse would swerve away from the sound. Bedlam erupted.

The horse reared over her, throwing its rider, and Lucien snatched Anne away from the horse's flashing hooves. He pulled her tightly against him. "Are you all right?" he demanded.

Struggling to get her breath, she pushed away enough to gain a little air. "I'm uninjured, my lord. What's happening?"

Sherbourne yelled, "Griffin, stop, you bloody scoundrel," and sprinted down the street chasing the rider who'd gotten up and fled on foot.

Lucien abruptly released her, pushing her toward Jenny. He grabbed the reins of the frightened horse and swung into the saddle. "Go home, Lady Anne. And put that dratted pistol away." He urged the horse into a gallop and raced after Sherbourne and the man they'd called Griffin.

"My lady." Jenny gripped her arm. "Are you truly unharmed?"

"Yes, just a little shaken."

"Whyever did you shoot at him?"

"It was either that or be run over. I had to divert the beast some way."

"And nearly got kicked in the head," Jenny scolded. She glanced around at the gathering crowd and lowered her voice. "We should get you home, my lady. You are a little untidy."

"Oh, dear, so I am," Anne said, straightening her hat that had been knocked askew by Lucien's rough handling and frowning at the debris thrown on her gown by the horse's hooves. "I cannot be seen like this." They hurried toward the carriage. Anne gave one wistful glance down the street. She would so like to follow and see what transpired, but the gentlemen were already out of sight. For once, she had no alternative but to follow Lord Ware's advice.

Chapter Twenty Eight

London, 1 July 1813

Lucien turned the corner at a mad gallop and spotted Sherry and Griffin fighting in the middle of the road about three buildings away. He reined the horse toward them, leaned over to grab the back of Griffin's coat, dangling the French spy in the air for a moment until his coat ripped. Lucien leapt from the horse to grab one arm while Sherry snagged the other.

"Spoil all my fun, will you?" Sherry asked. "I was looking forward to beating the stuffing out of him."

"The law will see that justice is done," Lucien said. "This is one hanging I may attend."

A crowd gathered, but uncertain what was happening, they were somewhat hostile until Sherry announced, "This scoundrel is a French spy." They were immediately offered all the help they could wish for in getting Griffin to Bow Street and his horse returned to Madam Burgess. Griffin would not be needing it again.

• • •

London, 2 July 1813

It wasn't until the following morning that Lucien arrived at the Chadley town residence carrying a parasol and was taken to Lady Anne in the family parlor. "Good morning, my lord." She rose and hurried toward him, holding out her hands. "You are truly unharmed? And Sherbourne? I received your kind message last night, but it is not the same as seeing for myself."

"We suffered no injuries worthy of note, my lady. You appear recovered from near disaster. I must say, you had me frightened right and proper when I saw those hooves so close to your pretty face."

"Why, Lord Ware, you shall make me blush."

"A fetching picture that would be. But not if it was sunburnt." He handed her the parasol.

"What is this?"

"When I returned to Burgess Millinery to collect my curricle, I found your parasol beside the road. It was rather banged up—the second one in a week—and after talking with Madam Burgess again to clear up a few questions, she assisted me in choosing a new one. I hope you like it."

"How thoughtful. It is lovely. I thank you, my lord." She smiled and set the parasol on the table. "I am surprised Madam Burgess was available. Is she not under arrest?"

"She was not aware of her son-in-law's activities. Nor did she realize he had kidnapped the señorita. She knew that Mr. Griffin had taken Rosa to the back room, allegedly to discuss her account, but he told her the señorita had left by the back door. She had no reason to disbelieve him—although we discovered she didn't like him much, claiming he was a cold and cruel husband to her daughter. The animosity appears to have gone both ways. He had nothing good to say about her, except he admitted 'that stupid woman,' as he called her, was not part of either the spying or the abduction."

"Thank goodness. I did not want to think badly of her. I so adore her hats and bonnets."

"Are you trying to persuade me that you were there yesterday to purchase a hat?"

"Yes…and no," she said, slightly hesitant. "I *might* have purchased one, but I confess it was merely an excuse. I thought you had gone to the millinery the day before, and I wanted to know what had occurred. I never imagined you would be there when I arrived." She urged him toward the setting of chairs and a small sofa near the windows. "Do be seated and tell me all."

He waited until they were both comfortably settled, she on the sofa and he directly across from her. "We have Mr. Griffin, the owner of the hat shop, and Oscar Hensley in custody. Hensley gave in immediately—told us everything he knew. Thomas Griffin—or whoever he is, for he is a native Frenchman—eventually caved under Rothe's interrogation and knowing that Hensley had already implicated him. Much of it we had sorted out on our own. The spy chain went from Hidalgo to Hensley to Griffin, who then forged the letters signing Mary Foster's name and sent them to Sally. As you know, Sally gave them to Nate and on to Pierre in France. It is surprising how many people were unwittingly involved—Mary Foster, Sally Woods, and Nate Barnes."

"But why was Rosa treated so horridly?"

"Griffin claimed he didn't know she was mistreated, but I doubt he ever inquired or cared. She could identify them all, and he never intended for her to go home. She was nothing to him."

"What a dreadful creature he is. How did you know it was him? Why did he run? Did he know you were after him? And what about the mysterious address? Is that where he lived?"

Lucien laughed aloud. "One question at a time, please." He explained how they'd traced the letters. "Once we had spoken to Mary, we knew someone in the millinery had forged them, because Sally was sending the responses to the shop. And Mary also mentioned the symbol on the shop owner's coach. If I had gotten a better look and realized it was a gryphon, we might have sorted this out sooner." Lucien stood and went to the window, staring out at nothing. "We had not even asked the owner's name. He was never a suspect, never considered important."

"You could not have saved Rosa," Anne said softly. "It was too late before you knew she existed."

He turned from the window. "That's true, but we might have saved Jonathan Dickson."

Lady Anne frowned and changed the conversation. "I do not understand why Griffon put the symbol of a gryphon on his carriage. It seems rather affected for a French spy who should wish to go unnoticed."

Lucien returned to his seat. “We didn’t ask him, but he may have thought it wouldn’t matter, that it was too small to be remembered. Having observed the man for several hours, however, I can tell you he has an arrogance about him. The gryphon may have been his way of saying I can do as I wish and not get caught.”

Lady Anne looked thoughtful. “A fatal flaw, an oddity of personality that helped bring him down.”

“As you say.”

“I wonder what made him become a spy,” she mused.

“He has always been one. He came to England five years ago for the sole purpose of marrying an English woman and using her family’s status as his cover. The spy operation we broke up was not his first gang of traitors. He gave us some additional names—which I assume means they have already fled the country—but Rothe and Bow Street will be looking for them.”

She sighed. “Such an elaborate scheme. I guess we shall never know who sent the note to Señorita Rosa that day…or what it said…unless it was sent by Griffin.”

“No, not him,” Lucien said with a grin. “You ladies were correct. It was Señora de Leon.”

“Truly?” she exclaimed. “Has she confessed?”

Lucien nodded. “After she came to see you, she was sure you had figured it out, and she confessed all to her husband. When Rothe asked to speak with de Leon yesterday to follow-up on your suspicions, the Envoy brought his wife to Whitehall, and she admitted she had written the note, asking Rosa to meet her at Madam Burgess’ millinery.”

“But why? Did she not know she was helping a spy?”

“Oh, yes, she knew, but she didn’t realize he’d planned a kidnapping. Griffin told her he was going to frighten Rosa and use threats against her to make Hidalgo spy for them.”

“And terrifying a young girl was acceptable to her?” Anne said indignantly. “I still don’t understand why she would want to help a French spy.”

"She didn't care about France or the war. She hoped Hidalgo would be caught spying, and with the embassy once again embarrassed, her husband would be recalled to Spain. She wanted to go home."

"That's it? That's all?" Anne blue eyes turned stormy. "Her selfish wishes were not worth a young girl's life."

"She had not counted on that. Hence, the sadness you witnessed. I have no doubt she is sorry," Lucien said, "but that cannot undo the harm she has done. And it doesn't help Hidalgo. The señora will get her wish to go home—diplomatic immunity will see to that—but her life will not be easy. I fear she has lost her husband's regard. He may even divorce her—unheard of in the Catholic faith—in an attempt to save his career."

"I cannot feel sorry for her."

"Nor can I. My sympathy lies with him…and Hidalgo, to be sure. Curiosity satisfied now?" he asked, giving her an amused look.

"The address," she prompted. "What was 98 Canton?"

"As it turned out, it was meaningless to us. It was the street corner where Big Toe picked up Fowler and Smith on the way to Seaford after abducting Señorita Rosa."

"Oh, not very helpful at all. Well, I shall probably think of other questions," she said, "but not at the moment. Oh, wait, yes, I do. I interrupted before you explained why Griffin nearly ran me down yesterday morning."

"He was just desperate to get away. His manservant had gotten a message to him that Sherry and I were looking for him, and Madam Burgess had told him we were at the shop yesterday. When he saw us at the shop door, he knew why we were there, fired a shot at Sherry, and fled." Lucien leaned forward and took Lady Anne's hands in his. "You arrived at just the wrong moment, my dear." He moved to the sofa beside her. "My heart was in my throat when I thought those hooves might trample you." His eyes sought hers and held her gaze. "I cannot allow anything to happen to you, dear

Anne. Which led me to the inevitable conclusion that I must keep you under a closer eye."

Lady Anne smiled gently. "Has it, my lord? How do you intend to do that?"

She looked so fetching that Lucien leaned forward, tempted to steal a kiss.

The Earl of Chadley entered the room with a loud clearing of his throat. Lady Anne pulled her hands away and sprang to her feet. Lucien stood beside her but retrieved one of her hands and kept a firm hold.

"I assume you are here about yesterday's incident at the millinery," Chadley said.

"Yes, sir," Lucien responded. "We were just discussing it."

"Did you catch the fellow? Was he responsible for the bounty?'

"Yes to both questions. His crimes are such he shall face the hangman noose, and word has already spread that the reward is withdrawn."

"Good, good." Chadley gave him a stern look. "I assume that means my daughter will no longer be risking her life every time she steps out of the house."

"I certainly hope so, sir."

"Very good. Well, then, I shall leave you to it."

"My lord, before you go. I desire to meet with you in private today." Lucien smiled down at Anne's upturned face. "With Lady Anne's agreement, I wish to plead my cause. I hope to gain your approval to court your very willful but charming and beautiful daughter."

Chadley laughed, his eyes twinkling. "Ask her, son, then come see me."

Lady Anne turned to Lucien and arched a delicate brow.

About the Author

After retiring from a legal career with the Juvenile Court System, J.L. Buck published sixteen urban fantasy/paranormal novels under the pen name of Ally Shields. In 2019 she turned her hand to her favorite genre and began working on the Viscount Ware Mystery series set in Regency England (1811-1820).

She lives in the Midwest with Latte, a mischievous Siamese cat, who often attempts to co-author her writing by taking over the keyboard or tries to distract her to come and play. When not writing or running two blogs, she enjoys her eight grandchildren (and a great-grandson), dinners with friends, reading (preferably on a sunny deck), travel (USA—she loves DisneyWorld—and abroad), and binge-watching any sub-genre of mystery shows.

Ms Buck loves to hear from readers and can be contacted through her website or social media (twitter: @janetlbuck or her pen name account: @ShieldsAlly). Follow her on BookBub.

www.ingramcontent.com/pod-product-compliance
Lightning Source LLC
Chambersburg PA
CBHW010539100726
47903CB00011B/3059

* 9 7 8 1 6 8 4 9 2 1 6 9 0 *